CW01667860

# Contents

*This book is dedicated to Ethel whose vision and enthusiasm started it all, and to Janet who has provided the basic information about mass catering, and with whom I have learned so much.*

# 1 The reasons why

Have you noticed that when God has something special to say to you, he often says it when you are least expecting it? It may be a very ordinary sort of day, and you are going about the routine chores, not looking for 'guidance', or even thinking of anything special, when WHAM ... something is said or done which means that life is never quite the same again.

I was not looking for 'something to do for God' as we pushed our prams home from the shops on that sunny spring afternoon. Ethel and I were chatting idly about how the pattern of our social life had changed, now that we had three pre-schoolers apiece.

'I enjoy going out for coffee, or an afternoon "cuppa",' said Ethel, 'but I do get a bit tired of all that baby-talk.' I grunted – partly in agreement and partly because my four year old had just ridden his tricycle over my foot! Ethel stopped dead, causing a collision between David's trike and her twin pushchair. 'Listen!' she said, disentangling herself and then almost steering the twins into the lamp post in her excitement. 'Why don't we have a coffee morning and invite all our friends who never go to church? We could have someone to speak on a really helpful subject from the Christian viewpoint and share what we believe, right there in our own homes!'

'Marvellous idea!' I was enthusiastic too. 'I'm sure that lots of people would like to hear something different and would come, even if they would never dream of going to church.' Then a thought struck me. 'But where would we hold it?' I queried.

'At your house of course!' Ethel seemed surprised that I had not thought of that immediately. 'After all, you have a large sitting room, and a playroom that we could use for a Creche.'

That was a different matter! After all, I had a two-month old baby and two small sons to keep me at full stretch. Surely I was not in any position to organise an enterprise like this. 'I'll have to think about it,' I said cautiously. 'I couldn't possibly do anything until Joanna has cut out her 10 a.m. feed, so let's leave it until the autumn.' It will be forgotten by then, I thought, and hastily changed the subject.

We might have forgotten, but God did not. Throughout the summer he repeatedly brought the subject back to my mind. 'But, Lord,' I prayed, 'there is so much to do with small children at home all day and I'm already involved in so many other Christian activities ...'

'You can find time for the things that you WANT to do,' came the answer. 'Trust me to help you to fit this in.'

'But, Lord, Ethel and I would be so unreliable. Six children under five years old between us! What happens if they are ill? We could be out of circulation for weeks and have to cancel the coffee mornings,' I argued. 'Anyway, who would come?' Then I became more honest. 'Lord, am I the type of person to do this?' I pleaded. 'After all, it is one thing to invite friends to a church service, or even to a meeting in someone else's house. But if it is held here, I'm labelled. My friends know that I'm "religious", but talking about you at a coffee morning – that is something else! They'll think that I'm really odd!' There was no answer to that.

In the early autumn, we spent a week-end with my sister in London. Her flat was steps away from a famous London church, and when the minister announced his text in the Sunday morning service I knew why God had taken me to that church, on that particular morning.

'Come, I will send you to Pharaoh, that you may bring forth my people ...'

I squirmed as I heard the excuses that Moses (and I) had made, and his final plea 'Oh, my Lord, send, I pray, some other person.' I knew when I was beaten. 'All right, Lord,' I said, rather ungraciously, 'but I just hope that you know how we're to do it, because I don't!' and I went home to set the wheels in motion for our first coffee morning.

That was the beginning of a new phase in our lives. Of course, Ethel and I make no claims to have been the originators of this idea. People have been hearing about God in other people's homes since New Testament times. In the twentieth century, Christians have been holding home-based meetings of one sort or another for decades, but during the last ten years the practice of using the home as a base for Christian work has gathered momentum. Doors have been opened for simple hospitality. Some women have invited just a few friends into their homes for a discussion, to hear a regular or occasional speaker, or to study the

Bible together. Others have worked as a team, giving coffee mornings in their homes, or sometimes arranging lunches or dinners in hotels or other 'neutral' places, all with one objective in view – to show that God does care for the individual today, and that he has demonstrated that care by sending Jesus Christ to this earth, and through him, offering 'new life' to all who will accept it.

But for all those who have shared their faith in this way, there are many more who would like to do so, but say that they feel so inadequate. 'How would you do this, and where would you find out about that?' they ask those of us who are already involved. 'What do you do when ... and if this happens, how do you cope?'

Within these pages we will attempt to give some of the answers. There is no set recipe, which, if slavishly followed, will guarantee instant success. Our God is a god of infinite and glorious variety, and he delights to meet people where they are, not where they ought to be! All he asked of me was my willingness to follow where he led; that is all he asks of anyone. Stop and read 2 Kings 6:24 – 7:9.

This story is a vivid picture of life today. People are spiritually bankrupt and starving, and they are trying things which in the past would have been unthinkable, in a vain effort to satisfy these inner needs. In the process they are tearing themselves and each other to pieces, and they don't know how to stop. And just like the lepers, who left the besieged city of Samaria, to find that the Syrian army had fled, 'we have good news, and we shouldn't keep it to ourselves'.

The chapters that follow, which draw on the experience of many women of all ages, suggest some of the ways that these women have discovered are effective in sharing that news. But just in case you are saying with Moses (as I was) 'I am nobody, how can I go?' let's get it quite straight in our minds just who Jesus was talking to when he said, 'Go, and make disciples ...'

# 2 But what about the church?

'Preaching should take place in the sanctuary, not in the sitting room,' boomed one very loyal member of a local congregation. 'Surely the church should be the place to which people come if they want to know about God. The clergy are trained to answer their questions; they have the resources to refer to and the time to do it. Are you not trying to do their job for them?'

This dear lady was certainly right on one point. The church should be the focal point for spiritual life in the community, but it is the people who go into it, rather than the physical building, who are responsible for showing light and joy to all those who live round about. And if the believers keep their faith within a building, then it will not spread very far. For, in the majority of cases, expecting unbelievers to go into a church service as a first step to finding God, is like asking you or me to go into a very exclusive club, where people speak in a special language and take part in rituals that only the club members know how to perform. The bravest of us would be horrified at the prospect. We'd be recognised as strangers; we would probably make fools of ourselves by doing the right thing at the wrong time, and what would be said, would be like mumbo-jumbo to us anyway. But supposing one of the club members asked us to her own house, explained her enthusiasm for the club activities and we saw for ourselves, as we got to know her better, what a valuable thing membership of that club would be ... well that would be a different story!

And so it is for those who know little of the Christian faith. Sadly, their minds are often filled with distortions and half-truths, and the church as an institution has no relevance in their eyes as a place to find the answer to life's problems. They may not even be aware of anything missing in their lives until they meet someone to whom Jesus is a living and vital reality, and then, perhaps, they may begin to get a little curious. But that is the key. They have to meet someone. And far too many of us, who are Christians, huddle together in our tight little 'In' groups, and like the salt in a certain brand of potato crisps, we stay in our little blue bags, and have no effect on the world around us.

Jesus did not do that. There were no churches for him to preach in. He went to the synagogue on the sabbath, certainly, to take part in the worship and to take his message to the religious people of his day. But he spent far more time down on the beach with the fishermen: chatting to the traders in the crowded markets, or meeting the needs of one individual after another. Much of his teaching was done in homes, and the company he kept brought scathing comments from the religious leaders of the day, who thought more of their own reputations than the needs of those whose lives were in a mess.

The first Christian disciples lived in the same

way. They became the talking point in Jerusalem, not because of the fine quality of their singing, or because of the magnificence of the building that they erected, but because of their completely different quality of life. They were excited about this Jesus of Nazareth: they really cared for each other and their joy and thankfulness was infectious. They had heard that the last request of Jesus had been that they should 'go and tell' and so they went right out and did it. And even in that male-orientated society, it was not just left to the apostles or even to the converted men. The women, too, had their part to play, and they did it effectively, just where they were, in their homes.

But what about today? The world and our way of life seems to have changed as much in the last seventy years, as it did in the previous nineteen hundred. And one of the major changes is that women, in general, are news. Women's rights, women's wrongs, equal pay for women and equal problems for women. Women have sailed around the world, climbed mountains, are leading political parties and rising to high positions in industry and the professions. The world is our oyster, or so it seems, but what about Christian women? What impact are we making in the last quarter of the twentieth century? To what use are we putting the much-vaunted 'freedom' that the women's libbers tell us is ours for the taking?

In our grandmother's day, women missionaries were trail-blazers, facing all kinds of challenges in the Thirld World, while their contemporaries in the 'Home Country' were still hemmed in by conventions and petty restrictions. Even now at the present time the only occasion on which many of us seem to stop and consider whether Christian women have any particular part to play in God's strategy for the world, is when the debate about the ordination of women swings into the spotlight of world news from time to time. And now that a decision about this has been shelved by the powers-that-be for the next few years, are we to sink back into our armchairs and say, 'What a pity! Now that I can't be ordained, I can't do anything of importance for God'? We should be hypocrites if we did! What difference would it make to the majority of us if a few of our number were called to serve God in the ordained ministry? Only a small proportion of Christian men are called to work in this capacity, and it would be the same for women. But just as in the book of Acts, so now, we are all called to be witnesses of what we know to be true, whatever our day-to-day occupation might be.

### '*It may be the twentieth century, but I'm not free*'

Free from what? Free to do what? What exactly is this freedom that we hear so much about today? According to the supporters of the feminist movement, we know freedom when we are working alongside men, doing the same job for the same rate of pay. But what kind of freedom is it that simply exchanges domestic responsibility for those of a paid employee? Of course, some women have to work outside the home and they should be paid fairly for the work that they do. But that has nothing to do with freedom. When you think about it, you have to recognise the fact that no responsible adult is completely free from outside demands, but Jesus offers us freedom that is different. A freedom that starts on the inside.

Sadly, so many of us fail to experience this freedom because we are hemmed in by other people's ideas of who we are and what we should be doing, instead of seeing ourselves as God sees us. He loves and accepts us just as we are. Our academic qualifications (or lack of them); the size of the family income, or how much we are like the ideal wife, mother and homemaker that we see portrayed in the media, counts for nothing with him. Just savour that thought for a moment – it can be the key to a whole new way of thinking. We do not have to keep up with the Joneses, whether they are the Church-Joneses, the neighbourhood-Joneses, or the media-Joneses! So we are free to be the unique and special individuals that God intends us to be, living in this world for a particular purpose.

God has a perfect plan for each one of our lives, and he tailors our circumstances to fit. So if you are (in your own eyes) an ordinary woman living in an ordinary house with an ordinary family, how does God see you? He sees you as a beloved daughter with her own unique gifts, opportunities and challenges. No one else has your neighbours; you live where you live for a purpose. The children that your children play with are not just 'chance acquaintances'; the play-group or school with which you are involved is 'special'.

Perhaps you feel, as I used to, that if you lived in a foreign country where those around you spoke a different language, it would be so much easier to 'witness' – once you could understand each other! After all 'they' would be so much more obviously 'heathen'. Perhaps from time to time, you receive a 'prayer-letter' from a missionary friend in some far-flung corner of the earth. Look again at the latest one. Just what have they written about? Their neighbours; their children's friends; the people that they come into contact with through their work – ordinary citizens of an ordinary country. Now look back over the last month of your life, and imagine that you are living in 'Outer Mongolia East', instead of Darkest England! Wouldn't that chat that you had with your depressed next door neighbour have been an item for prayer in your 'letter home'? And what about that lonely old lady for whom you shop from time to time, and the Committee of the school Parent-Teacher Association to which you have just been elected? Try writing that imaginary prayer-letter, and see how many opportunities to share God's love exist right now, in your present circumstances. And you are free to accept or reject them, because that is God's way.

Free to accept or reject! So how are we going to use this fantastic gift of freedom? Should we be content to drift through life, icebergs on the sea of God's frozen assets, always looking at the restrictions of our circumstances, rather than the opportunities that each special phase of life brings with it? Or should we allow ourselves to be melted by his love, and face up to the challenge and the immensely exciting privilege of being used by God? The whole adventure can begin with four simple words 'Over to you, Lord!'

# 3 Over to you, Lord

There's no doubt about it, Moses was a reluctant messenger! Even though God spoke to him personally, he tried, in every way that he knew, to get the job of leading the Israelites out of Egypt handed on to someone else. The lepers that we read about in 2 Kings 6 seem to have had mixed feelings too. Their first instinct was to grab all that they could for themselves, but then they remembered their fellow Samaritans. It is interesting to see how their feelings of responsibility towards their friends received a hefty boost when they realised that punishment was likely to follow their failure to tell.

***Look at your motives***

We serve God for a variety of motives, and not all of them are very worthy. Sometimes we undertake a task because it is a way of gaining recognition among our fellow Christians. Or perhaps we feel a need to 'do our own thing' and so take on a particular activity to fulfil a need that *we* have. Then there are those who are 'born volunteers' – naturally nice folk who feel impelled to offer to do a job that no one else wants because 'somebody has to'.

So why are you prepared to say 'Over to you, Lord'? It may be for any of the reasons that I have suggested, or a different one that I have not thought of. But the only motive that pleases God is that of loving obedience. We love him and so we want to please him: he asks something of us and we cheerfully obey. This means that we do not obey only because we have weighed up the pros and cons and decided that this job is important and so it warrants *our* spending *our* precious time on it. Nor do we feel that it is worth doing only because we will be reaching those who are powerful or influential (although of course we may be) and it is therefore sufficiently glamorous to flatter our ego. If God has told us to do it, then the smallest job, done quietly, at his direction, is *the* important thing for us, and that is all that we have to take into account.

### *Look at your circumstances*

Each one who reads this book is an individual, with her own needs, abilities, opportunities and circumstances. I am assuming only four things.

First, that you are female.

Second, that you have seen your own need for forgiveness and a new life, and have asked Jesus Christ to supply that need.

Third, that you feel his prompting to share your faith with others as you invite them into your home, and that you are willing to do so – for the right reason of course!

And last of all that you have a home (which may be anything from a residential caravan to a castle) into which to invite them. Beyond that – anything goes.

You may be single, married, looking forward to your first baby, your next grandchild, or anything in between. You may live in the country, the city or the suburbs. You may work outside the home full or part-time, or you may be home-based. Your husband (if you have one) may share your faith or he may not. None of these things, in themselves, need form a barrier; they will simply act as markers, to indicate which way God is likely to be guiding you.

*Look at your options*

There seem to be four main ways that women are using their homes for God:

1. Hospitality
2. Evangelistic meetings
3. Bible Study Groups
4. Prayer Groups

*Hospitality*

This is the first, and perhaps the most obvious way. It ranges from the simple inviting of a neighbour in for a cup of coffee, right through to taking a needy person in as part of the family for a period of time. Hospitality provides a bridge between the church and the world outside, a refuge for the lonely and troubled, a nursery in which those who are young in the faith can begin to grow, and a workshop in which God can begin to shape individuals, and fit them together as a loving caring unit.

*Evangelistic meetings*

Basically, this is hospitality with a speaker. Of course you do not have to hold a formal meeting before you can share the good news about Jesus, but it is a good way of speaking to a number of people at one time, in a more direct way than is often possible in casual conversation. Coffee mornings or afternoon teas for women, and evening get-togethers for husbands and wives, or working women, when coffee and other light refreshments are served are the most popular ways of doing it, although some folk have held buffet lunches or fork suppers at home, as well.

The details vary, but the basic ingredients are the same – a home, a speaker with a living faith and the ability to speak about it in everday language and people who are willing to listen.

### *Bible Study Groups*

People *are* reading the Bible today. The old excuse that it is too old-fashioned and difficult to understand has been swept out of the door with the coming of modern translations, and people are finding that it really does contain 'Good News'. They are getting together in two's, three's or larger groups, to find out what God has to say about himself and the way that we should live. Lives are being transformed as Christians grow in their faith and unbelievers discover that the Bible *has* something to say about them and their problems.

### *Prayer Groups*

These often go hand-in-hand with Bible Study groups but not always. Some women have been called by God to give themselves to prayer in a special way. Alone, or in groups, they are giving time and concentrated effort to pray for the nation, their own town or local church situation and the power of God is being released in a very definite way. Their prayers are being answered and they know it.

So these are the options. And just in case this

all sounds rather overwhelming, let's remind ourselves that very few (if any) women would be called to serve God in all four of these ways at once!

In the Acts of the Apostles, we have many examples of the Holy Spirit sending one apostle in this direction and another apostle in that. Read Acts 16:6–9 and you will see what I mean. God has a specific work for each individual to do and that alone is her task. The important thing is for each one to take the time to find out what he is asking of her, at the particular age and stage which she and her family are at now and to do that.

But just how do we 'find out'? Paul's Macedonian vision was gloriously positive and occasionally God does speak to people in the same way today. More often, however, we have to pray, perhaps talk to other people and then look at the signpost of circumstance. Taken together, these things will usually point the way forward. Which is the way for you? Well, let's look at hospitality first, since that is a possibility for most of us.

If you are at home all day, casual entertaining of friends and neighbours to coffee or an afternoon 'cuppa' may well be part of your normal life-style already, especially if you have young children. This is something that you can do even if your husband does not share your faith. If you have felt that the 'social round' is rather a waste of time and so tend to avoid it, ask the Holy Spirit to bring people to your door who are really in need, then stand back and see him at work.

If you are single and at work all day, or a mother of school-age children and either working full or part-time yourself (or find that the majority of your friends are doing so) you may find opportunities to be hospitable confined to evenings or week-ends. For many of us, anything that is done in the evening means that husbands will be affected and therefore he will have to be in agreement, so you will need to discuss it with him first. Then if God is speaking to you as a couple, you may want to consider opening your home on a regular basis to entertain single folk, other couples, or even families, both from the church and from your neighbourhood.

Coffee mornings with a speaker are ideally suited to women with pre-school children. Yes, I know that at that stage of life you feel that you have more than enough to do, but this is the one period when your contemporaries are readily available to come and listen. When children start school, so many women return to work, that even if *you* are still home-based, many of your neighbours and friends will not be, and the potential for this kind of activity is reduced.

This does not mean, of course, that there are no older women running coffee mornings or coming to them – far from it. There are needy folk in every age group and although in some instances a group may cater mainly for young mothers, in others, women of widely differing ages get together and benefit just because they *are* so different and have such a wide range of experience to share.

And what about Bible Study and Prayer Groups? These can be a mighty weapon, in God's hands, for women of any age. Obviously those who are not involved in full-time work are much freer to serve God in this way – and surely this is a factor that many more of us need to take into account if we are free to choose what we do with our days. But if we offer the time we have available to God, he will use even the smallest amount if we are prepared to let him.

He will ... if we will! That is the key. We tend

to make it so complicated when it is really very simple. We do not need a large or immaculate house or unlimited time. We do not have to be a trained Bible teacher, fabulous cook or a model housekeeper before we can do any of these things. All we need is a loving concern for those around us, obedient hearts and an absolute dependence on the Holy Spirit. Without him we can accomplish nothing: with him we can do anything. Over to you, Lord!

# 4 Angels unawares?

'I don't need a book to tell me how to entertain my friends,' said Jenny. 'It's something you *do*, not something you read about.'

'Yes, but what about the uninvited guests?' asked Ann. 'I love to have a meal or coffee with friends that I've made a date with, but how do you cope with those who just 'turn up'? Living almost next door to the school is a very mixed blessing. Marcia drops in before I've washed up the breakfast things sometimes; Jan watches me cook lunch at least once a week, and a wet afternoon is murder – almost half of the third-year Mums seem to take shelter in my kitchen. I find it really hard to get the chores done. Is it ever right not to invite an unexpected visitor in, do you think?'

'I think that hospitality is a spirtual gift like any other,' said Mary firmly, 'and if you've got it you entertain anybody and everybody, and if you haven't, you don't! Anyway, we couldn't possibly have anyone round at the moment. Every room in the house needs decorating, and the loose covers on our chairs are absolutely threadbare.'

Well ... what do think? Is there a difference between hospitality and entertaining? Do you need a special sort of temperament and talent – to say nothing of masses of space and a bottomless purse? Should Christians have first call on our time and resources, or those outside the church? And what about the wear and tear on our possessions; the pressure that extra people in the house will put onto our own family relationships, and the inroads it will make on our meagre stores of time and energy?

We often speak of hospitality as a virtue of the East, and a law of the desert. Even today, in many Eastern countries, it is unthinkable that a stranger should be allowed to pass through on a journey without being offered food and shelter. But is it just a cultural thing? Should it be a principle of life for Western Christians, or an optional extra? What does the Bible have to say about it?

### *The Bible teaches it*

Care and concern for the needs of others, demonstrated by hospitality, is a golden thread running right through the Bible from Genesis onwards. Abraham started it; the Levitical Law demanded it; the prophets commended it and Jesus himself spoke about it. One of the distinguishing marks of the early church in Acts was their joyful sharing of hospitality, and the epistles repeat the theme.

Everybody was included. Abraham put himself out on a hot afternoon for strangers (and found that he had entertained not men but angels); the Levitical Law insisted on a square deal for non-Jews and Isaiah tells us that to care for the hungry, helpless, poor and destitute is not only God's will but is a sure recipe for personal blessing. Jesus, too, had a passionate concern for the needs of the underdogs of society (read Matt. 25:31–44 and Luke 14:12–14, if you need reminding).

Isaiah also points out that we have a very definite responsibility to our own relatives (Isa. 58:6-9), and in the epistles, Christians are reminded of their responsibility to care for each other and to give mutual help and encouragement to other believers, as well as to look after the needs of those outside of God's family. A hospitable heart was even one of the qualifications required for a potential church leader – I wonder how often the modern church takes that factor into consideration today?

### *Hospitality or Entertaining?*

In the Pocket Oxford Dictionary, the word 'entertain' is listed in between 'enterprise' – 'a difficult undertaking' (which entertaining often is!) and 'enthrall' – 'to captivate' (which is often its aim!).

'Hospitality', on the other hand, nestles between 'hospice' meaning 'a shelter' and 'hospital' which is a 'place of healing and restoration'. The actual definition of 'hospitality' is 'the friendly and liberal reception of guests or strangers', but as Christians we can offer something more than refreshment, entertainment and liberal friendship, because we can also share what we know of the one who is a shelter from the storms of life and gives healing for minds and spirits.

So there is a difference between entertaining and hospitality. The one who entertains thinks 'things are more important than people'. The house must be decorated, the furnishings complete – the object is to impress and enthrall. The hospitable hostess does not try to impress but to serve.

The one who entertains says in effect, 'This is

mine; aren't I lucky; wealthy; clever? Don't you envy me?' The hospitable hostess says, 'All that I have is in trust from my Master, and I gladly share it with you. Please make yourself at home.'

The one who entertains implies, 'Look how well I cope with homemaking; what an efficient person I am.' The hospitable hostess smiles, 'I need your help. Please contribute – I can't manage it all on my own.'

Entertaining looks for rewards in terms of compliments and return invitations. Hospitality gives, without any secondary motives, out of love for the Lord.

But is hospitality a spiritual gift or a natural talent? There is a sense in which some Christians have a particular 'gift of hospitality' given to them by the Holy Spirit, and for them, hospitality and service of others becomes their main sphere of ministry, every bit as valid as a gift of teaching, preaching, prophecy, or any of the other gifts mentioned in the Bible.

You may know someone like Charlotte. She has seven children, a large house to run single-handed, and a husband with a demanding career that necessitates his being overseas a great deal. Consequently, Cha is rarely able to get to meetings, and her life is very much centred on the home. She cannot go out to the world, so the world comes to her. A tiny flatlet at the top of the house provides a 'Prophets Chamber' for visiting ministers and missionaries. Children flock in to play with hers; Sunday is a day when the 'singles' in the church are lovingly drawn in. That home is a living demonstration of God's love. Has Cha a spirtual gift? Certainly!

I cannot point you to a passage where the word 'hospitality' is mentioned within a list of spirtual gifts, but both Paul (in Rom. 12:7, 8) and Peter (in 1 Pet. 4:10) mention someone who 'serves' as exercising a gift given by the Holy Spirit, and in both cases it either precedes, or immediately follows, an injunction to hospitality, and after all, what is hospitality but service to others?

If we enjoy home-making and all that goes with it, *we* may think of it as a natural ability, but all our talents are given by God, and when we offer them back to him, he can work through us to achieve results in the spiritual realm. We have only to ask ourselves three questions. First, am I willing to use this gift for God? Secondly, are there any wrong attitudes in my heart towards others or wrong-doing that I cling to? (If there is, the channel of my life will be blocked, and the Holy Spirit will not be able to flow). Last of all, although I may have a natural ability in this area, am I totally dependent on God to transform my home into his power-house?

But perhaps you are saying, 'I'm not particularly domesticated, and I'm very busy with other things – does that mean that I can be excused offering hospitality?' A thorough study of the Biblical passages that touch on the subject would suggest not. Read Romans 12:13; 1 Timothy 3:2; 1 Peter 4:9; Hebrews 13:2; Matthew 25:31-44; Leviticus 19:32-34; and Isaiah 58:6-9. Paul does not tell the Romans to 'practise hospitality – if you have nothing else on next Sunday', nor does Peter remark that the Christians scattered through Asia Minor should open their homes to each other 'if they should happen to feel like it!' In fact, since he tells them to do it 'without complaining', one gets the feeling that they were expected to do it however they felt!

So all Christians are to show hospitality to strangers, to the outcasts, to fellow Christians and to their own relations, but many of us will not be doing this exclusively, but occasionally and in addition to other things.

***Counting the cost***

Whether we are offering hospitality on an occasional or frequent basis, there is a price to be paid. First of all there is a cost in terms of family relationships. We often laughingly say that an Englishman's home is his castle, and within that castle we may feel secure and in command of the situation. But let down the drawbridge so that all who wish to may cross over and see what happens!

You see not all visitors are charming and helpful; not all children can be relied on to wash their grimy hands *before* you have cleaned the basin instead of afterwards. And when husbands are late home on the very night that they *promised* to be early, and small children reduce the house to its normal chaotic state just before guests arrive (because *you* were busy in the kitchen) gaps may show up in your spirituality that you have tried to ignore for years.

Children will have to learn to share – their parents' attention; their toys; maybe even their rooms. And husbands and wives have to learn to achieve the delicate balance of time given to others, while still maintaining communication between themselves. Of course, these can all be opportunities for learning and growing. But as we offer hospitality we should beware of treating those outside our family better than we do those within it.

Then there is the wear and tear factor. Cups do get broken, floors do get muddied and upholstery does wear out more rapidly if lots of people sit on it. Happy-go-lucky housekeepers may find this kind of damage easier to bear than their more perfectionist sisters, but the key to coping is not in our nature but in the way that we regard ourselves.

In Biblical times, the slave was a fact of life. He or she was bought and sold like any other commodity, and all that a slave had in terms of earthly possessions belonged to his master. The apostles recognised that they had been purchased by Jesus – the only difference between themselves and ordinary slaves was the currency that had been used in the purchase. And so they frequently referred to themselves as 'servants'. Do you see yourself as a servant of Jesus Christ? If you do, then you will have to recognise his claim on all your possessions. Your car; your stereo; your carpets; and your furniture – all are his and lent to you to be used on his behalf. To see your house in this light brings a whole new sense of freedom. Of course, this does not mean that you are careless with your master's goods: after all, if you are looking after something for a friend, you tend it even more carefully than if it belongs to you. But you can have the same attitude as Sally and John who, over the years, furnished their home with antiques; most of them junk-shop finds and all lovingly and knowledgeably restored. This meant that hours of work had been poured into each item, and their value had been considerably increased. Then Sally and John became Christians and opened their home for God to use.

'Surely you're not going to have people lounging all over those beautiful chairs,' wailed her mother. 'Think of all the time and money that have been invested in them.' Sally smiled, 'Our furniture is the Lord's and he will take care of his own,' she said. And he did. In spite of all the people who came in and out of their home, no irreversible damage was ever done.

And finally – is it ever right to say 'No'? If, like Ann, at the beginning of the chapter, you never seem to have an uninterrupted moment – what then? There may be times when it is right to say 'No'. For instance, when your children are facing important examinations, and need your help with revision, or perhaps simply your loving attention or a listening ear, then the drawbridge may have to be raised temporarily. Or there may be occasions when you have to withdraw for a while, in order to give concentrated effort to another area of Christian service.

But in the normal pattern of life, if you are burdened by constant callers, why not do what the Schaeffers have done at L'Abri, the Christian community that they founded in Switzerland. God placed this philosopher, his wife and four children in an obscure village in Switzerland. Then one by one, he brought people from all over the world to their home. The Schaeffers have never advertised, or gone out of their way to invite people but they have prayed that God would bring to their home those folk that he wanted to be there, and keep the others away. And this is what has happened.

You may like to pray a similar prayer and then accept those who come as gifts to you from God and love and serve them for his sake.

# 5 Practically speaking

'I love having visitors when they're actually here,' sighed Sally, 'but the "befores" and "afters" are murder! A dinner party takes me days to prepare and hours to clear up. The kitchen always looks as if a bomb has hit it when I've been cooking.'

'Me, too,' Marilyn agreed. 'I don't know how Jenny has the energy to fill her house with people, Sunday after Sunday. What kind of day of rest is that? Anyway, what's the point of entertaining relations and people from the church. You can't say many of them are needy. Surely we should be concentrating on people outside the Christian family.'

'I wish we knew some people to invite,' said Rosemary. 'We've lived in our present house for six months and I've spoken to one of my neighbours twice, and the other one not at all. Our street is absolutely deserted during the day; everyone seems to be out at work except me. And very few of our church folk are my age. We've had one or two invitations to Sunday tea, but one visit per family seems to be the limit, and it was all very formal. I just don't know how to break through the barriers.'

Sally, Marilyn and Rosemary were discussing the whole topic of hospitality, but these particular comments seem to sum up the three main problems associated with this particular ministry:

1. *Time* – where to find it and how to use it in the best possible way.
2. *Whom to invite*, and how to make the time that you spend together really worthwhile and free from stress.
3. *How to make friends*, both in and outside of the church, especially if you are new to the area or shy and unsure of yourself.

Let's consider them one by one.

***How do you find the time?***

Whole books have been written on time-management and yet most of us are still not very good at it. Time is, of course, one of the most precious commodities that we have, and rich or poor, we all have the same raw material at our disposal – twenty-four hours in a day and seven days in a week. Each day's ration has to be put to good use (or is lost beyond recall) because we can neither store time up from yesterday, nor have an advance from tomorrow! Even so, if we spend 8 hours out of the 24 sleeping (which is a generous ration for many adults) and 8 hours at work, 5 days a week, we are still left with a balance of 72 hours, to invest as we please. Even those mothers of young children who reckon that they work an average 12 hour day, 7 days a week, have 28 hours unaccounted for. Where *do* they go?

One of the first steps towards solving the 'vanishing time syndrome' is to buy a notebook and simply write down how you spend each waking hour, dividing the day into half-hour periods. If you do this for several weeks, you will see a pattern emerging, and will probably find that your time distribution is very uneven – some things taking far more than their fair share, while others are almost squeezed out.

Having assessed the situation, you then need to decide on your priorities. Dr Ted Engstrom, who leads 'Managing Your Time' seminars in the United States (and whose book *Strategy for Living* is excellent if you really want to get to grips with this subject) has reduced this process of sorting out priorities, to a slogan:

'Goals, priorities, planning, living'

*A goal* is our response to what we believe that God wants us to do and to be. It is specific – a particular activity or project – and something that we *can* accomplish. In other words, it is within our capacity to do and we shall know whether it has been done or not. We may have one goal or several.

*Priorities* are needed when we have more than one goal. Setting priorities helps us to sort out which goal is the most important, otherwise one just gets in the way of another.

*We plan*, when we analyse the best way to reach those goals, and as we start working towards the goals by following our plans, we start 'Living'. Does it work in practice? Wendy (among many others) would say that it does.

She came back from her summer holiday last year determined to be more disciplined in her use of time. Her church was planning an autumn of outreach to those who were not committed Christians. Wendy and her husband felt a real need to develop a greater unity with their Christian friends, as well as spending more time with their immediate neighbours, in order to build bridges of shared interests and better understanding.

Consequently, Wendy's goals (written in the order in which they occurred to her) read like this:

1. Take part in the Outreach programme.
2. Entertain at least two families from the church each month.
3. Invite everyone that I know living nearby to coffee, two or three at a time.
4. Enrol in an evening class that will enable me to make new friends.
5. Get to know God better for myself.
6. Spend at least one evening each week doing something with John (her husband).
7. Allow time each evening to read and pray with the children.
8. Get on top of the housework.

She then felt rather daunted! All of these goals were good, but it was obvious that they could not all be accomplished at once. So the next step was to decide priorities. Having prayed about it, she marked the most important goals with an 'A', the next most important with a 'B', and the least important with a 'C'. Her new list read as follows:

A – Get to know God better for myself.
A – Spend at least one evening each week doing something with John.
A – Allow time each evening to read and pray with the children.
A – Entertain at least two families from the church each month.
B – Take part in the Outreach Programme.
B – Invite everyone that I know living nearby to coffee, two or three at a time.
B – Get on top of the housework.
C – Enrol in an evening class that will enable me to make new friends.

Wendy explained why she had graded things as she had.

'The first three A's are obvious. You can't lead another person closer to Jesus than you are yourself, so my own spiritual life must be built up. My other prime responsibilities are John and the children. It was difficult to know whether entertaining church families or being involved in outreach should be A's or B's, but if we are to work within the church effectively, we need to be closer to our co-workers, so I felt that one step led to another. If the house gets in too much of a muddle I can't cope with other things, so that was awarded a B, and I think that the evening classes may have to wait.'

It may seem very time consuming to plan in this way and then to take the necessary steps to see that the plans are worked out in day-to-day living, but the time is invested, rather than spent, and really does pay dividends. So if you are a Harassed Harriet, why not try it? You've nothing to lose and possibly a great deal to gain.

### *Whom do you invite?*

We have deduced already that the Bible tells us to open our homes to all. The needs of the social misfits and the spiritually bankrupt are fairly obvious – but are we sensitive to the claims of our own relatives and fellow Christians? It is sad but true that in many families, relatives do not get on well together, but the Bible has strong words to say about those who try to shirk family responsibility.

Have you heard the true story of the old lady who wanted all her grown-up and successful children to come to her birthday party, but they refused, saying that they were all too busy to come? She then asked her neighbour to send word that she had died and was to be buried on her birthday. The family all came – to what they expected to be a funeral – because they thought that it was more important to show respect in death, than love in life.

Then there are those with whom we worship and work in the church. How well do you know those with whom you exchange a few words each Sunday? Do you have any idea of the spiritual and practical needs with which some of them are wrestling? Do you care about the needs of the one-parent families, the teenagers from non-Christian homes, or the growing pains of those young in the faith? Or do you leave all that kind of thing to the minister and other church leaders? And what about the minister, elders or deacons in your church? Do you notice when they are 'down' and do something that might lift their burdens and spirits a little?

'Well it wasn't a very uplifting evening last time we tried it. Margo moaned about the young people; Sam droned on about predestination, and Bill and Sue hardly spoke.' Have you had an evening like that and vowed never to repeat the experiment? Well try again, but this time, pray about it beforehand. Ask God to give you his love for each individual, and a sensitivity to their needs. Ask that each one may be ministered to by the Lord and that a sense of his presence will fill the whole house. Then every minute will be infinitely worthwhile.

'Yes, but ...!!' Perhaps you are like Marilyn and Sally, and find the sheer practicalities of preparing meals and coping with any more than the members of your own family very wearying. Maybe you look with awe, tinged with envy, at those who do it with apparent ease! Well let's get one thing straight to start with – there is always some effort involved. But it can be greatly reduced if you deal with the greatest enemy of 'hospitality with less effort' – your pride! Admit that you cannot do it all with one hand tied behind you, and you are at least ten steps further forward. You might like to write these six reminders on a piece of paper and put it where you will see it regularly.

1. *Forget your pride – and remember that if a room is tidy it looks clean*

So it is not necessary to spring-clean before visitors arrive, in fact some 'less-effort' hostesses make a policy of having a good clean after they have gone! This is not an exhortation to slovenliness, but a reminder that if you are pushed for time, a quick flick with a duster, toys tidied away and cushions shaken up, usually works wonders.

2. *Forget your pride – simple meals can be special if they are served with imagination*

Try serving shepherd's pie with a border of mashed potatoes and the centre filled with sweet corn and peas, or carrots and French beans. Learn to cook rice (if you don't know already) and serve it from a ring mould. Look out for scallop shells and use them as dishes to serve fish; use coloured paper napkins with matching candles and even beans on toast has a festive air! There are so many ways of adding interest and colour to your meal table and they need not be costly in time or money. And while we're on the subject of simplicity, do be sensitive. If your guests' main meal is eaten at midday, it may be more appropriate to invite them for evening coffee and dessert, or savoury snacks, than to a full blown dinner which they would not normally have. Try always to provide food that can be eaten without embarrassment (spaghetti and the like can be tricky here unless you know each other very well, or are Italian!) and *do* enquire whether there is anything that they cannot eat. It is much better to know beforehand than to serve their least favourite food (my husband cannot eat onions, so I know what headaches this little point can cause).

3. *Forget your pride – and never say 'no' to offers to help*

If a guest offers help beforehand – accept it. Try pot-luck lunches or suppers – they can be great fun and ease the burden on the hostess considerably. The congregation of our church is divided into small groups for Bible study and pastoral care. When this scheme started we invited all the couples in our group to have lunch with us one Sunday and to bring their children – 12 adults and 9 children. I provided the main course, three of the wives brought desserts, another provided sweets for the children to share after the meal and another supplied soft drinks. This sharing of the catering made the whole undertaking easy, and one that we shall certainly do again.

4. *Forget your pride – and learn from the expertise of others*

If you have a friend who caters easily and you find it hard – ask her advice. Keep a file and make a note of labour saving methods – try new ways of doing things and always take the easy way if there is one. If you are not a confident cook, decide on four basic menus (one for each of the four seasons so that you can use seasonal and therefore less expensive food) and serve those until you can put them together without a second thought. After that you can branch out to more adventurous fare if you wish – but remember a meal is never improved by giving yourself a nervous breakdown over it beforehand.

5. *Plan ahead – and add to your file recipes that can be prepared in advance*

If you have a freezer you have a very definite advantage, and are probably already in the habit of doubling quantities when you make things like pastry, pancakes, cakes and stews, where to cook twice as much (and then freeze half for future use) certainly does not take twice the time. Another great time-saver, if you have a freezer and can use a car for grocery shopping, is to buy your non-perishables and freezables in one big shop each month. (This assumes, of course, that you have your housekeeping money on a monthly basis.) I do this and the whole operation probably takes me twice as long as a weekly shop and I then have to buy only fresh eggs and vegetables and perhaps some meat for the rest of the month.

If you have no freezer there are still recipes that can be pre-prepared and stored in the refrigerator for 24 hours; and we can all keep the ingredients for a couple of basic meals in the pantry ready for the unexpected visitor. I have a couple of 'iron-ration' meals which can be conjured up in a very short time from tins and packets, and whenever I use up those ingredients I replace them immediately so that I can always rely on having something in the cupboard.

6. *Clear up as you go*

Pre-preparation means that at least some of the cooking utensils can be washed up and out of the way long before the meal is put on the table. If you serve a starter, or fruit juice before the meal and have older children able to help – how about training them to clear these things away and wash them up while you are dishing up the main course? Meat plates and main course cutlery can be left soaking while you are enjoying your dessert and hey-presto, at least half the washing-up is dealt with, before the meal is over! I can't honestly claim that this ideal state of affairs has been reached in our house yet – but I'm working on it.

***But isn't all this terribly expensive?***

It could be if you insist on every meal being a mini-banquet. But if you make a determined effort to keep things simple and allow others to contribute, then it need not be. And God is no man's debtor. Jesus multiplied the loaves and fishes, and many know from their own experience that God has a wonderful way of replenishing empty larders with unexpected gifts, when the food that was there has been shared for love of him.

***But how do you make the friends in the first place?***

In all our considerations so far we have assumed that people are ready and eager to come into our homes when invited, and that we have a wide circle of acquaintances and friends, both in and outside of the church. But what do you do, if, like Rosemary, you know very few people and are at a loss to know how to make the initial contact? Does it mean that hospitality is just not your 'scene', or is there some solution? In the next chapter we will consider how bridges can be built to real and lasting friendships, both in and outside of the church.

# 6 Building bridges

***Building bridges in the church***

We have to admit that in some churches, little hospitality is practised. Sometimes, the fellowship seems to be divided agewise with very little movement between the groups, and in such a church, if there are not many folk of your own age around, you can be in for a hard time as a newcomer – unless you are an unusually good mixer.

In other churches, the divisions fall according to activity – the choir members are on christian name terms and so are the Sunday School teachers. The deacons and their wives all get on well together (hopefully!) and the committee of the Women's Meeting all appear to know each other very well. But without a role to play, especially in a large church, it's perfectly possible to worship there for months and not to do more than exchange a few words with those sitting near to you. What can be done?

First of all, a quick reminder that those who are well integrated in a church need to be aware of their responsibilities. If you are one of the 'In's', why not try to speak to at least one new person next Sunday (or someone you hardly know)? Take time to introduce them to others who live in the same neighbourhood; offer to collect them for a Bible Study or Young Wives Group perhaps. It may seem a small thing to you, but it can be a life-line to a newcomer.

And if you are one of the 'Out's' – or feel that you are – pray about it. Ask God to sit you beside the person who needs *you*, next Sunday. It may not be someone of your own age, or anyone with obvious needs. But smile and speak, trusting the Holy Spirit to give you wisdom. Don't always wait for others to speak first; they are probably shy too! When you find out someone's name – write it down. There is nothing so inhibiting as to have been told someone's name and to have forgotten it by the next week. You feel embarrassed to have to ask again, and so you tend to avoid your new acquaintance, rather than getting to know them better.

Then ask God to show you where you can offer your services. 'Oh!' you may say, 'that would be no solution at our church. There are plenty of gifted Christians to run everything.'

Don't you believe it! Even in a large community of Christians, it is almost always the faithful few who do the bulk of the work, and any offers of help are usually joyfully received. Speak to your minister about it – and if you haven't the courage to bring it up at the church door after service, ask when it would be a convenient time to telephone. You hate the telephone? Then write him a note, indicating the areas of church life where you feel that you could be of most use. You may be able to help with the creche, do some visiting amongst the elderly, offer secretarial skills, or act as relief pianist for the Sunday School. God gives his children gifts so that they can minister to others. So ask him to take away the fear of a rebuff and guide you to the 'friends and the job' that he has designed for you.

### *Building bridges in the community*

'You are the salt of the earth' said Jesus – salt to act as a preservative in society; salt to add pungency to life; salt to make others thirsty for spiritual values. But in order to have any of these functions, salt has to be sprinkled onto the substance with which it has to interact. While it is confined to its tin or packet it has no effect. And so it is with Christians. While there *are* those who find it hard to establish meaningful relationships within the Church, there are far more who are happy within the safety of the Christian community, but are at a loss to know how to share their faith and thus be 'salt' to those who live around them.

The famous British 'reserve' and spirit of 'not wanting to seem pushy or interfering' is often barrier number one. If that is surmounted, barrier number two tends to rear its forbidding head.

'We haven't got much in common. We can't join in with their social life. We're not interested in Bridge; we don't "do the Pools" or go down to the pub; we don't want to spend Sunday on the golf course! We just don't have the same aims and ambitions any more.'

Fair enough! Certainly we are told to live in the world but not to be pressed into its mould. But what did Jesus do? He went to where the people were. Of course he spent time with his disciples, but he also attended supper parties given by healed lepers, reformed tax-collectors and repentant prostitutes for their friends from the shady side of the street, who definitely were not reformed characters – yet! They needed to meet Jesus and he did not summon them to the synagogue, but went to the places where they felt at home. Jesus did not compromise his message. He did not leave his holiness outside as he stepped over these dingy thresholds. But his was no repressive sour-faced influence, but one that was full of hope, joy, love and positive goodness.

Hope, joy, love and positive goodness. Is that what *you* take to a party? Or is it negativism, disapproval, apologetic religiosity and compromise? I am not under-estimating the problems. There are social occasions which we could not attend as Christians, and we have to tread a very fine line, directed always by the Holy Spirit. But in spite of that, and the differences that we may see in the lives of those around us, there *are* many points of contact.

We are all sinners in need of forgiveness – some of us have recognised that already, others have not. That is the only difference between us in the eyes of God. We are all loved by him; if we are enjoying that love we should be praying for those who are not, rather than criticising them.

On a day-to-day basis, we all belong to a village, town or city and all want to see our local amenities fairly administered. We may be parents with an interest in schools, and all the social and sporting links that come into our lives as the result of our children's activities. We probably have some sporting or cultural interest of our own – all potential bridges if only we will build them with God's help. So let's think of the ways that we can turn blueprints into reality.

***Pray***

Do you know the names of the people who live in your road? Write down as many of them as you can remember. Ask the Holy Spirit to bring to your mind the names of other people among your acquaintances whom he is preparing to hear God's message. Make a list as the names come to you. Pray for them daily, and expectantly. Be watching and waiting for God to show you the next step in getting to know them better.

### *Get involved*

During the year of Queen Elizabeth's Silver Jubilee I got to know people living along our road who had been nothing more than familiar faces to me before. Like many other people we celebrated Jubilee Day with a children's street party, games and competitions and there was a new sense of belonging and sharing which did not fade away completely afterwards.

This kind of togetherness is easier to establish in a village or small area, but it can be done in the rather faceless suburbs and new housing estates that surround many of our larger towns.

*Look at the needs around you*

Caroline lived on the edge of a new housing development. As she watched the houses being completed and their new owners moving in, strangers to each other and to the area, she wondered what she could do to help to make them feel at home. Eventually she had an idea. She remembered all the things that she had wanted to know when she had come to the town a few years previously. Where to find a reliable plumber and other handy-men; which of the local shops were particularly good for 'special' items of shopping; when and where the buses went; which doctor and dentist were good with children; and so on. She typed out some lists of her own personal recommendations, and those of her friends, and added other useful local information. Then she invited those people living in one street or part of a street to her house to have a cup of tea and to meet each other. Two or three of her friends from church came on each occasion, and Caroline was amazed at the response. In spite of the fact that by then the houses had been occupied for up to three or four months, many of the newcomers had not met each other, and were delighted that someone had taken the initiative and broken the ice. After tea and biscuits had been served, Caroline explained her 'useful' list (which included church and Sunday School times) and she and the other old-stagers were bombarded with questions. As a result of these get-togethers, several of the new folk joined in with the Christian activities in the area, and many new friendships were formed.

*Be part of what is going on*

If you have young children it is often easier to make friends as you meet other mothers at baby clinics and play-groups. Many churches run their own play-groups and Mother and Toddler Clubs for those who are too young for play-group proper and these provide an excellent meeting ground. Many libraries run story times for toddlers; some towns with heated indoor pools have swimming classes for pre-schoolers; there are parks with informal clubs where small children can work off surplus energy on the playground apparatus while their mothers chat. So if you are in that age group, look out for opportunities such as these to widen your circle of friends, and weave an additional strand of new experiences into the lives of your children as well.

*Start something new*

Jenny and Helen faced a common problem of

young parents living far away from relatives – they lacked baby-sitters. They decided to form their own group, but deliberately invited only six of their 'church' friends to join them. They then looked for the rest of their members among neighbours and acquaintances from some of the organisations I've just mentioned. One person brought along another, and soon they had a thriving group of eighteen women, some of whom were getting to know committed Christians for the first time in their lives.

So much for mothers of pre-school children. Now what about those of us with children at school or even living away from home completely? It is quite true that it is less easy to get to know others at this stage in life, especially as many women return to work, either full or part-time and so have little time or energy left to socialise.

*Build on your own interests*

Janet had this problem. She lived in the centre of a large town and had few neighbours. But she became active in the Parent-Teacher Association of her children's school and as she worked alongside other parents, sharing their common interest in the improvement of their children's educational facilities, she made many new friends. She found that her seemingly 'isolated' town-house was ideally situated for casual visits from exhausted shoppers and before long she was able to extend that hospitality to a soup-and-cheese lunch (after which someone gave a brief talk) on market day, when people came into town for shopping.

Other women have made new friends by joining evening or daytime classes in subjects that interest them, taking up a sport, offering to help at the local hospital, W.R.V.S., or one of the many other organisations which are always in need of volunteers. They have proved that a common interest, and a willingness to be friendly were two of the basic ingredients needed to build the bridge between themselves and their local community.

This third and other essential is:

### *Be available*

'I didn't like to bother you; you're always so busy!' Have you had this said to you? This 'too busy' syndrome is one of the curses of modern life. Many of us are whirling round so fast that our would-be friends just cannot catch up with us.

Some missionaries in Thailand had this problem. None of the local people ever came to visit them, and Rachel and Graham wondered why. Then they realised that the Thai people would sit on their verandahs in the early evening, doing absolutely nothing – just sitting there and perhaps calling a greeting to passers-by. Rachel and Graham copied this practice of sitting on the verandah, but in true Western fashion they tried to *use* the time – so they wrote letters, read books or did other small chores. And the Thai people still did not come; they thought it impolite to disturb these 'busy' people. It was not until the missionaries simply sat down and did nothing else, that the visitors started to trickle in.

Now we do not have verandahs or the same Eastern customs, but we can be aware of the 'too busy bug' and deliberately make time to be available, trusting God to use it as he sees best.

### *So I've built bridges – now what?*

This is where many of us come unstuck. We make the friends; we invite them to our homes but when it comes to putting our faith into words our mouths remain obstinately shut. We read with envy of Christians who lead complete strangers to Jesus Christ on the train, or set the entire shop alight with spiritual talk by a casual comment in the butcher's queue! Why is it that none of *our* friends ever ask a leading question or appear to have any pressing needs? How do '*they*' do it?

As with so many things in the Christian life there is no magic formula. Many people appear content on the surface and yet underneath are desperately seeking for 'something' and when Christians are living close to God, others do notice a difference. A prayer that we might all pray each morning is 'Lord, please give me one opportunity to share my faith today. Show me what to say; don't let me miss the chance when it comes.' It does not have to be a sermon or even a 'sermonette'. Just two or three words can plant a seed.

In the same way, a carefully chosen selection of Christian books and magazines that are kept in an easily accessible place can be very useful. As you drink your coffee or eat your meals, the conversation may be ranging over the delights of making things, for instance, and perhaps you have Edith Schaeffer's book *Hidden Art* to hand. Many creative people would enjoy that, and if you lend it, you have a splendid opportunity to talk about the ideas expressed in it, when it is returned. Match your book to your friend and another seed is planted. Pray much, and the seed will be watered.

And then may come the time to recognise that God is leading you one step further. Would you be willing to consider another way of sharing? Would you be prepared to offer 'hospitality with a speaker'? In other words, to hold an evangelistic meeting right there, in your own home? You would – if you knew how to go about it? Then read on!

# 7 One step further

It is one thing to joyfully (or nervously!) accept the fact that God is leading you to open up your home for him to use in this way, and quite another to know what to do next. Of course, God will guide you if you ask him to, but he does require active co-operation from us, so what are the first steps that you will have to take?

There are four very basic things to consider:

1. A Place – where you will have it.
2. A Partner – who will help you to run it.
3. People who will come.
4. Prayer.

### *Prayer*

The first three items on the list are like the legs of a stool. If one is missing, you might be able to balance on the other two for a short while at least. But a three-legged stool without a seat is just a bundle of sticks and no use as a piece of furniture at all. And in the same way, any undertaking for God, which is not brought to him, detail by detail, will accomplish nothing of lasting value.

Prayer is never easy. Very few of us give it the prominence that it should have in our lives, and the very 'busyness' of our doing things, so often crowds it out, leaving us spiritually poverty-stricken. So start as you mean to carry on. Ask God to give you an absolute assurance that you are doing what he wants you to do. He may not speak quite so dramatically to you as he did to me (some of us are more stubborn than others!) but he can and will confirm his guidance in many different ways, and you will need that inner certainty when things get difficult, you make mistakes, or the first flush of enthusiasm wears off.

### *A Partner – or more than one*

The next thing to pray for is one person – or several – who will share your vision and work in partnership with you. When Ethel and I started our coffee morning, we were a double act right from the beginning, because of the way that God had spoken to us. Other people have arrived at the same destination by other paths. Marcia, Jane and Carol started to meet once a fortnight for a time of Bible study and prayer together. After a while, God spoke to them about inviting their neighbours along as well, and so there they were, with a ready-made committee of three.

Dorothy tackled things differently. She heard about what others were doing in their homes, but she had a problem. She lived in a country district with no neighbours within shouting distance, and certainly no Christian friends near by. So she wrote to the wives of seven Christian businessmen that her husband knew, who lived in the surrounding villages and the near-by town. She outlined what she had in mind, and asked them to come to coffee with her and discuss the idea. All seven did so. They were enthusiastic about the plan and so Dorothy had a committee of seven, who each had a responsibility for her own area.

'But why', you may ask 'do you have to have other people to help you if you are just going to invite a few friends to a meeting in your own home?' Strictly speaking, of course, you do not HAVE to do anything. In at least five or six instances that I know of, people have launched out on their own, humanly speaking, and God has blessed what they have done. But all of them agree that as they look back, they would have preferred to have someone with whom to share the burdens and the blessings, had they had the choice. And it is this sharing factor that is so important. Someone to pray with, someone to make suggestions, someone else to keep you from going off at a tangent, to help with all the practical details, and most of all to share your vision of what can be done.

### *People to come*

'My friends will come to a meal or to coffee, but who will come to someone else's house to hear a talk about religion when they would never darken the doors of a church?' You will be surprised! People come for all sorts of reasons. Young mothers will come in order to get out of their own homes and to meet others. Some will come because they are lonely or depressed, others will come because they are really wanting to know why they are in this world, and where they are going. You may wonder if you know enough people yourself to support such a venture; if this is the case, why not do as Dorothy did and invite your Christian friends living locally to come to coffee and share your vision with them. Ask them each to bring a non-church going friend with them to the meeting that you hope to arrange. They in turn will bring *their* friends, and the whole thing snowballs. Your second option is to travel along a more direct route.

This is the way that Mary did it. She lived in a village. Her home and about thirty-five others had been built in the grounds of a demolished manor house – a community within a community. When God spoke to her about opening her home for a coffee morning, she began her preparations rather reluctantly. A comparative newcomer to the village, she knew of no one to act as her 'partner' and she knew relatively few of her neighbours. She wondered what to do. Should she write her invitations and just pop them through the doors? She hadn't time to do anything else, she reasoned; she worked part-time as a clinic doctor and life was hectic enough. To knock on every door and speak to everyone would be an impossible task. However, she could not feel at ease about the impersonal approach, and eventually she mustered every ounce of her courage and went out visiting. To her amazement she was made welcome everywhere she went, and twenty-five women crowded into her lounge for her first meeting.

Monica did a similar thing, knocking on every door in the block of London flats in which she lived, offering an invitation and an explanation in person. It is this second thing that is the hardest to do – offer an explanation – and yet it is very important to make it quite clear what kind of event it is that you are inviting people to. Otherwise, they may feel that they have been lured along under false pretences.

When I invited someone along to our meetings for the first time, I used to say something like this: 'We're having a coffee morning on such and such a date, and we would love you to come. Mrs Jenkins is speaking about her work with Battered Wives and the difference that her Christian faith makes to her job.' If my guest-to-be looked doubtful, or made some comment like 'I'm not very religious' or 'I'm afraid I don't get along to church these days', I would always add, 'Well, all sorts of folk come; some go to church but lots don't. So give us a try, and if you decide that it's not your "thing" when you've been along once, then feel free to say so. We shan't be embarrassed.' (This last bit is very important if you don't want them to avoid you in the supermarket for the next few weeks!) In my experience most of them came and very few failed to come back.

And so we have seen the need for Prayer, Partners, People, and finally:

### *A Place to meet*

Most people meet in a home, at least to begin with, and the most likely home will be yours, if you are the initiator of the scheme. But if you do have a choice, what should govern your decision? If one member of your committee has a large house it may seem the obvious place to go, even if it is a little way out of your area. But if most of the women who come live in an ordinary semi – think carefully. Will they feel at home? Will they make the extra effort to go that little bit further away from home? If the majority of your guests are young mothers with push-chairs or prams to cope with, ten minutes walk is about the most that they can face, especially if they have to get home again in time to prepare lunch for other members of the family.

So look at your guest list carefully. If they have cars or have a good bus service available, and come from a wide area, a town centre meeting place may be best, as Janet found. Then think about space. Of course you will need enough room for people to sit in reasonable comfort, and ideally a separate room for a creche. But a home, even if it is a little cramped is usually better than the greater space (and more impersonal atmosphere) offered by a church or village hall. The warmth of the welcome and the friendliness of the group is far more important than the depth of the carpet pile or the high gloss on the furniture. Some people find it a good scheme to alternate between two homes to spread the load on the hostesses and the size of their area. This is a matter of choice, of course, but if you do this, do remember that people are amazingly forgetful and quite likely to end up in the right place on the wrong day, or vice versa, unless you make sure that you give them everything in writing. (And even then, it is wise to leave a notice on the front door of the 'other' venue, for the odd hopeless case, who will get it wrong whatever you do!)

# 8 On your mark

So God has given you the 'go-ahead'; you have a friend or friends to share in the enterprise with you; a home to meet in and people lined up to invite. But is there anything else that you need to do before you hold your first meeting? There are certain practical things that you can learn as you go along, but you will save yourselves a few headaches and a lot of time if you think some of them through beforehand. So why not get together with those who are going to help – and

## *Hold a planning session*

### *What equipment will you need?*

It may seem to be stating the obvious, but you will need enough cups and saucers for the numbers that you are intending to invite, and not every hostess will have enough. So decide who will supply the extra cups, if needed, and remember that small children will need a small quantity of squash in an unbreakable container. If you are thinking of using disposable cups for coffee, the insulated polystyrene ones are much easier to hold than the more flimsy variety and less likely to be mashed to a pulp by an eager toddler's iron grasp! The only eatables necessary are biscuits, and although chocolate ones are very popular with small children, they are also extremely messy , so it's probably wiser to stick to plain ones. A couple of vacuum flasks are useful so that milk can be pre-heated ahead of time and if you have very large numbers, an urn or boiler which will heat up large quantities of hot water. For most groups starting out though, a couple of electric kettles will be sufficient.

Then you will need to check your seating capacity. How many people can you seat in your sitting room? Will you need to import extra chairs from neighbours or dig out the upright garden chairs from the shed? Floor cushions can be very useful if your guests are nimble and able-bodied – they won't be so popular with the slipped-disc brigade!

The creche will need equipment too. If you have young children of your own, you may feel that you have quite enough toys around the house to occupy an army of visitors. But do remember that some pre-schoolers can be very rough with toys and it is very hard on your own children to see their prize possessions being trampled underfoot. So either decide with them, beforehand, what indestructible toys may be brought out for 'coffee morning' and what will be safely packed away, or keep a small selection of 'special' toys (which may be passed on by friends with older children or picked up at Jumble Sales) for the creche only. This will have a novelty value for your own children too. And one final word of warning on the subject of toys. If you have 'crawlers', 'toddlers' and 'almost-fives' together in the creche, check your toys for the 'swallowable' parts. Lego and similar toys with small parts should be kept well above floor level, or your creche helper may be faced with Joy's predicament. She turned round from soothing a fractious baby with one hand and breaking up a fight with the other, to find the 'quiet' eighteen month old stuffing himself with small soldiers as fast as he could!

### *Who does what?*

In an ideal situation, there are enough people to take on one job each, and to regard that as their special responsibility. You may not have enough helpers to do this, but do divide the jobs up as evenly as you can, and make sure that each person understands what is expected of her. These are some of the jobs that will need doing:

(a) Hostess
(b) Kitchen staff – to make coffee, serve it and wash up.
(c) Creche
(d) Invitations – written and delivered
(e) Secretarial – letters to speakers, etc.
(f) Treasurer
(g) Librarian – if you have a selection of helpful books to loan.

#### *The Hostess*

This job almost always falls on the shoulders of the person in whose home the meeting is held. She welcomes the guests as they arrive, introduces them to one another and does all the normal 'oiling of the wheels' that she would do when any visitors come to her home. She will probably do all the initial organisation of chairs and the kitchen, well before guests arrive, but if at all possible, she should be freed from actually making and serving the coffee. Once people are in the house, her main job is to look after those who have come and make them feel welcome and at home.

*Kitchen Staff*

When Ethel and I started our coffee morning, my next door neighbour offered to be entirely responsible for the coffee. She brought the extra cups that were needed, supplied the coffee, biscuits and orange squash and arrived ten minutes early to make the coffee. She then washed everything up afterwards. You may not have anyone able to take over to quite that extent, but there needs to be one person actually making the coffee and another one or two to hand it round. Again, with small children in mind, it may be a good idea to put everything onto a table and allow people to help themselves, than to be carrying trays of hot coffee around a crowded room. Some washing up can be done as cups are emptied, but there will always be some to be done after the meeting. If you have one person responsible for clearing away dirty cups and starting the washing up, you will probably find that you have plenty of volunteer labour to help her.

*Creche Aunty*

If you are running a meeting attended by young mothers, do have a creche if it is at all possible. Some people have found that to have it in the house next door, or just along the road is a good plan, as the mothers cannot be disturbed by junior's yells. On the whole though, a separate room in the same house as the coffee morning is the most common arrangement, and you will need at least one helper to look after the children.

Some groups have done as we did – have one person who undertakes the creche as her 'job', calling on others for assistance if the numbers of children get too large. The advantage of this system is that the children get to know her and are therefore more willing to leave mother's side. (Do bear in mind though, that this means that she will never hear the speaker and can feel rather 'out' of things. Making a tape recording of the talk, which she can listen to later, is one way of putting this right.) Other groups have worked out a rota so that several people do it between them and perhaps are on duty once a term.

If you *can* persuade the children to go into the creche so well and good. (Serving their drinks and biscuits in 'their' room and having an attractive selection of toys are a help in this.) But if the clingy ones refuse to be parted from Mum, don't insist. If they are clingy, they are usually also fairly quiet, and if supplied with a couple of picture books will often sit mouse-like on their mother's knee. It is far better to have your friend listening to the speaker, accompanied by her toddler, than it is for her to stay away because he won't be parted from her.

*Secretary*

Someone has to be responsible for the paper work. Speakers will have to be booked, by letter or by telephone, and reminded of the date just beforehand. If you decide to have printed invitation cards or programmes, these will have to be ordered, and invitations will have to be written and delivered. (Whether you decide to have specially printed cards or not, some form of written reminder is almost essential.) Often the Secretary looks after arranging the speakers, and someone else takes on the task of getting the invitations out. It all depends on the woman-power that you have available, but do make sure that those doing the jobs know exactly where their responsibilities begin and end or you may end up with two speakers arriving to speak when no invitations have been sent out, or vice versa!

If you can enlist this amount of help then you are fortunate. but many groups have functioned very well with a committee of two or three. Just adapt these suggestions to your own needs and plan accordingly.

*What about money?*

Coffee mornings need not be expensive to run. Your basic needs will be money for refreshments, postage and telephone calls. You may decide to give a small gift to the speaker if she lives locally: you should certainly offer her her fare or money for petrol if she has had to travel from out of town. Often the Secretary looks after the money side of things as well, but if you have someone willing and able to be Treasurer so much the better. She will need to keep a note of what is put into the kitty and what is spent, and look after the float.

***Where does the money come from?***

Usually those Christians who are committed to the venture give when they meet to pray and plan. You may like to have a bowl out on these occasions so that people can contribute quietly if they wish to do so.

Whether to allow the guests who come to the meetings to give money is rather a vexed question. We did not accept money from anyone at the meetings at first and then several people said that they wanted to give something towards the refreshments and really pressed the point.

Eventually, we simply left a bowl out on the table, and those who wanted to give something did so, while others did not. Money matters were never discussed unless the guests brought it up and everyone seemed happy with this arrangement.

***How often should we meet?***

This depends entirely on how much the committee can cope with, and how often your guests are free to come. Most groups operate within term-time only, and find that to meet once a week is necessary if they are doing a series of Bible Studies. If you want to have a speaker every time, a weekly meeting will probably over-stretch your resources, but mothers with pre-school children seem to like to meet reasonably frequently, and fortnightly seems to be most popular with this age group. Some groups have found that a monthly meeting keeps people interested, without demanding too much of them, in terms of time; others meet less frequently still, perhaps once or twice a term.

It is better to meet a little less frequently and cover every meeting with prayer, using the time in between to deepen relationships with those who come, than to be so rushed by a weekly commitment that the committee rarely pray together and you begin to regard your guests, not as friends, but as 'meeting fodder', because you only ever see them in a crowd.

# 9 Get set

Once you have decided how often you will meet, you will have to plan a programme. Whom do you ask to speak and what should they speak about? Where will you find the speakers and what makes one suitable for this kind of meeting and another not?

We shall be thinking about the speaker in more detail later on, but for now it is sufficient to say that he or she should be able to speak about his or her faith in terms that an ordinary person can understand. An informal chat is needed rather than a sermon and for this reason 'professional preachers' may not be your best first choice. The subject that you choose and the speaker whom you invite to your very first meeting needs especially careful consideration. Remember that the people you invite will not know what to expect and they may be rather wary, or afraid of being 'got-at'. So aim to set them thinking and asking questions rather than trying to present them with the whole counsel of God on that first day.

### *Know your audience*

You need to suit your programme to the needs of those who come, and answer the questions that they really are asking, rather than the ones that *you* think they *ought* to be. So the first essential in programme planning is a realistic assessment of your group. Are they women with a background of occasional church attendance, or was their wedding day the last occasion on which they stepped over the church threshold? Are they predominantly young-marrieds or have you got a cross-section of ages? Are some of them divorcees, widows or separated from their husbands? What problems are they coping with in day-to-day living? Jealous toddlers, rebellious teenagers? Elderly and frail relatives? Perhaps they have a husband who is out of work or grappling with business worries? Have the Mormons or Jehovah's Witnesses been visiting in your areas recently? Do you live in a multi-racial community, or are your neighbours more likely to be suffering from 'new town blues'? These are all details in the overall picture that you have to consider.

### *Know your aims*

The other essential thing is to know what you are aiming at – for if you aim at nothing you are sure to hit it! Presumably your aim for this group is to lead the women who come into a personal relationship with Jesus Christ and then to help the immature Christians to grow stronger in their faith. But you have to recognise the fact that the majority will probably consider themselves Christians already, either because they were born in a so-called 'Christian' country, or were christened as infants, or went to Sunday School as a child, or 'try to live a good life' – there are some very confused people around today.

***Lay the foundations***

So your first, very delicate task is to clarify what a Christian really is, and the fact that Jesus Christ can be a living reality in the life of ordinary people.

How can this be done? There are various possibilities. You may like to tackle it from the children's viewpoint and have a series of talks on 'Teaching our children about God'. The great advantage of this approach is that no one feels 'got-at', and they can admit their ignorance of how to put these things across to their children, without it being too personal. Under this general heading you can consider: 'Explaining God'; 'Who was Jesus?'; 'Which are the important Bible stories?'; 'When should we start to pray?'; 'Children in church'; 'Explaining about death'; 'Making the festivals (Harvest, Easter, Christmas, etc.) real'. As you can see, there is enormous scope here.

Then there is personal experience. Think of the problems that we all have to face in family living and to which people really do want to find out if God offers a solution. We started our coffee morning programme with a series on 'Teaching children about God', and the next term followed this with 'Coping with Crisis' when we asked a widow, an unmarried daughter caring for her elderly mother, a woman whose husband had had a nervous breakdown, another whose husband had been made redundant, and a mother of handicapped twins, to speak to us. They were all committed Christians and their theme was how God had enabled them to cope in these crisis situations.

Another area where faith and day-to-day living

can be linked together is when Christians speak about how their faith affects their job. Have you got a Christian doctor, dentist, social worker, factory worker, businessman, or school teacher living near you? If they can be free for an hour during the day, what they have to say can be of great interest.

Then you might like to have a number of people speaking about 'Why I go to church'. This could be an opportunity for your minister to explain why he does the job he does; it could allow a Sunday School teacher to tell your group the value she sees in Christain education for the young, and perhaps two ordinary church members of different ages could round things off by explaining what the church means to them. Plenty of possibilities here!

***Don't be afraid of the Bible!***

So much for testimonies. They can be very valuable, but there are other things that need exploring. Many people are utterly ignorant about the Bible and what it says, and having suddenly met people for whom it is all important, are genuinely interested to know what the Bible teaches. What does it have to say about family life, money, the future, worry and anxiety, social issues and so on? Don't be afraid to go back to the Bible and aim to encourage people to buy a modern translation and start finding out some of these things for themselves. Make it easy for them by having some inexpensive Bibles available for sale (your local Christian bookshop will probably be delighted to supply them to you on a sale or return basis) with helpful explanatory notes or booklets. If you can establish what a Christian is, some of the basic things that she believes, and that God speaks to us through the Bible, you have laid a firm foundation for future growth.

### *Should you always have a speaker?*

Not necessarily! In some ways, speakers are an easy option, because all the hostess has to do is invite her, introduce her and thank her! In a way, the responsibility for the spiritual content of the meeting rests on the speaker's shoulders (although let it never be forgotten that the committee should have a total commitment to prayer support before, during and after the meeting). But variety is good, and there are many helpful filmstrips, some accompanied by tape-recorded commentary which bring a point of view home in a very telling way. Tapes, too, can be used in smaller groups, especially as a discussion starter, but do make sure that you listen to the tape beforehand, and that your equipment is in good working order and can be clearly heard all round the room. If you use a longer tape as the main talk, do have something on which people can focus their attention – otherwise concentration can lapse. Imagine that you had a tape from a missionary for instance. You might pin a map of the area in which she was working on the wall above the tape recorder, or stick a collection of pictures of the country or the missionary at work onto a board. Little touches like this can make the vital difference between a memorable meeting and one that you quickly forget.

### *Are discussions a good idea?*

The short answer is 'sometimes'. The group will need to get to know each other and begin to feel relaxed before they are able to share their thoughts, so save a whole morning of discussion until you have been meeting for some while. It can be a good idea to have an opportunity for questions at the end of a talk, although this needs sensitive handling by the hostess. Sometimes, questions and general chat can detract from a very challenging talk, and in this instance it is better to close with a brief prayer, thank the speaker, and encourage her to mingle with the guests, so that individuals can put their private queries if they wish to do so.

A morning of discussion can be a useful way of summing up the questions raised by a session of talks, or even one talk in particular. Do remember though, that it needs careful preparation with a brief general introduction to explain the subject and then specific questions for the group to consider. And if it is not to be just 'our opinions', you will need to have a note of the Bible verses that relate to the subject, so that God's standard is made clear. Since many people lack the confidence to open their mouths in a group of a dozen or more, it is a good idea to divide into three's or four's and move the chairs into clusters, so that every one can be encouraged to have their say. Each small group will need a leader who has seen the questions beforehand – not so that she can lecture the group with her findings, but so that she can help the others to come to their own conclusions. An egg-timer or kitchen 'pinger' set for five minutes can be used as a signal to move from one question to the next and ensure that each question is tackled and no time is wasted. The leaders may like to report back the findings of their group to the whole meeting at the end of the morning – if you do this, limit the report to one question per group or it may be rather repetitive.

### *Subjects or speakers?*

Which comes first? Do you look around and see what speakers are available and then plan your programme around 'their' subjects, or do you plan your subjects first, and then prayerfully consider who should be asked to tackle them? Both methods are used, but I firmly believe that the second method is the right one. Admittedly, it can be difficult to know what the needs of your group will be if you are planning your meetings a long while in advance, and the Holy Spirit can over-rule so that a long-booked speaker turns out to be just the right one for that particular point in time. But most speakers would much prefer to know what you are aiming at and how you see her talk fitting into the general scheme of things, than to be told, 'Oh, speak on anything you feel led to. I'm sure the Holy Spirit will bless'!

***Write to your speaker***

It may seem easier just to pick up the telephone and ask your selected speaker to come on the date you have chosen, but on the whole, it is better to write. This gives the speaker time to pray about your invitation and means that she has a record of the date, time, place and subject on which she is being asked to talk, which she can refer to later. Or at least that is what she should have! Look at these two sample letters and decide which one you would prefer to receive.

*Either:*

Dear Mrs. X,

I am the Secretary of the 'Pause for Thought' group which meets on Thursday mornings, twice monthly, at 46, Elm Tree Close. We wondered whether you could come and speak to us in June. If you can come, please would you let me know the title of your talk? I look forward to hearing from you.

Yours sincerely,

*Or:*
Dear Mrs. X,

I am the Secretary of the 'Pause for Thought' group which meets on the first and third Thursday mornings of each month in term-time at 46, Elm Tree Close. We meet for coffee at 10.30 a.m. and invite a speaker to chat informally for about 15-20 minutes on a topic of Christian concern, usually starting about 11 a.m. We finish the formal part of the proceedings promptly at 11.30 a.m. although some people do stay on longer to chat.

We have about 20 folk who come more or less regularly, and the majority of them are young mothers with toddlers, with perhaps five or six in the 30-45 age bracket. We do have a creche but there are always one or two tots who insist on staying with their mothers.

70% of the people who come are not committed Christians and rarely, if ever, attend church. Those who do, worship at our local parish church. We are very excited by the fact that two of our 'regulars' were converted last week, and so we are aiming to help them (and the other Christians) to grow in their faith as well as introducing the others to a personal faith. Our theme for next term is 'Why I believe', and we should be very glad if you could speak on 'Why I believe the Bible'. The two previous speakers will be tackling, 'Why I believe in God' and 'Why I believe in Prayer', and the other two topics we shall cover are 'Heaven and Hell' and 'The return of Jesus'. Big subjects, I know, and difficult to cover in the time, but if you assume total ignorance and just cover the basics, you'll be aiming at the right level.

We should be so glad if you could come on – June or – June, 1980, and will be praying for you as you consider whether this is right for you.

[Don't put that bit in unless you intend to do it!] If you are able to come I will contact you again nearer the time and send you directions of how to find Elm Tree Close. I enclose a stamped addressed envelope for your reply.

Yours sincerely,

You may feel that I have overdone the details in the second letter, but speaking from experience, I can assure you that those are the things that a speaker *needs* to know if she is to prepare adequately.

If the speaker accepts your invitation, keep her letter carefully and during the week before her intended visit, telephone her (preferably) or write, to make sure that she has remembered the date, that she knows how to get to your meeting place, whether she needs meeting from a bus or train, and whether there are any questions she wants to ask.

Is it worth going to all that trouble for a small group of people? Of course it is! Your speaker will appreciate the care that you have taken, and, even more important, will be able to give of her very best, as she prepares and finally speaks. And that, after all, is the whole object of the exercise!

# 10 Go

'It won't be so bad once we've got this first one over,' I groaned to my husband when the day of our first coffee morning dawned and I awoke from a dream-filled sleep, with butterflies in my tummy and a longing to be miles away, mixed with excitement and anticipation.

'The first time that you do anything is always the most difficult,' he replied, trying to be comforting and only half succeeding. 'You'll learn by your mistakes.' And so we did.

I used to be under the impression that if I am doing what God has told me to do, things ought to proceed pretty smoothly. I have now learned differently. The devil doesn't like it when we step out in faith with God and he lets us know it. The minor disasters that tend to occur and the doubts and fears that press in should be a comfort (in a funny kind of way) rather than an indication that we have got our guidance wrong. After all, Satan is most active when he feels threatened. The sure antidote to panic is to remember that *we* are not required to convert anyone. All that we can do is to prepare the way with our practical arrangements, our own spiritual preparation, and our prayers, so that the Holy Spirit can work in his own time and in his own way.

All the same, the devil will try to put a spoke in the wheel and he is not fussy about the methods that he uses. Sometimes it's the mundane practical details that get snarled up, and at other times it is people who cause the problems. Your experiences will not be identical to mine, any more than I have had to cope with every problem that other groups have faced. But these are some of the lessons that others have learned – to be forewarned is to be forearmed!

***Lesson One**: Other people's children always do the unexpected*

I would have said that our house was fairly toddler proof when we started the coffee mornings. After all, my own children were $4\frac{1}{2}$ years, $2\frac{1}{2}$ years and 5 months old respectively. But what I had forgotten was that although *they* knew that the dog and the cat were quite harmless and would tolerate gentle loving, other people's children were either prone to love the animals to death or to scream at the sight of them. So after that first morning, when the dog hid in a cupboard and the cat nearly left home for good, the pets were put into the garden or shut away in a bedroom, out of kindness to them and to us.

It had never been necessary to remove the key from the door of the downstairs cloakroom either. Angus and David had never shown any inclination to lock it. But one small girl, with a passion for privacy, locked herself in, right in the middle of the talk – which, incidentally, was being given by her mother! Her screams completely drowned the whispered commands of the 'Creche

Aunty' to 'turn the key darling, or take it out and push it under the door' and it was only with great difficulty that we persuaded Rachel to open the small window and allow herself to be lifted out. (Her mother, meanwhile, continued her talk, completely unaware of what was going on.) At the end of the morning we had to employ the services of the daintiest mother present to squeeze in through the window and retrieve the key – thus allowing everyone else to get at their coats. After that the key was placed on a hook high up on the door frame on coffee morning days, so that the adults could have privacy, but the children were safe.

***Lesson Two: Start and finish promptly***

There will always be one or two people who arrive at least ten minutes before the stated time and others who will rush in ten minutes late. It is hard to know what to do with the first group (especially if you are still getting things ready) and it is tempting to wait for the late-comers, or offer to stop and make a cup of coffee once they do arrive. But restrain yourself. If you get into the habit of 'waiting a minute for Mary because she's definitely coming', people will drift in later and later and it becomes increasingly difficult to finish on time.

Most people find it practical to start serving coffee as soon as the first guest arrives. This acts as an ice-breaker. Another useful ploy is to put some magazines of general interest out on a table or window-sill so that if you are really unable to sit and chat, you can encourage your 'early bird' to relax and look at a magazine until other people come in. As for late-comers, keep them seats by the door, *never*, reproach them for being late and offer them a cup of coffee *after* the meeting. In this way the proceedings can get under way with a minimum of disruption.

***Lesson Three:* Lots of people need help in forming relationships**

I don't know whether it is just in Britain that people can spend hours in each other's company, sitting side-by-side, or facing each other with knees almost touching, and never say a word. But you have only got to travel by train to know that it is true. And a group of people drinking coffee in your sitting room will tend to act as if they're on a train unless *you* do something positive about it. So don't be afraid to perform some introductions and not just the 'Jane, this is Mary' variety, but 'Jane, this is Mary. She has a daughter at the Community Centre Playgroup too'. This gives Jane and Mary a peg on which to hang their conversation. Obviously, one person cannot keep the entire conversational pot boiling and this is why it is important that those who know each other should not get into a huddle in the kitchen, but be circulating within the group. It gets easier as the weeks pass and people begin to know one another, but often there will be newcomers (you hope) and those who are very shy and this need to help people to mix is one that has to be constantly borne in mind.

***Lesson Four:* Christians are needy too**

In the past there has been a dangerous tendency within the evangelical wing of the Christian Church to concentrate all our efforts on bringing people to the point where they find a personal faith. Once they have committed their lives to Jesus Christ we have labelled them 'saved' and assumed that they could now be left to their own devices while we turned our attention to the next 'seeker'.

This, of course, is quite wrong. The point of personal commitment is just the beginning of a new life and a Christian needs to grow spiritually from that day onwards. Sadly, some Christians never grow beyond babyhood, and others get stuck in spiritual adolescence, with unresolved conflicts and personality problems hidden under a thin 'Christian' veneer. So don't expect perfection from anyone!

If you bear this in mind, you will be disarming one of Satan's most potent weapons, for if he can cause petty jealousies, hurt feelings and misunderstandings among any group of people (and women, for some reason, seem to be particularly susceptible to this ploy) he will do so and wreak absolute havoc in the process. So as those of you who are Christians meet to pray and work together, you need to bear four things very firmly in mind:

(a) Each one who comes to the group wants to be valued for the person she is now. Perhaps there are those who have few obvious talents, or an irritating personality; never mind. God loves her as she is – will you?

(b) Each one who comes to the group needs to feel that her contribution is important, even if all that she does is to come. Many people have hidden talents, which, if recognised and brought into use, can be an enormous blessing to the individual concerned, as well as to the group as a whole. So don't let the very capable two or three do all the work, but accept offers of help, and look out for things that the 'quiet ones' can do; then encourage and praise all the way.

(c) Each one who comes to the group is on a voyage of discovery – about herself! You may feel that you know what makes you tick, but do you? 'I never knew that I had a temper until I had three children under three years old,' confessed Ethel ruefully, 'and I never realised how little patience I had until I tried to work with Cherry.' And so say all of us! God uses close encounters with others in his family to smooth off rough corners and to make each one of us more like Jesus. It can only be for our good if we remember one thing. *Never grouse about one Christian to another.* If you have a complaint about the way a fellow Christian has behaved, pray about it. Look at your own attitudes; you will usually find that you, too, are at fault somewhere along the line. And if you still feel that the matter needs dealing with, *go to the person concerned*, and humbly and lovingly, tell her how you feel. (On the other side of the coin, if you hear directly or indirectly that you have offended someone else, go and talk it over with them.) Oh yes! I know that it is hard to do, and if you are on the receiving end of the criticism it is hard to accept. But left unattended to, it can cause bitterness and dissension, and a venture for God can be ruined, just by gossip and in-fighting.

(d) Each one who comes to the group needs hope and purpose, for the future. No one, from the leader to the very quietest newcomer, is self-sufficient. Everyone needs loving; everyone needs caring. prayerful support. Do Christians ever get depressed? Yes they do. Do Christians ever feel that they are unlovable and unprofitable servents? Yes, of course. We have only to read our Bibles to know that. And it is often those who are in the forefront of the battle and who seem so strong in the faith who are most in need of someone to say, 'I want you to know that I'm praying for you – is there any special need at the moment?'

### *Lesson Five: Pity the poor speaker!*

'Someone who is in the forefront of the battle!' That just about sums the speaker up. And it is so easy to think that because someone can put her thoughts into words, and share those words with other people, she has 'arrived', and belongs to a race apart. What rubbish! That process of putting thoughts into words will have taken her hours of prayerful consideration, and she may well step over your threshold with a dry mouth, butterflies in her tummy and knees that feel scarcely capable of supporting her.

Perhaps you are tired, anxious about the morning ahead and have problems with your mother-in-law – she may well be in just the same position. So even though you have briefed her well in your letter of invitation, don't just give her a cup of coffee and leave her to the chattering throng. Show her where the bathroom is and ask if she would prefer to chat with folk beforehand, or have a few minutes to collect her thoughts in the peace and quiet of the bedroom. Try to have someone available from amongst your helpers to pray with her and answer any questions that she may have. And when the meeting proper begins, introduce her in a way that helps your guests to relate to her, rather than reading out a list of her accomplishments (if she has any) which makes her sound like 'Wonder Woman'! Keep the introduction brief so that she has time to give her talk and thank her warmly afterwards. Let her know beforehand whether you intend to close in prayer, whether you would like her to do so, or whether you usually go straight on to questions.

And before she goes, give her her expenses if she has had to travel *any* distance. A book token or a gift voucher is very nice but garages are awkward about exchanging those for petrol, and they certainly aren't considered legal tender on the train! So do take the trouble to check up what the fare will be by ringing the station beforehand, or work out petrol costs at so much per mile. The average car does between 25–30 miles to the gallon, so look at current pump prices and take it from there. Some speakers may decline their expenses and that is their privilege, but always offer them and *never* say, 'What do I owe you?' That is something that you should know.

***Lesson Six:* *Prayer changes things***

You will have undoubtedly prayed about the coffee morning or meeting beforehand, you should certainly pray about it afterwards. But what about while it is going on? This woman is mad, you're probably thinking, how can I be doing all the other things that she suggests *and* pray as well? You can't. Well, you can't do more than fire the occasional 'arrow' prayer heavenwards, anyway. But what about some of the elderly folk in your church who are unable to get out much. Would they pray, right where they are, while the coffee morning is in progress? If you can enlist prayer support like this, I can assure you that it does make a difference. I have spoken at many meetings where it has been a battle all the way. I have spoken at a few where I have had such freedom of expression and known such a sense of God's presence that the room has almost seemed to hum. And when I commented on the atmosphere afterwards, I have been told – 'the prayer battery was at work'.

If you do ask people to pray, make sure that they have plenty of background information – without betraying any confidence of course. Tell them who you expect to come, their needs, any special problems and the speaker's name and subject. Afterwards, let them know how things have gone, and make them feel part of this venture for God, as indeed they are.

# 11 Caring enough

There is a great temptation to feel that having invited friends to your home (or taken them to someone else's) to hear the good news about Jesus, you have 'done your bit' and can then sit back and relax. In fact the reverse is true. Once they have heard what God demands of them, they are accountable to him and you have a great responsibility to water the seed that has been sown, caring for them in practical ways and being available to answer questions as they arise. In other words to 'follow-up'.

'What do you do to follow-up the guests who come to your coffee mornings?' This was the last section on the questionnaire which many groups filled in, in order to provide me with information for this book. But this question was left blank by several groups. Others wrote, 'We don't do enough of it'; 'We're discussing how to do this effectively'; 'We feel that we fail in this area'; and other comments along the same lines. Why is this so? What is so difficult about spiritual horticulture? Why do we not see the seed growing into fruiting, healthy plants that go on to reproduce themselves?

Perhaps one of the reasons why we often see comparatively little fruit is because we don't *expect* to see much. We give lip-service to the fact that Jesus can and does touch the lives of people today but add mentally 'but I can't imagine it happening to so-and-so'. All through the gospels, Jesus hammers the lesson home that faith is *vital* if we want to see his power released. Look at his dealings with the two blind men (Matthew 9:27–31). 'Do you believe that I can ...' he asked them, 'Let it happen, then, just as you believe.' If he said that to you, how much would happen?

'Dream great dreams! Plan great plans, and pray great prayers,' says Luis Palau, the South American evangelist. Basing his thinking on John 14:12–14, he points out that Jesus has promised that *all* his disciples have the potential to do even greater things than he has done (in extent) and that anything that glorifies God can be asked for with absolute certainty. 'The Father is glorified through the triumphs of the Son, brought about by the prayers of the disciples.' What potential!

So faith and prayer are two essential factors in follow-up – and perhaps can be compared with providing the correct soil and plenty of water for a germinating seed in the garden. But just as young plants have to be staked and protected from extremes of temperature, so there are certain practical things that can be done too.

First of all we need to remember that individuals must never become a statistic on your invitation list. If they come to your home once a fortnight (or whenever), that is no reason for letting other social contacts lapse, however busy you may be. Invite two or three folk from the group to come in for a cup of coffee in the intervening time, so that you can all get to know each other better. Be ready to accept invitations too – if you are willing to be interested in their concerns they will be interested in yours. True friendship is never one-sided.

The whole undertaking of visiting and being visited should not fall on one person. Christians who bring their friends should be encouraged to accept their responsibility to follow them up, as well as to develop friendships with others in the group.

In Jean's group each of the committee takes a section of names on the invitation list as the group for which she cares. She delivers the invitations, pops in casually to see that all is well if a 'regular' is missing, arranges transport for anyone who needs it and takes an interest in any newcomers from 'her' area, taking the initiative in introducing them to others if required. If there can be a sense of caring developed and practical Christianity demonstrated, this often speaks louder than a thousand words.

In Evelyn's village the Christians have done this in a very real way. Mary has a car and is willing to take people into town for shopping when she goes; to supply transport for a hospital appointment; or get a prescription to the chemist. Joyce's children are at school and so she is willing to baby-sit with pre-schoolers if Mum is ill or simply needs a few hours off. She has even been known to take a fractious baby into her own home for a couple of nights to give an exhausted mother a chance to sleep. Jan has a freezer and always keeps an emergency supply of ready-cooked meals which she takes to anyone who is under pressure through illness or other circumstances, and Sally is the laundry lady who is called upon in similar circumstances. June has a warm and friendly personality and pops in to visit newcomers with details of the area's activities soon after they move in, and so it goes on. These

Christians radiate the love of their Lord and their friends are intrigued and challenged as a result.

'There are a number of folk who have been coming along for ages and we *still* haven't seen any response!' sighed Sally. 'How *can* we get people to make a real commitment to Christ? There must be some way of pushing them past the point of "almost decided"!' Sally was letting her enthusiasm run away with her. She needed to be reminded that 'a man (or woman) convinced against his will, is of the same opinion still'! and that it is the work of the Holy Spirit alone to convince an individual of her need of God and to bring them to a point of conviction and conversion. There is a danger of 'picking unripe fruit' if we try to push someone into a decision for which she is not ready and which is not therefore truly hers. She may appear to agree just to please you, but no true spiritual growth will result. On the other hand, a real work of the Holy Spirit may be slow, but it will last.

Take Margery for example. Pat met Margery when she was desperately lonely and so hard pressed by the demands of four small children that she was contemplating suicide. Pat invited her along to the local coffee morning and Margery quickly found a host of new friends and her interest in spiritual matters was roused. For several months she was one of the most regular attenders, then her husband began to object. Roger was a scientist, hard-headed and factual in his approach to everything and he was proud of being an atheist. He poured cold water on Margery's growing excitement about Christian things, and eventually she began to refuse the invitations that she had previously accepted with such enthusiasm.

Pat was disappointed but undeterred. She remained friendly but made no reference to her faith, unless Margery brought the subject up. She prayed and waited. Three years passed and Pat began to feel discouraged. Her prayers for Margery dwindled. And then it happened. A town-wide evangelistic crusade was held and on the very last night, Margery went along. No one invited her; no one went with her. On that night, Margery committed her life to Jesus Christ. Pat was delighted but also alarmed. Roger had decided to emigrate. Margery was due to leave for Canada with the rest of her family in less than three months' time. How could such a spiritual babe possibly survive an upheaval like that? Well, she could and she did. Margery was baptised before she left England and when she arrived in Canada she found a Bible-based church. She was quickly drawn into the family of God there and in spite of her husband's continued opposition, grew and flourished as the months went by. Eventually, her children came to share her faith and Roger's atheism slowly changed to open-mindedness. She was in God's hand and no one could pull her out again.

Margery is a rather unusual example of a new Christian who was given extra strength for extraordinary needs. Because she left her familiar surroundings so quickly, she did not fall into the trap of regarding the outreach group as a substitute for a church, which ensnares some young Christians. She *had* to find a church, but does everyone?

We have not discussed the relationship of a home-based outreach group to the local church and clergy and this does need to be considered. Some groups are, of course, a direct arm of a local church, known as such by those who come, and supported by the prayers and interest of the minister and other members of the congregation. When this is the case, new converts are usually channelled into the church quite naturally and their 'infant-care' is shared by the whole church fellowship. This is right and should always be the ideal that is aimed at. But what happens when a group of Christians have got together on an area rather than a church basis, and perhaps some of the churches in the area are more dead than alive? What dealings (if any) should you have with the clergy then, and where do you send the new converts, if Christians within the group attend different churches?

The first thing to remember is that Christians are to show love and courtesy to one another. So if you are working in a small community like a village or a local housing area, it is only polite to inform the ministers of your local churches about the vision that God has given you. If you are working on an interdenominational basis, you need to stress that you see yourself as building a bridge between the churches and those you invite, and assure the ministers that converts will be channelled into the churches and no 'sheep stealing' is intended! If you operate on a town-wide scale, holding a large meeting in a central location, then you would be wise to contact all the clergy and ask them to make the meeting known among their own congregation. This often has the added bonus of bringing along women who may be regular church-goers without having a personal relationship with God.

All Christians need to put down roots within a church fellowship, and a home-based outreach meeting is no substitute for that. The leader of the group needs to encourage converts to get settled in a spiritual home quickly and the first step in doing this is to discover whether they have had any previous church connections. If they have, then the local church of that denomination should be the first one to be considered, even if you don't go there yourself. But what should one do if that church has little spiritual life in it (as far as one can tell) and the minister takes a non-Biblical standpoint? The first answer is pray! If the new convert wants to go there, leave it to the Holy Spirit to open her eyes to what is missing. If, on the other hand, she has no special preferences (as most often happens) or would prefer to come with you, take her along and if your particular form of service does not meet her needs, link her up with another living fellowship which does.

But what about the new Christian whose husband makes it difficult, if not impossible, for her to get to church at all? How can she be encouraged and helped to grow? *Step one* is to keep the ideal of church membership constantly in mind, even if it is not possible at a given time. *Step two* is to arrange a time when a more mature Christian can do some basic Bible study with her, possibly on a one-to-one basis, so that she receives a grounding in the basic doctrines. *Step three* is to assemble a small library of tapes and books that beginners can benefit from and can borrow, return and discuss, at times which do not clash with the demands of husband and family. A wife in this position longs to share her new-found faith with her husband, but she needs wise counsel. It is not a good witness for a wife to be constantly dashing out to meetings and making her husband feel rejected and alienated. Nor is it wise to nag him about his sinfulness or lack of interest in God. A wife who is *more* loving and caring is going to make far more impact than one who constantly criticises and seems to find her new-found friends more attractive than those who should have her first consideration.

So follow-up your contacts, feed your young Christians and expect great things from God. And never forget that although you cannot do the work of the Holy Spirit for him, you *can* and should be an effective channel for him to use.

# 12 Digging deeper

Most of us find it fairly easy to invite someone to a coffee morning or other type of meeting, where we can all sit back comfortably, just one of a number, and listen to someone else doing the talking, and many people are pleased to come. But when we mention 'Bible Study', we often get a different reaction.

The shy ones may be terrified of having to *say* something, and hastily find something else to do on that morning. The less-intellectual may feel that the Bible is far too difficult for them to tackle and the 'know-it-all Nellies' often dismiss the Bible as a load of legends anyway. Even the Christians in the group may have their reservations. They know that it is important to progress from listening to others share their discoveries about God, to really digging into his word for themselves, but they are afraid that if they had to lead a Bible Study group, they might let God down by not knowing all the answers.

If you are feeling like that – take comfort. Many others who have felt exactly the same before you, having taken the plunge, would say – like the hardy bathers on a British summer day – 'Once you're in, the water's lovely!'

It had been a long, hot day at the Worldwide Evangelisation Crusade Missionary Training College in Tasmania. Marie, the Principal's wife, had been hard at work preparing meals for fifty people, canning fruit, jam-making and looking after her two small daughters. The chores were almost finished and all that she wanted was a refreshing shower and a few minutes peace and quiet before bed.

The doorbell rang, 'There's a lady to see you Mrs. D.' The student who had answered the door, popped her head into the sitting room, and Marie sighed.

'Oh, not now! Can't she come back tomorrow?' she asked wearily. The student shrugged, 'She was very insistent that she saw you tonight ... said that it's rather urgent ...'

Marie groaned inwardly and went to invite her guest inside. Joan was in trouble. The wife of a local butcher, she had a colourful reputation in the town and her marriage was cracking up fast. She came to Marie for help and was told that the answer to her problems could be found in one place – the Bible. Would she be prepared to study and find the answers that God offers if Marie helped her? Joan agreed that she would. Together they studied the Bible and within a few weeks, Joan had committed her life to Jesus. The change in her life was startling!

Thrilled by her new discoveries, she gossiped the gospel over the garden fence as she delivered the meat, and her customers were intrigued. Soon Joan brought Pat along for Bible study, Pat was joined by others and over the next two years the group grew by leaps and bounds – twenty ... forty ... sixty ... seventy, and still they came.

Eventually, a house could not contain them all and they had to meet at a church with lots of classrooms and divide into a host of small groups.

Marie used a book on basic doctrine for her textbook in the early days, but then the book went out of print and she had to prepare her own studies. Working just one week ahead, she prepared the study, and duplicated notes so that each woman had her own copy. The system was that the passage for the week was split up into daily readings with two or three questions assigned for each day. Each individual did her own studying during the week and then at the weekly meeting the answers to the questions were discussed. After the group members had shared their findings and raised any queries that they might have, the group leader summed up and set the scene for the following week's study. The Holy Spirit really got to work.

On the mainland Australia's Christian Women's Conventions International have devised a similar system. They called it *Know Your Bible Course.* This course was aimed particularly at Christian women, to help them grow and mature, while Marie's *Geared for Growth,* was especially useful in evangelistic work (although, since the Holy Spirit is not bound by 'courses', both approaches benefited Christians and non-Christians alike). Now both of these Bible study courses are being used in many countries of the world, and these methods of individual study, backed up by group discussion, are having far-reaching effects.

That is one example of what God has done because one woman put aside her own convenience to help another woman study his word. There are, of course, many people who have done the same, and, using different systems and methods of study, have seen non-Christians find a faith and committed Christians grow stronger. But which method is the best for your group? If you are already involved in an outreach meeting, should Bible study form part of your overall strategy, or is it something to be used 'instead of' rather than 'as well as'?

If you have a nice tidy group of non-believers, active seekers, new converts or aged saints (!) it is relatively easy to find an answer, because everybody needs the same approach. Unfortunately, life is rarely that well organised and so usually you will be catering for a mixture of these individuals, plus others who cannot be classified.

You may find it best to have a separate Bible Study Group meeting on a different day and at a different time from your regular meeting for perhaps a six or eight week session and then a break. This is a particularly good idea if your 'speaker' meetings are infrequent and you have longish clear spells in between. It also has the obvious advantage of sorting out those who are really interested from those who are not.

The disadvantage is that some people may find it hard to allot that extra time, while others will be wary of committing themselves to a weekly meeting.

The alternative is to integrate a Bible study with your programme of other meetings. When groups meet fortnightly, they often have a speaker once a month and a Bible study on the alternative fortnight. They find that people who would not come along to a series of Bible studies accept them if they are part of an overall series, and in the course of discussion often reveal needs which would never be aired in front of a speaker. When this approach is used, some groups ask the speaker to tackle a certain subject and then they do a Bible study on the same subject at their next meeting. If you try this, do remember that you are bound to have some at the Bible study who did not hear the speaker and be ready with a brief resume of the talk for their benefit. And realise that if you want to use the 'homework' approach, you will have to embark on a weekly meeting, as a monthly gap is far too long.

### *What method and materials would suit us?*

We have already discussed the factors that you have to consider when you are choosing speakers for a group, and the same things apply to your choice of subjects and materials for a Bible study. A most helpful book on the whole subject of Bible Study Groups is Tom Rees' *Breakthrough.* This gives many suggestions and actual examples of different methods that have been used with various groups, ages and backgrounds, and is well worth reading. In addition, several different organisations produce helpful notes and study outlines, and these are listed at the end of the chapter.

The basic material that you must have is a Bible. For a group with little knowledge of the Bible, a modern version, and preferably identical copies so that page numbers can be given, is ideal. In this group it is a good idea to major on one passage so that people are not embarrassed by not knowing where to find minor prophets or even major ones. It is important too, to avoid theological language and keep the whole study simple and applied to every day living and problems. And do not fall into the trap of deciding what the Holy Spirit should say and then manipulating the questions so that you make sure that he says it.

### *The Leader*

Being the leader does not mean that you should be able to answer every question. In fact, skilful leaders speak rarely and direct the group in such a way that they are hardly aware of it. The best approach is the one that says, 'Let's learn together' rather than 'I'm the teacher, you're the pupil'.

### *Preparation*

Preparation is essential. Your own spiritual preparation begins with prayer – for yourself; for those who come; and for the presence of the Holy Spirit to make the passage studied living and vital to all those who attend the meeting. Pray expectantly – believing that God *will* meet needs, solve problems and bring more people in.

Prepare the passage to be studied. Many of us fall into the trap of thinking that if we have an outline prepared for us, all we have to do is to flick through the questions the night before and all will be well. That is *not* the purpose of an outline. It is only intended to guide the leader and must never replace her own careful preparation. If the rest of the group are doing homework so must you – only more so. Look up references in several versions and compare them. Check up any doubtful points in a commentary or Bible Dictionary. Sort out in your own mind:

What the passage says
What the passage means
How the passage applies in practical terms.

### *Presentation*

1. Begin with a short prayer asking God to speak to you through his word.

2. Read the passage aloud. If it is very long, read the section to which the first two or three questions apply, and then read the next section before tackling subsequent questions.
3. When you pose the question suggest two minutes of silence while people consider their answers and then ask for contributions. It is sometimes helpful to ask a specific person to start the ball rolling on a given question, but don't let one person monopolise the discussion.
4. Keep an eye on the clock and make sure that all the questions are covered. You can always go back to discuss detail if there is time. How long should a Bible study last? An hour is a good length of time, but take into account the fact that some people's concentration span is more limited than others, and the creche helper cannot cope indefinitely. It is better to be too brief and have them wish it was longer than vice versa.
5. If there are conflicting points of view expressed about a question and there is no obviously 'right' answer, don't allow an argument to develop. Simply summarise what has been said and pass on to the next question.
6. Don't let the group get too large. A dozen is about the maximum for this type of study group and eight is considered ideal. Work on the divide and multiply principle, as the group begins to grow, start to train an assistant leader. Pray and prepare the studies together for a few weeks, take it in turns to lead the discussion and when the numbers warrant it, divide. It is not necessary to meet in two different places, unless you have people coming from a wide area and it is therefore more convenient to do so. You can meet in the same house, using different rooms and perhaps come together at the end of the hour for a brief summing up and closing prayer. At the end of a series of studies get together and highlight the

main themes, asking people to share what they have learned. Do not forget that what a person discovers for herself is far more important than what you tell her. And she will remember best what she puts into words. So lead from behind, expect to learn yourself, encourage everyone who comes to take part and see what God can do.

---

Many groups and societies provide excellent material for Bible Study Groups. Most will send lists or samples on request (but remember a stamped addressed envelope). Here are the names and addresses of some:

1. '*Geared for Growth*'
   The Word Worldwide,
   'Pleasant View',
   Prescot Road, Melling,
   Liverpool
   L31 1AR

   or

   The Word Worldwide,
   10 Prince Albert Road,
   Glasgow
   G12 9NW

   The individual study and group discussion method, started by Marie Dinnen. Especially geared for outreach groups.

2. '*Know Your Bible*'
   c/o Mrs. E. Bewsey,
   Morningside,
   Guildford Road,
   Cranleigh, Surrey
   GU6 8PG

   A similar system, but especially helpful to young Christians.

| | |
|---|---|
| 3. The Scripture Union,<br>130 City Road,<br>London<br>E.C.1<br><br>280 St. Vincent Street,<br>Glasgow G2<br><br>YMCA Buildings,<br>Wellington Street,<br>Belfast | Variety of aids for all age groups. |
| 4. Emmaus Bible School,<br>10 Hatley Road,<br>Bitterne,<br>Southampton<br>SO2 5NU | Intended for individual correspondence course, but supplied at Group Rates for 5 or more people when the leader marks the course. |
| 5. Fishers Fellowship,<br>96 Plaistow Lane,<br>Bromley,<br>Kent | Very comprehensive range of 60 study papers. |
| 6. Church Pastoral Aid Society,<br>Falcon Court,<br>32 Fleet Street,<br>London<br>E.C.4 | Excellent Falcon booklets on The Creed, The Lord's Prayer, and other subjects. |
| 7. Universities and Colleges Christian Fellowship,<br>39 Bedford Square,<br>London<br>WC1B 3EY | A useful how-to-lead a Bible study leaflet plus various outlines. |
| 8. Campus Crusade for Christ,<br>105 London Road,<br>Reading,<br>Berks. | Excellent series of booklets. |

| | |
|---|---|
| 9. The Navigators,<br>86b Coombe Road,<br>New Malden, Surrey<br>KT3 4RB | Wide range of aids, including well known memory system. |

# 13 The listening ear

One of the results of the exodus of women from their homes into the world of paid employment is that there are few people around to listen any more. And as the availability of listeners decreases, the numbers of those who desperately need someone to talk to about their problems, increase. Of course, there are the voluntary groups like the Marriage Guidance Council and the Samaritans, whose trained counsellors do a great deal to help people whose affairs have reached a crisis point, but many people will not turn to 'official' bodies like these until they are absolutely desperate, and maybe not even then.

Women (rather more than men) seem to need to talk a problem through. My husband gets quite exasperated with me at times because I want to discuss a given situation at great length, looking at umpteen possible courses of action and ending up by deciding on the solution that we had mentioned first. He, on the other hand, has accepted the first solution and has dismissed the matter from his mind. So women need to talk, and if you are known by your friends to be a Christian, who appears to them to have discovered some of the answers to life's problems, they are likely to want to come and talk to you.

Does that thought please or horrify you? Do you avoid close contact with the bereaved, the lonely and the sick, just because you don't know what to say? Do you find yourself weighed down by the problems of others and avoid their confidences if at all possible? Or perhaps you feel willing to listen, but quite unable to offer advice.

There are those who have a particular ministry of counselling and this is their gift. They don't need encouragement from me, but could well benefit from in-depth training to enable them to exercise that gift to the full. But the rest of us do have a responsibility, as Christians, to listen, to care and to help where we can, and it is a privilege that should be treasured rather than a penance to be endured with gritted teeth.

'Oh but ...' you may say, 'I have no training, no wisdom and very little patience! I can't solve my own problems half the time, so I certainly couldn't advise anyone else. I'd probably make a delicate situation worse if I put my oar in. I'd rather leave that sort of thing to those who know what they're doing.'

But if *you* are the one that your friend trusts and turns to – what then? Unlikely as it may seem to you at this moment, you could find yourself faced with a problem like Barbara did.

She was having lunch with her family one day when the doorbell rang. In the porch stood Maggie, tears streaming down her bruised face. Once inside, the sad story tumbled out. Her husband had just given her a vicious beating because, unknown to Maggie, their toddler had whiled away part of the morning by painting a pattern on the bathroom floor with her mother's nail varnish. Bob blamed Maggie for not supervising Susie more carefully, and had expressed his displeasure by emptying their meal into the dustbin and blacking both of Maggie's eyes.

Barbara was horrified. She had no idea that such things were going on right under her nose, and apparently it was not the first time that Bob had abused his wife in this way. Usually he simply put the bruises where they did not show! Maggie wanted help, and although she was not a committed Christian herself, she had come to the one person she knew who, as she put it, 'seemed to know where to turn'. Barbara felt completely out of her depth. But she could not turn her friend away, and as she talked to Maggie, and went, on her behalf, to others for advice, she began to understand what Paul meant when he told the Galatian Christians to 'share each others troubles and problems, and so obey our Lord's command' (Gal. 6:2, Living Bible).

Barbara learned a great deal from her dealings with Maggie. She discovered things about herself (including needs in her own life) and the way that she reacted to other people. She learned some of the ways that she could offer help. And since many of these things are principles which apply to anyone who is offering help and advice to others in trouble, let's look at them in more detail.

### *The Counsellor as a person*

The first thing that Barbara had to accept was that she was not an amateur psychologist, but an instrument in the hands of God, available for him to use, as much or as little as he chose.

She quickly realised too, that she needed a far greater love for other people, especially towards the obvious wrong-doer like Bob, and that this was not something that she could work up herself, but a gift that she had to ask God for.

As time went on, Barbara also came to see that deep problems like Maggie's would not go away in a week, or even a month, and that helping her meant a long term commitment to prayer and caring. Feeling very aware of her own inadequacy, Barbara turned to her pastor for advice. He impressed upon her that she must really lean on the Holy Spirit for wisdom and insight, and that as Maggie shared her problems, Barbara must listen to her, while also listening inwardly to the promptings of the Holy Spirit. Barbara asked for suggestions about books to lend – the pastor handed her one book: the Bible. 'There are other books, of course,' he said, 'but this is the most effective tool in the hands of any Christian counsellor. If you want to help anyone else, you must be familiar with the remedies that it offers.' Barbara went home and did some studying for herself.

### *Relating to other people*

Barbara would freely admit that she is one of those people who is rarely at a loss for words – and she had to learn to hold her tongue. Maggie's greatest need was to have someone who would listen, and to accept her lovingly for what she was – a confused and unhappy woman with her fair share of faults but her own particular gifts and good qualities too. This, Barbara found relatively easy to do. What was far harder was to repent of her own instinctive rejection of Bob. She came to realise that she had to see him as God saw him, a sinner, certainly, but one for whom Christ died. Her initial (and rather un-Christian!) reaction had been to advise Maggie to leave home, taking her daughter (who was the idol of Bob's life) with her, and thus to teach him a lesson. But Maggie was made of gentler stuff. She was prepared to stay, but she wanted life to be different. Barbara had to learn to keep her advice to herself, and to offer help to Maggie only in the areas in which she asked for it.

### *Sharing God's point of view*

As she searched the Bible for help to offer others, Barbara discovered a very interesting fact. The basic principles of counselling are set out as early as the second chapter of Genesis. When God put Adam and Eve in the Garden of Eden, they had the perfect environment in which to live as they had been designed to do. God laid down certain ground rules (Gen. 2:15) and if these were obeyed, a meaningful and happy life would follow. But when Eve and then Adam decided to disregard God's rules, guilt came into their lives and they immediately tried to cover their nakedness and vulnerability (Gen. 3:6). When God called them to account, Adam blamed his nakedness for his fear of God, rather than recognising the underlying cause – his disobedience. God confronted Adam with his basic sin of disobedience, and instead of recognising it and repenting of it, Adam promptly tried to pass the buck.

Barbara had to realise that Maggie's primary conflict was not with Bob, or with an unhappy marriage, but with God. By trying to live life by her own rules rather than God's, she was like an engine, out of gear to start with. When she had shared this with Maggie, Barbara had to try to help her to recognise that Bob was in the same position, and that his unreasonable anger and violence stemmed from the underlying problems of his conflict with God. The next step was to show Maggie the remedy for sin that the Bible talks about and how she could apply it to her own life.

This sounds very simple, and of course it is not. A problem as difficult and deep-rooted as Maggie and Bob's eventually needed expert help from a Christian psychiatrist and even then, in Bob's case, progress was painfully slow. But the fact remains that under the leading of the Holy Spirit, and with the support of others who could advise her, Barbara was able to give a very real measure of help to her friend. At the right time (and when Maggie was willing) she was also able to put her in touch with other, more expert guidance.

### *Spiritual midwifery*

'How can you be so *sure* of your Christian faith?' This question (coming as it did in the middle of idle chat about potty training) floored Anne completely. Here was the opportunity that she had always wanted – a chance to share her faith with someone who really wanted to know. This was the time to witness with a capital 'W' and she was at a loss for words.

This is the one form of 'counselling' that we all want to do, and the one that is most likely to come our way. There is only one problem which is common to everyone, sin, and we are privileged to have the answer. And yet we often feel terrified to try to share that answer because we are afraid of making a hash of it.

We may have watched over the awakening spiritual interest in a friend with as much care as any doctor at an ante-natal clinic, but when it comes to delivery time we long for someone else to come and be the midwife.

How would you have answered Anne's friend? Would you have had an explanation ready? Although the Holy Spirit can and does give inspiration on such an occasion, there are certain things that we can do to prepare for an opportunity like that:

1. Know what the Bible has to say about man's need of God, and God's remedy for sin. Learn the relevant verses that speak of sin, and salvation, and if you can't quote them word for word, know where to find them in the Bible and keep a Bible handy at all times.
2. Be ready to explain what God has done in your life. After all, that is what the word 'witness' means – telling what you know to be true. Many of us feel that unless we have been rescued from a life of vice or crime, we've nothing much to share. But most people live very ordinary lives and they want to know whether God can make a difference in a life like theirs. So tell them and give them a chance to respond.
3. Know how to explain how one actually becomes a Christian. Many people hear about the Christian faith, they may even know Christians whom they respect and admire, but when it comes to experiencing this new life for themselves, they just don't know what to do.

There are many booklets that explain the basic steps that we need to take in order to become a Christian. One of the most widely used is *Four Spiritual Laws* published by Campus Crusade for Christ. These are small enough to slip into a pocket or purse; you can show it to the enquirer, read through it with her, and then ask whether she is ready to pray the prayer of commitment at the end. If she is, you can do it there and then. If not, you can give her the booklet to take away.

'That's all very well,' you may argue, 'but I don't carry a mini-library around with me! Can't I lead someone to Christ without a booklet to refer to?' Of course you can (although a New

Testament takes up very little room and the *Four Spiritual Laws* booklet is so small that you could have one in every pocket and not notice it).

One way to explain it is as easy as A.B.C. – '*A*dmit your need, *B*elieve that Jesus can meet that need, *C*ommit the *C*ontrol of your life to him.' Memorise the appropriate Bible verse for the A.B.C. and away you go. God does not tell you that you must be successful, but he does ask that you should be obedient. We are commanded to be witnesses, but only the Holy Spirit can use that witness to change human beings. So you can obey and then relax. Someone has described it like this, 'Success in witnessing is sharing your faith in the power of the Holy Spirit and leaving the results to God.' Can you do that? Of course, and so can I.

The *Four Spiritual Laws* booklet available from:

Campus Crusade for Christ,
105 London Road,
Reading,
Berks.

For details of counselling courses and other helpful literature, write to:

Crusade for World Revival,
P.O. Box 11,
Walton-on-Thames,
Surrey

Care and Counsel,
146 Queen Victoria Street,
London,
EC4 46X

For further reading:

*Restoring the Image* Roger Hurding (Paternoster Press)

# 14 Branching out

Nearly all of our considerations, so far, have been related to witnessing to women. This is not because I have anything against men – far from it – but, because, not every woman has a husband who shares her faith, or, for that matter, a husband at all. For this reason we have given a great deal of time and space to thinking of what a woman can do, whatever her marital status.

However, there is no doubt that the ideal method of evangelism reaches all the members of a family and most important, meets the needs of husbands and wives together. I don't know why, but it happens very often that if a woman is converted, she often has a problem in sharing her new-found faith with her husband. If, on the other hand, her husband responds first, the whole family tends to follow suit in a very short time. Something for the women's lib. to ponder perhaps!

With family evangelism in mind, many groups have seen their aim as being to make initial contact with the women in their area, but to bring in the husbands as soon as possible. Not an easy task, but one that is infinitely worthwhile.

How has it been done? The simplest way, and the first step, is for Christian couples to welcome their non-Christian friends, business colleagues and neighbours into their own home. You know the story of the Gospel Blimp, in which the Christians in a mythical American town decided to have an evangelistic outreach. They hired an enormous hot-air balloon which towed banner texts across the sky, showered tracts down on the local inhabitants, and filled their ears with broadcast hymns and sermonettes. The net result was to infuriate a lot of people. Then a Christian man accepted his neighbour's invitation to go fishing and more was achieved in pointing that neighbour to Christ in one day, than had been done in weeks of 'Blimp' ministry. This is a parody of course! There is a great deal to be gained by a concentrated town-wide evangelistic outreach, undertaken at God's direction and in his strength. But the ground has to be prepared first. And this means that men, as well as women, will have to take time to build bridges and make friends, be available and open up their homes.

The next step has been for groups to give coffee evenings, lunches, buffet suppers or dinners, to which husbands and wives are invited together to hear a speaker. These are sometimes held in homes (if there is room) or, more often, on neutral ground like a restaurant, community hall, or a church lounge. The latter is not, strictly speaking, 'neutral' territory, but is the obvious place for a church based group and it can be appropriate for other groups when, for instance, a redundant church has a spacious hall which is known to be used for a variety of purposes.

At one time, restaurants and hotels were the first choice for organisers of this kind of function.

The food and other details were all seen to by the hotel staff, and all the committee had to do was agree on the menu, sell the tickets, fix up a speaker and welcome the guests. But inflation hits us all, and rising costs mean that for the majority of groups 'do-it-yourself' is now the only feasible plan. While the thought of planning and preparing a meal for 100 or more guests may turn the blood to ice in your veins, don't dismiss the idea out of hand. There are many advantages, quite apart from reducing costs. Working together is a marvellous way of forming bonds within a group and an event such as this offers scope for a variety of skills. Cooks are needed and so are those with organisational ability. People who can make table decorations and arrange flowers have their part to play, but those who feel that their contribution is 'only washing-up' or 'shopping', are equally important.

What are the possibilities open to a committee who want to organise an event for 'husbands and wives'? If you live in a town where many people work locally, a lunch in a central venue can be a good idea. If you do this, remember that since many people have a limited time away from work, it is best not to have elaborate food. A simple meal of soup, cheese or cold meats, rolls and seasonal fruit is relatively inexpensive, easy to prepare and quick to serve. The speaker must be disciplined and speak only for the allotted time, and it is important to let him start his talk promptly.

In the evening you have the choice between a coffee evening, which can probably be held in a home quite easily, a fork or buffet supper, or a full-blown dinner. Whichever happens to be right for your group, there are certain practical considerations to take into account, especially if you are doing your own catering.

### *Begin with prayer*

Before you begin to plan in detail, realise that the practical and the spiritual aspects cannot be separated. All of your practical arrangements, and especially the catering, need to be prayed over, just as much as the more obviously spiritual side. Good organisation is not enough by itself. It is a sign of your love and care when you consider the comfort of your guests, and when refreshments, however simple, are carefully prepared and lovingly offered. And the way in which you do this can add to or detract from the atmosphere and the spiritual effectiveness of the event.

### *You will need a Chief-Charlie*

One person needs to take overall responsibility for the function. She will delegate most of the jobs, but it is essential that one person knows what is going on in every department, and liaises with those who are responsible for the various jobs.

Here is a check-list of things that need to be done:

(a) Arrange date and book speaker.
(b) Hire of hall.
(c) Hire of cutlery, glass, etc., or loan of it from individuals or a church. (If you can get it all from one source it saves a lot of sorting out afterwards).
(d) Seating arrangements, laying of tables, table decorations.
(e) Flower arrangements for the room.
(f) Public address system and background music (if any).
(g) Cloakroom needs – supplying clean towels, spare soap, etc. if needed.
(h) Decide who is to greet the guests as they

arrive; meet, look after and if necessary supply overnight accommodation for the speaker; say grace and give the vote of thanks.

(i) The bookstall: At a daytime function a bookstall is often useful and appreciated. (Some people have found that a 'Book Party', with an author or publisher to speak, has also been very popular, especially towards Christmas).

(j) The meal itself: This is the responsibility of the caterer. Her job is to organise, but not to do all the work herself. A caterer needs to have a cool head, a well-organised mind, an ability to get along well with others, experience of coping with numbers, and most important of all, a genuine liking for the job!

She plans the menu, organises the shopping, cooking, serving and clearing up afterwards. She will decide how the guests will get their food (self-service or waitress service). How dirty plates are to be disposed of, when coffee is to be made and who is to serve it; who is to wash up and when. (She will also check that the extras for the tables are available – items like salt and pepper, ashtrays, napkins, place cards (if used) and programmes of future events).

We have found that a team of teenagers have worked as willing waiters and waitresses, under the direction of the caterer, and that even if you are having self-service, helpers are very useful to whisk away dirty plates, serve coffee and help with the clearing up.

The two major items that need further nsideration are the venue and the meal itself.

### *Choosing the venue*

We have already considered some of the options. When you are deciding, check on the following:

Is there ample parking?
Is it easy to find – you do not want half your guests circling vainly round the one-way system trying to get to you!
Is it warm (in winter) or well ventilated (in summer)?
Is the decor reasonable (or can you make it so)?
Are there adequate chairs and tables available to cope with the numbers you intend to invite?
Is there a public address system, or can you rig one up if necessary?
What about the shape of the room?
Will your speaker be able to stand so that he can be both seen and heard?
Are there cloakroom facilities and what about the kitchen?

### *The meal itself*

Your actual choice of meal is governed by three main factors:

(a) The woman-power you have to do the work.
(b) The facilities that you have in which to prepare and serve it.
(c) Your budget.

#### *Woman-power*

The caterer will need her own team of helpers and her first option is to choose a meal which has a variety of dishes and to ask each member of the team to prepare such things as quiches, cold desserts and salads in their own homes and bring the food to the hall all ready to serve. This is a good idea if 3 or 4 people are planning to cater for say 24-30 guests.

An alternative is for each couple to prepare enough food for themselves and the guests that they are inviting and to bring this with them. The food is then pooled. This is truly a pot-luck supper and should probably be advertised as such. It is ideal for a small informal occasion.

The other possible course of action is for one or two people to buy all the necessary ingredients and then a number of helpers prepare it all centrally. This does not mean that the preparation has to be done at the hall; any home with a good-sized kitchen can be used. If large numbers are being catered for, this is often a more economical method, both in terms of time and money.

*The facilities*

If you are planning to cater for a number of people, then the kitchen facilities at your chosen venue are very important. The immediate reaction of some people is to say – 'we must have a cold meal; hot ones are far too difficult to do'. But if you have a reasonable number of electric points, and a cooker with an oven, it is perfectly possible to prepare a hot meal for 100 people and to keep and serve it piping hot.

If you are thinking about a cold meal, bear in mind that salads often require a lot of preparation and chopping and that this has to be done on the day. This can, however, be a good choice in summer when the salad vegetables are plentiful and relatively cheap, and the weather will, you hope, be warm.

In the cooler weather, it is worth considering serving a hot meal such as a casserole and rice which can be prepared a day or two in advance and heated up when needed. All the initial preparation can be done at home; the rice cooked and cooled and the casseroles given their initial slow cooking period. If you are really pressed for oven space, bring the casseroles up to simmering point in big pans on top of the cooker on the evening and transfer to heated dishes just before serving. Make sure that your plates are well warmed (but not so hot that your guests cannot carry them without oven cloths!) and if any of your number have heated serving trays or even a heated trolley, these can be valuable aids to achieving that 'piping hot' standard that should be your aim.

If you use convenience foods, be imaginative! Catering packs of soup mix, for example, are often very good and can be made even better by the addition of that 'little extra' before serving. Single cream, top of the milk or grated orange rind adds zip to tomato soup; chopped chives, parsley or chopped watercress goes with chicken soup, and sherry and lemon juice gives a fillip to mushroom, as does chopped cucumber and wine vinegar to vegetable.

*The cost*

How does one pay for an event such as this? This can be a vexed question. A few groups feel that no mention of money should be made and that they should look to God to supply their finances through the gifts of his people. Other groups feel that the cost should be kept to the minimum, but that some charge for tickets should be made. Couples who are inviting guests then buy the requisite number of tickets for themselves and their friends. In addition, if the function is announced publicly (at a coffee morning, for instance) regulars may wish to purchase their own tickets and come along, not specifically as someone's guest, but in their own right because they already feel part of what is going on.

How is the cost of the tickets calculated? There are two ways of doing it. The first way is to decide on the cost of the ticket first. You then make a note of all your essential expenses. You will usually have to pay for the hire of the hall, you will certainly pay for the speaker's expenses and you may need to allow for hire of extra glasses, plates and cutlery. Then there are the hidden extras like napkins, table decorations, flowers, candles and little luxuries like 'After Dinner Mints' – if you decide to have them! Each group will have a different list of priorites. When you have decided what yours are, you can calculate like this:

Maximum possible number guests: 100
Maximum price of ticket: £2 per head
Total budget = £200

| | |
|---|---|
| Hire of hall | £20.00 |
| Speaker's expenses | £15.00 |
| Hire of crockery | £15.00 |
| TOTAL | £50.00 |

The caterer is then asked to decide what kind of food and extras she can provide allowing £1.50 per person.

The alternative is to decide on your menu first and ask the caterer to cost it. You then add on the extras and work out the cost of the ticket.

For example, imagine that your caterer says that your chosen menu would cost £5 per head:

Number of guests expected: 100
Cost of food and drink per head: £5
Therefore food budget = £500

Extras:

| | |
|---|---|
| Hire of hall | £30.00 |
| Hire of cutlery | £15.00 |
| Speaker's expenses | £25.00 |
| Flowers, candles, napkins | £30.00 |

Therefore total budget £600.00
Cost of ticket: £6 each

***Useful Quantities***

At a coffee evening, coffee and biscuits, or possibly a dessert or gateau are all that is needed.

*Instant coffee:* 57–85 gm (2–3 oz.) coffee to 3.41 litres (6 pints) of water provides 24–26 servings. This quantity requires 1.14 litres (2 pints) of milk and 452 gm (1 lb.) of sugar.

*Ground coffee:* 226–283 gm (8–10 oz.) coffee, in 3.41 litres (6 pints) of water with 1.7 litres (3 pints) of milk gives 24–26 servings. 452 gm (1 lb. of sugar) is required. Catering coffee bags are useful and can be bought in 3-cup bags.

*For 25 people you will need:*
Soup – 4.55 litres (1 gallon)
Long grain rice – 908 gm (2 lbs.)
Lettuce – 3–4
Cucumber – 2
Tomatoes – 1.36 kg. (3 lbs.)
White cabbage (for winter salads) – 680 gm ($1\frac{1}{2}$ lbs.)
Potatoes (for potato salad) – 1.36 kg (3 lbs).
Cheese and biscuits – 680 gm–910 gm ($1\frac{1}{2}$–2 lbs.) cheese, 452 gm (1 lb.) butter, 908 gm (2 lbs.) biscuits.
Tea – 57 gm (2oz.) in 4.55 litres (1 gallon) pot needs 852 ml ($1\frac{1}{2}$ pints) of milk, 452 gm (1 lb.) sugar.

*Rosemary's Rice*

This is an excellent method of ensuring fluffy single-grain rice every time!

Wash the rice thoroughly and then soak it in cold water for one hour. Bring a large pan of salted water to the boil and when it is boiling vigorously, add the washed rice. Boil rapidly for four minutes only. Test and if the grains are soft, with just a slight central firmness, strain. Put a pat of butter into the saucepan, return the rice and cover the pan with a clean dry tea-towel. Replace the lid firmly and stand in a warm place (but away from direct heat) for five minutes.

If you wish to serve the rice cold, it can be left in the saucepan to cool and then turned onto a serving dish and 'forked up'.

There are several cookery books which give excellent recipes for catering for numbers. Among these are *Summer Cookery* (Cordon Bleu) and *Cooking for Crowds* (Penguin). Many other books contain one or two recipes for buffet suppers for 10–12 people.

# 15 Learning to serve

Jesus said, 'I am among you as one who serves' (Luke 22:27), and if God has called you into a position of responsibility within his church, he has done it so that you can serve others, and not for your own self-gratification. The whole purpose of this book is to help those whom God has called to serve him in a particular way, to do so, but no book can contain the answer to every question or do more than touch on the experiences of a limited number of people. There are always new lessons to learn and new approaches to problems to be explored, and this is why it is helpful for those who have a similar vision to get together and help each other.

In the mid-1960s, some American women came to England with their husbands on a business trip. They were full of excitement about what God was doing in reaching women through coffee mornings and other similar meetings in the States and they shared this vision with English Christians whom they met. The initial flicker of interest grew into a steady flame and soon the organisation known as

Christian Lunch and Dinner Clubs was born. Over the years it has acted as a link for groups already in existence, whether they are holding Coffee Mornings, Lunches, Dinners, At Homes or Bible Studies, and has helped and encouraged those who want to form new groups. Each group functions quite independently, but can ask for help and advice from the Executive Committee and the Council of Reference. None of these women are salaried workers, but, coming as they do, from all the major denominations, can share their wide experience of speaking to and leading groups. They give their time out of love for the Lord.

C.L.D.C. holds an annual Training and Fellowship day in London, which is open to all those who are interested, and the magazine, which is published three times each year, gives news of what the different clubs are doing so that others can pray, and acts as a channel for new ideas.

Another group who exist primarily to help women to witness more effectively, whether it is at home or within the church framework, is Women's Action, one of the arms of the Church Pastoral Aid Society. This is primarily an Anglican organisation and groups are to be found in many of the evangelical Anglican churches, but their literature, Bible study aids, tapes and training days are available to everyone.

'But', perhaps you're saying, 'I'm not an "organisation" type,' or, 'I live miles from London', or, 'I'm too tied by a young family or other commitments to get to a central Training Day'. 'Is it worth doing anything locally, and if so, who would come?'

The answers to those questions is, 'Indeed it is', and 'You'll be surprised!' Although I, and many others, have benefited greatly from the help and encouragement given both by C.L.D.C. and Women's Action (even though I'm not an

Anglican) there is no doubt that there is great value in Christians from one locality getting together for mutual encouragement and prayer support. Time and money is saved since little travelling is involved, and those who have no idea what is going on, right on their own doorstep, have an opportunity to hear and become involved.

There are many ways in which this can be done, and (in my own home area) we tried three basic approaches.

### *A Quiet Day*

This is aimed at building up Christians in some aspect of their faith, and most important, to enclose a period of time when they can be still and hear God speaking to them in a particular way. The whole object of a Quiet Day is to *be* quiet, and so the place in which you hold it needs to have enough space for people to get away by themselves for personal prayer and meditation. We held one such day in a home out in the country, where those who came could wander in a large garden, or sit and look out over the fields and woods. On another occasion we used a church hall for the formal part of the proceedings, and the church itself was open for an extended lunch hour for those who wished to think and pray.

#### *The Programme*

What sort of programme do you provide on a Quiet Day? You will need a speaker, or someone to lead a session of meditation on your chosen subject. It may be helpful to have a discussion or question time, and perhaps a period of united prayer. Most people find three or four hours of total silence a bit overpowering and need some direction of their thoughts for at least part of the time. If you are running a creche, both the helpers and the children will need a break in the middle of the day. So you might arrange your programme like this:

| | |
|---|---|
| 10.15 | Coffee and chat. |
| 10.45 | Talk, guided meditation or Bible Study. |
| 11.30 | Quiet for personal prayer or reading. |
| 12.00 | Discussion in small groups. |
| 12.45–2.00 | Lunch and an opportunity for those who wish to do so to chat, while others can go to a 'silent' room and eat there if they wish. |
| 2.00 | Second talk or meditation. |
| 2.30–3.00 | United prayer, questions, or further period of quiet. |

We have found it best for people to bring their own lunch and for the organisers to provide tea or coffee at appropriate times. Timing is, of course, flexible, but usually needs to fit in with school hours. Topics for the day could be: Worship, Prayer, Guidance, Suffering, Coping with Strain and Stress, Bereavement, the work of the Holy Spirit, and many others that help us to understand more about God and his dealings with his children.

*The People*

Circulate all your local churches with news of what you are doing. The pastor's wife or leader of the women's work in a particular church is often the best person to contact. You may be surprised how many women from churches of all types will be attracted by the thought of a time to be quiet. And if you are thinking of running a creche, do impress upon people the need to let you know the numbers of children expected. Otherwise you may find yourself in the same position as we did, when we expected three toddlers and found ourselves with twenty plus.

### *The information and outreach day*

This is a day geared particularly for the interested but uncommitted. The church-goer who may need an opportunity to think through what she does believe, and could certainly do with some help in putting those beliefs into words and sharing them with others.

The general pattern of the day could be the same as for a 'Quiet Day', with a speaker, but with more time for questions and discussion, and perhaps a brief talk about what people are actually doing to share their faith locally. We held a day like this with the general title of 'A Faith to Keep and Share' when our speaker talked first about what we believed and secondly, how we might share those beliefs with others. As she left, one lady shook the speaker by the hand and said, 'I've often wondered why I found it hard to talk about my faith. I've realised today that I don't really have a faith to talk about and I'm going home to think it through.' And that wasn't planned as a directly evangelistic occasion!

### *The training day*

If you have several small groups meeting around the town (or in a number of villages) for Bible Study, Prayer or Outreach, why not get together for a Training and Fellowship Day? If you are few in number you can probably meet in a home, but again, there is often a heartening response from churches if you let them know in good time, and then larger premises may be needed.

In planning such a day, be practical. Ask people who know, *from personal experience*, something about the different topics that you want to cover, to share those experiences with you. You will probably want to start with a time of worship and perhaps have a fairly brief devotional talk to remind yourselves that it is the God whom you serve rather than the service itself, who must have first place in your life. Then get down to the nitty-gritty. Have sessions on 'How to lead a Bible Study'; 'How to lead a Discussion Group'; 'How to Counsel' – in fact any of the topics that we have thought through together in this book and any others that are relevant to your local situation. Don't take yourselves too seriously. If you have dramatic talent in your midst, some skits on 'What not to do' will probably be remembered long after the lectures have been forgotten. Leave plenty of time to ask questions, hear what other groups are doing (each group might be asked to give a progress report) and share points for prayer. Then PRAY. There is immense value in dividing into small groups at the end of the day and bringing each others needs to God.

In a few areas, a Training Day like this has resulted in a newsletter which is duplicated and circulated among the groups to keep them in touch with each other during the year. Others have appointed a Prayer Secretary to whom particular needs can be telephoned at any time, and who will then pass them on to the leaders of other groups for prayer backing. One or two areas have compiled their own Speakers' List (do ask speakers for their permission to include their names before you do so, if you follow suit) and details of suitable premises that can be hired for 'big occasions' and other helpful information.

We have all got so much to learn, and we never reach the point when we know it all. So look out for opportunities to share with others the lessons that God has taught you, and never be afraid to ask for help and advice.

In these ways we can help and encourage each other, not only to serve Jesus Christ, but to do so more effectively.

For further information:

Christian Lunch & Dinner Clubs,
Mrs. J. McKechnie,
21 Glebe Hyrst,
Sanderstead,
South Croydon, Surrey
CR2 9JG.

Women's Action,
Church Pastoral Aid Society,
Falcon Court,
32 Fleet Court,
London
E.C.4.

# 16 What, me up there?

'I'll do anything you like behind the scenes, but don't ask me to say anything in public!'

'I think I'd *die*, if I had to stand up in front of a lot of people – or even a few!'

'Can you imagine *me* giving a talk? I'd open my mouth and a squeak would come out. I know it would!'

These and many similar comments came bubbling out in a discussion about how one prepares to give a talk. Almost all those present were emphatic that they just could not do it. This is one area of Christian work in which there are certainly not 'too many chiefs and too few Indians' – in fact, quite the reverse.

Why is it that the thought of giving a talk fills so many of us with horror? If we have some item of exciting news to share with our friends, we have no difficulty in finding words then. So why is it that we draw back from sharing the most important news of all? There are all sorts of hidden reasons. Fear is one of the most common. Fear of failure, fear of ridicule, fear of being misunderstood, of making fools of ourselves. And entangled with fear, is pride. Then there is false modesty. Some Christians take a positive delight in belittling themselves, and quote verses from the Bible about humility and man's inability to please God, in his own strength, at great length. 'Apart from me you can do nothing' (John 15:5) they say, laying all the stress on the last four words, and living as if they are indeed 'apart from Christ' instead of rejoicing that 'I can do all things in him who strengthens me' (Phil. 4:13).

Strangely enough, there were those in the early church who had the same problem, and it was not just the women. Paul had to say very firmly to Timothy, 'I remind you to rekindle the gift of God that is within you ... for God did not give us a spirit of timidity, but a spirit of power and love and self-control. Do not be ashamed then, of testifying to our Lord ...' (2 Tim. 1:6–8).

I am not deducing from this, that all Christians are called to be preachers, or even public speakers in a general sense. Some people are, and for them it is a gift of the Spirit and they have a great responsibility to exercise it prayerfully and wisely. But we should all be able to 'testify to our Lord'; that command is not limited to those who find it easy to 'speak'. In fact, some of the most powerful testimonies that I have ever heard were those given by people who were far from fluent, and obviously nervous. I attended a day conference some years ago, when one woman was so moved by the experiences that she was trying to share with us, that tears trickled down her cheeks as she spoke and her voice was almost inaudible at times. But I still remember what she said now, whereas much of the rest of that day's messages have been forgotten.

How can you prepare to 'testify', so that you are ready to do it, if God asks you to do so?

### *Get used to the sound of your own voice*

This may seem to be one of the biggest hurdles to get over, and yet it isn't really that difficult. Start small. Ask a question in a discussion group. Read out the verse, or the passage for the Bible study. If you are asked to announce a future meeting or welcome the speaker, accept. Agree to close the meeting in prayer (you can write your prayer out beforehand if it helps). As you gain confidence, you might be able to give a book review (again, you can write it out first) or take part in an Any Questions team or Brains Trust panel. Read aloud and tape record your voice. Ask an honest friend how you sound when you take part in a meeting and listen to others, assessing whether they speak clearly and learn what you can from them. Think about going to an evening class on public speaking where you can all learn together.

As a young man, Luis Palau, the South American evangelist, saw the possibilities of television for spreading the good news about Jesus long before there was any possibility of his using the medium. He read an article in a magazine about how well-known people prepared themselves for a television broadcast and decided to do some homework. He locked himself in his bedroom with a tape recorder and a mirror and set to work to learn how to speak to a camera. Eventually, the opportunity came for him to speak on television and when it did he was ready – a little nervous, certainly, but prepared to take the opportunity that God had given him.

### *Get your testimony organised*

The Bible tells us that Satan is overcome by the blood of the Lamb *and the word of our testimony* (Rev. 12:11). Imagine that! You can help to defeat

Satan by explaining to others what God has done for you – even though it may seem undramatic and ordinary in comparison to some people's 'gutter to glory story'! What is the reason for sharing our 'testimony'? We have already seen that it helps to defeat Satan, but we also want it to glorify God. And it will do both of these things if it has a life-changing effect on someone else. So we need to know in what direction our testimony is aimed, if we are to hope to achieve a 'direct hit'. A friend of ours, Dave Ames, has written a very helpful leaflet on the do's and dont's of this type of speaking and he suggests that there are no less than eight possible goals for us to bear in mind. We may be aiming:

(1) To demonstrate that the gospel is not simply a matter of intellectual assent, but a personal, practical and very real encounter within a person.

(2) To convict those out of harmony with God's plan. (Of course it is the Holy Spirit who does the convicting, but you can provide him with good ammunition!)

(3) To create a hunger for a deeper, more effective Christian life. (Again the Holy Spirit's work. See above.)

(4) To demonstrate how scriptural principles were applied to specific situations and to encourage others to search the Bible for solutions to their own problems.

(5) To prepare members of a group for a specific teaching. (In other words, your experience might illustrate what the main speaker has to say.)

(6) To encourage others to see their own spiritual growth as a message that they can share.

(7) To unite Christians by demonstrating that we all have similar conflicts.
(8) To demonstrate that God answers prayer.

Which of these areas do God's dealings with you touch on? Different experiences in your life will have different functions in this respect.

If you are sharing the story of how you received Christ as your Saviour, Dave Ames suggests that your talk should have three basic sections:

(1) Your life and problems before knowing Christ. (This is only intended to set the scene and not to give a complete criminal record.)
(2) How you came to know Christ, including:
  (a) How he got your attention. (What were the needs or the circumstances that made you look for 'something more'?)
  (b) What *specific* steps did you take? (Could someone else follow them?)
(3) The difference that Jesus Christ has made in your life.

Testimonies that illustrate other steps along the spiritual pathway should have the same basic format:

(1) The problem and the reasons why you couldn't cope on your own.
(2) How God helped you to solve that problem.
(3) The difference in your life as a result.

If a particular verse of scripture helped you, say so, with the reference, but don't hop about all over the Bible. It's far better to talk about one or at the most two verses that other people can remember and apply to their own situation, than to dazzle them with your Bible knowledge.

*Don't spoil it*

1. By telling too much. Most testimonies have to be kept brief, unless they form the main talk of the meeting. So don't confuse the issue by including too many details – either of circumstances or sins of the past.
2. By telling too little. People want to know what the problem was and what steps you took to resolve it. Could someone else, in the same situation, follow your example? Is your explanation clear enough?
3. By preaching. There is no need for you to tell others what they should do. If your testimony is clear, they will be able to see the right way to go, just the same as if you want to demonstrate that a crooked line is wobbly, you simply have to place the straight edge of a ruler beside it.

*Be careful*

1. Not to criticise others – either individuals or churches.
2. Not to use Christian jargon that an outsider might not understand.
3. To be positive and smile! If God has done great things for you and you are glad – show it.
4. To learn the verses that you want to refer to and their references.

*Write it down*

Although many people find it hard to do, it is an excellent discipline and aid to brevity if you write down what you want to say, word for word. If you are just giving a brief testimony you may want to memorise the whole thing; not so that you repeat it off parrot fashion, but so that you have the basic framework firmly in your mind. If you are giving a longer talk, you will probably want to reduce it to note form with headings of the various points underlined in red, so they catch your eye as you glance at your notes. NEVER read a talk. Once your basic outlining is done, go over it until you can remember the sequence of thoughts with hardly a reference to your notes, but have them there. They are a comforting safety net!

Write your notes in a spiral bound notebook that can lie flat in your Bible. This will prevent you from having to chase fluttering pieces of paper around the platform or across the sitting room floor. It also means that the talk is kept safely, in case God has a use for it a second or even more times.

*What else can I talk about?*

Within the framework of home-based meetings, personal experience scores again and again. We have considered testimonies in some detail, and this idea of sharing your own experiences can cover a wider field than personal problems solved. If you have survived the pre-school stage of family life with your sanity intact, you have probably discovered some basic principles for making life enjoyable at that stage. These can be explained and illustrated from your own experience. Many jobs or hobbies are of general interest too, and illustrate spiritual principles very well. I have heard a talk on pottery, for instance, in which the speaker demonstrated how it was done, and as she worked, spoke of God as the Master Potter. You can doubtless think of many other possibilities.

*Be prepared*

It is one thing to think through what God has done in your life, or what he has taught you through a job or a hobby, and to write it down, in full or note form, but that is by no means the end of the preparation. In fact, it is barely the beginning.

Although I would encourage everyone to prayerfully think it over whether she should be serving God in this way, either frequently or occasionally, each actual invitation to speak, or share in a meeting, needs to be carefully and prayerfully considered, and sometimes it is right to say 'No'. If you say 'Yes', you need to pray about the meeting and what God wants you to say *on this particular occasion.* You may be sharing something that you have spoken about before, but ask God how you should present it to this group. What shutters will they have in their minds, which may shut out what you are trying to say. Familiarity with the Christian message, ignorance, fear of being 'got-at', materialism – all these and many others can form very effective shutters against God's word. You need to anticipate these shutters, prepare your talk accordingly, asking God to open their eyes and their ears.

Then there is your own preparation. God cannot use an unclean channel for his Spirit and you need to spend time asking him to search your heart and cleanse you from any hidden or unconfessed sin. Ask for love for, and sensitivity to, the needs of the audience to whom you go, and never try to appear perfect. Although we need to have experienced the truth of what we are sharing with others, for ourselves, we never finish learning from God. And to say humbly, 'God has showed me this; I am learning to obey him in it, but I still get it wrong sometimes and have to ask his forgiveness', is not dishonouring to God. It simply shows us to be what we are: 'One beggar showing another beggar where to find bread'.

# 17 What happens when women pray?

Hospitality, home-based evangelistic meetings, Bible Study groups and now ... prayer groups. Is there some significance in the fact that we are considering this last of all? As Christians we say that we believe in prayer, that we can attempt nothing without prayer, that God answers prayer, and yet what happens when the pressure builds up and we are short of time ... prayer is often the first thing that we cut out.

Prayer is an enormous subject. Shelves of books have been written about it. Hours of sermons have been preached on it. And as we have seen throughout this book, prayer comes first, last and in the middle of any service that we do for God. When I think of any kind of home-based outreach, I always picture a house whose foundation consists of the call of God, and the roof is made of prayer. These are two absolute essentials. But in this chapter I want to share some of the things that I have learned from women who have been called by God to give prayer for others a priority position in their lives and Christian service.

It was 1968 in America, Evelyn Christenson had been requested to do a project for her denomination's involvement in the Crusade of the Americas. 'Working with women in your own church, would you discover in a six-month period what happens when women pray?' they asked her.

'I'll take that little task,' Evelyn replied cheerfully. It seemed a small job – until she started! Then she found that when it came to group prayer, many women knew a lot *about* prayer, but they did not know *how* to pray with others. The 'small task for six months' turned into a life-changing adventure as they learned how to put theory into practice. You see, they discovered that the most basic lesson of all was that we can read about prayer, talk about it, listen to sermons and tapes about it and give a great deal of thought to it. But nothing happens until we get down on our knees and actually begin to pray, whether it is alone or in groups. Once they started to pray, Evelyn and her friends discovered that there are:

### *Conditions for Prayer*

When we pray, God has promised to answer. But there are conditions. Psalm 66:18 tells us that, 'If I had cherished iniquity in my heart, the Lord would not have listened' (RSV). And that does not just refer to murder, adultery, lying and cheating. God hates jealousy, pride, self-satisfaction, self-pity, pretence and all the other hidden sins which we often fail to recognise in ourselves, but are thoroughly effective in blocking up the communication channels between ourselves and him.

James remarks that 'the prayer of a *righteous*

man (or woman!) has great power in its effects' (James 5:16 RSV). Notice the word 'righteous'. We have to keep our lives clean by coming to God for forgiveness, every time he points out a wrong attitude or action and by forgiving others. It is only then that we can pray with confidence, knowing that he is hearing us.

James also lays great stress on faith as a prerequisite for answered prayer. In the first chapter of his epistle he says:

> 'When you pray, you must *believe* and not doubt at all. Whoever doubts is like a wave in the sea, that is blown about by the wind. A person like that, unable to make up his mind and undecided in all he does, must not think that he will receive anything from the Lord.'
>
> *Good News Bible*

Many people are puzzled about how to pray about a matter, believingly. Does it mean that we say, 'Father, please do this or that' asking for the thing to be worked out as we want it and then 'believing' as hard as we can so that it will happen? NO! The Bible tells us to 'let our requests be made known to God' (Phil. 4:6), not to dictate answers. The first that even newcomers to prayer can do, is to say 'Father, here is the problem. In my human wisdom it seems that this is the right thing to ask for. But I want your will to be done in this situation and if I have got it wrong, please work it out your way. I am willing for your will.'

That is kindergarten level. Those who have gone on a little in the school of prayer are beginning to grasp an exciting fact. It *is* possible to be shown God's will for any given situation, if they will only wait quietly in his presence until he indicates to them how to pray. This is not easy, nor is it quick. Jesus has promised that his sheep would hear his voice and that they would know that it was him speaking, but we have to learn to shut out other distractions and listen. Costly, time-consuming; but what a privilege! The Creator of the Universe is willing to speak to us direct and to allow us to have a part in bringing about his purposes on earth. Whatever discipline or sacrifice may be involved in learning to pray like this, it is infinitely worthwhile.

### *Companions in Prayer*

One of the beauties of intercessory prayer is that we can pray at any time, anywhere and by ourselves or with others. One bed-bound invalid has whole segments of the day divided up into fifteen or thirty minute sections, and 'books' prayer space for her church, various friends, missionaries and local and national affairs. But as Evelyn Christenson and many others have discovered, there is great power in united prayer. Jesus promised, 'whenever two of you agree about anything you pray for, it will be done for you by my Father in heaven' (Matt. 18:19), and people are finding that promise to be true today.

Have you a prayer partner? If your husband shares your faith, then you probably pray over problems and matters of family concern with him. (If you do not, then this is the place to start.) But there is a very special joy in sharing your needs with a Christian friend and knowing that she is praying for you as you do the same for her.

How do you find such a person? I had felt the need for a prayer partner for some months and had a particular friend in mind with whom I knew that I could be completely honest and open. But she was terribly busy and I was not sure if she would welcome the idea – besides, I am a creature of impulse and so I wanted to be sure that it was

God's prompting and not just my own thought. I prayed, asking that if this was God's will, he would pop the same idea into my friend's head, without me having to say anything.

Several months passed and the matter slipped to the back of my mind. Then one day, Janet said, 'I've been reading *Born Again* by Charles Colson, and there was one thing that impressed me particularly – that idea of prayer partnerships. Do you think that *we* could ...?'

People put the idea of prayer partnerships to work in different ways. We meet once a fortnight for lunch and a time of sharing and prayer. We each have a notebook in which we keep a note of prayer requests that we make and answers that we receive. Prayer becomes exciting when we can see specific results. If one of us is speaking at a meeting or doing something else for which she needs particular prayer support, the other prays at the time, on the day. If emergencies crop up, the telephone keeps us in touch.

Some people rely on the telephone for their prayer and sharing. Others meet, in two's, three's or even more, every week. Some covenant to pray for a particular need at the same time each day, so that although they are not together in body, they are in Spirit.

A further development of this idea is the prayer chain. One person acts as co-ordinator and undertakes to man her telephone for a certain period each day. During that time people can 'phone in prayer requests and when she receives one, the co-ordinator 'phones the first link in the chain. She prays immediately herself, for that need and then contacts the second link, and so on down the chain. All that prayer chain members have to do is to keep all the prayer requests that they receive confidential – no gossiping – pray themselves and then pass the requests on to the next link immediately. Simple but so effective. It is a wonderful way of mobilising a large prayer force very quickly and exciting results have been seen.

### *Challenge to Pray*

In 1911 a young Russian woman was extremely concerned for her father's safety during a period of political instability in Russia. She went to a monastery of the Russian Orthodox Church and asked the godly monks there to pray for her father's safety. While praying for her father, one of the monks had, what he believed to be, a God-given insight into the future. Among other things, he told Barbara that he had seen Russia in the grip of a godless ideology; that in the last days, Germany would be divided into two and that America would feed the world. He also said that Russia and China would destroy each other and that Britain would lose her empire and her colonies and would come to almost total ruin but would be saved by praying women. All this is reported by Lance Lambert in his book, *Battle for Israel*, and although, as he points out, we should not accept such things gullibly, without carefully considering and testing them, it is amazing how much of this (unthinkable as it was in 1911) has actually come true.

Mother Barbara is still alive and living in Jerusalem, a remarkable Christian woman now in her eighties. She believes, apparently, that Britain will probably be the only surviving light in an ever-darkening Europe. Kept that way by praying women? Well, God is certainly raising up groups of women all over the world who feel a great burden to pray for their government and their nation and Britain is not being left out. Up and down the country, small groups are meeting to battle things out in prayer. What do they do?

They meet, usually once a month, for three or four hours in the middle of the day. Most groups are small with a maximum membership of ten to twelve – this encourages everyone to take part and enables people to know and care for each other really well. They go without lunch so that the whole time can be given to prayer and listening to God. Faith explained it to me like this:

'We start off by reading a psalm or some other part of the Bible which reminds us of God's might, power and glory. We spend some time in joint praise and worship and then we ask God to search our hearts and show us if there is any hidden sin in our lives which needs to be confessed and put right. The next step is to wait quietly before God, asking him what he wants us to pray about. We don't come with a long prayer list and rush straight in; we wait – perhaps for ten minutes or longer, and then the group is asked what God has put into their minds. Often several people will have thought of different aspects of the same subject, and when we are agreed on the topic, we pray about that for as long as the Holy Spirit gives us things to pray for. Then we may move onto another topic. We always finish by thanking God for the answers that we know he will give.'

*Commitment to pray ... for what?*

What do these prayer groups actually pray for? The personal and practical needs of individuals, certainly, but there is also a great emphasis on praying for God's work wherever it is taking place, giving especial thought to the needs of the church, the community and the country.

In at least one town in England, the crime rate has dropped rather than risen in the past year or two. The police are congratulating themselves on doing a good job (as indeed they are) but they are unaware of a secret weapon which is being employed on their side – a small group of Christians are meeting regularly to pray for the town.

There is at least one active prayer group praying for the members of the government and legislation as it is debated in the House of Commons. Some people are prompted to pray especially for the trouble spots of the world – Africa, the Middle East, Ireland, the Communist countries. Others have prayed particularly for industrial relations or for prominent people in their own locality. Most groups have had the experience of being led to pray for a number of areas over a period of time, but often only one or two things during one prayer time. There is a great value in focusing on one topic and really praying it through.

Many parents are deeply concerned about the problems and standards in our schools. In some places God is drawing women together to pray for their children's school – just three or four women with children at the same school meet to pray for the staff, the children and problems as they arise.

At one school, the Head of Religious Education had been far from helpful over the years, and the truth had not always been taught in Religious Education classes. The prayer group had prayed about this for a long time but nothing seemed to happen. Then one day, by chance (humanly speaking!), one of the mothers in the prayer group noticed that a new head of the Religious Education Department was being advertised for in the national press – the present teacher was retiring.

Immediately, she telephoned the rest of the group, asking them to pray and asking if anyone knew of a suitably qualified committed Christian who could be urged to apply for the post. Just one name was suggested – one among the dozens who would apply. The prayer group met and prayed. Their nominee applied. The women kept on praying. He was short-listed and called for an interview. Encouraged, they kept on praying and on the day of the interview he was offered the job.

That is one example out of many many that could be given of what happens when women pray. Lives *are* changed; the purposes of evil men *can* be thwarted; wrongs *can* be righted. Today, God is looking for an army of ordinary women who are ready to face up to the challenge and pay the price in terms of time and dedication.

For further reading:

*When Happens When Women Pray* Evelyn Christenson (Victor Books)
*Battle for Israel* Lance Lambert (Kingsway Publications)
*Hush! Hush!* Jill Briscoe (Pickering & Inglis)
*The Ministry of Intercession* F. J. Huegal (Bethany Fellowship)
*Rees Howells Intercessor* Norman Grubb (The Lutterworth Press)
*Pray in the Spirit* Arthur Wallis (Kingsway Publications)

These last three books and helpful tapes on intercessory prayer are available from:

Mannafest Media,
(Youth with a Mission)
Box 44,
Crawley,
Sussex

# 18 Consider him

'I am among you as one who serves' said Jesus. 'Your attitude must be like my own.' It is so easy to start out with a rush of enthusiasm, catching a vision of what can be done with a home which is entirely at his disposal. But after a few months, if things begin to get tough, are we going to become 'weary and faint-hearted'? Fed up with the people and the pressures? Surprised because it isn't all easy? Hating the servant's badge that we put on so eagerly at first? It can happen. And the most effective defence against it is to take as our watchword these two words 'Consider him'.

'Consider him, who endured such hostility against himself, so that you may not grow weary or faint-hearted' (Heb. 12:3). 'Consider him'. If, in the midst of all the busyness of our Christian service, we lose sight of the one for whom we are doing it all, then we are wasting our lives. Work should be a natural overflow from a loving relationship, and only that kind of service will stand the test of fire. And make no mistake; you will be tested, just as he was.

Jesus is King of Kings and Lord of Lords, but on earth he had no great title. He was known simply as 'Jesus of Nazareth' (and at times by far worse names!). Having left heaven's glory, he had no luxurious home – in fact for most of his ministry he had no settled home at all. While others went home to bed, he went to the Mount of Olives.

He had no money, no influential friends, no great education or well-paid job. He did not organise great rallies – but such was the quality of his life and teaching that people flocked to be with him and hung on to every word that he spoke. He did not call the religious leaders of the day to prayer meetings – but when the disciples saw the quality of his prayer life and the priority that he gave to it, they said, 'Lord, teach us to pray'.

Jesus always did his Father's will, and communicating with God in prayer was more important to him than sleep, healing the sick, or even preaching. He was never disturbed by pressures of time, flattery or difficulties. He knew where he was going. His goals were clear. When people begged him to stay in one place when he knew that it was time to move on, he did not give in to public pressure (Luke:42). And he had a burning sense of the urgency of his task. 'All of us must quickly carry out the tasks assigned to us by the one who sent me, for there is little time left,' he said (John 9:4 Living Bible).

He was prepared to be helped by very unlikely people. No one was shut out on grounds of birth, intelligence, social standing or religious affiliation. And he knew what it was to feel tired and spiritually drained. Worse still, he was misunderstood, disappointed and let down by his friends.

'Will you also go away?' he asked the disciples.

'To whom shall we go?' asked Simon Peter.

Brave words! And yet while Jesus sweated blood on the night before his execution, Peter and the others slept. When it came to the final crunch, they all ran for their lives and Peter cursed as he denied all knowledge of him.

'Simon, do you love me?' asked Jesus when he had risen from the dead, and things had been put right between them.

'Yes, Lord,' he answered.

'Take care of my lambs,' said Jesus.

You see, love is not just an emotion to be enjoyed, but an attitude to be acted upon. If we say that we love this Jesus, then it should result in actions. Feeding the lambs means getting the food from the Shepherd and distributing it to others.

Hard work; self-denial; self-giving! Does this seem to paint the picture of a very tough life? Well, the Bible makes no bones about the fact that the Christian life will be a battle. The enemy is real, and he will do his best to throw us off course. He gets at us in so many ways. We may intend to 'consider him' and have that attitude of heart which sees money, influence, social position and possessions as quite secondary to our relationship to God and obedience to his will. But the prevailing atmosphere of materialism and compromise is an insidious thing, colouring our thinking and deflecting our purpose, here a little, there a little, until almost without realising it, our lives can lose their 'cutting edge', so that we become indistinguishable from those living around us.

Even in the church he worms his way in. It is so easy to rely on methods, organisation and big names to achieve God's purposes, instead of the Holy Spirit. And if God should lead us to do something a bit different ... the opposition from those inside the church can be every bit as vigorous as from those who do not profess to be

Christians, and it is far more painful. If you come under fire because you are doing something that has not been done in your church before, be patient! Try to understand your critics' point of view; pray about their objections, but if God assures you that he has spoken to you, do not allow yourself to be deflected. Hebrews 12 reminds us to 'try to stay out of all quarrels ... look after each other ... watch out that no bitterness takes root among you' (Living Bible).

It is costly to give yourself to others. If you open your home, your own spiritual life has to be real. There is no room for pretence and shame in inter-family relationships if outsiders are watching. You will have to grow, and all growth is painful. We are such very earthen vessels. But 'look to Jesus'. He laid down his life for others right through his ministry and finally at the cross. Never think it was easy for him. But he did it for love of us and 'for the joy that was set before him'.

We do not *have* to follow suit. We can choose. We can either cling onto our 'rights', putting our own comfort and convenience first, or we can lay down our lives in service to him and to others. Those who choose the second path know the hurts and the struggles of the battle. But they also know his company, his joy, his peace, his strength.

I know which path I'll walk along – with his help. How about you?

A Prayer:.

Use us, Lord, to touch many other lives for you.
Whether by the word we speak,
The prayer we breathe,
Or the life we live;
And every life we touch, may your Holy Spirit bring to life.
Through Jesus Christ our Lord. Amen.

CW01667999

Au champ de l'univers, tu cueilleras
ce que tu sèmes.

Proverbe persan

Un bon livre est un jardin que l'on
transporte avec soi.

Sagesse d'Orient

# Contes des sages jardiniers

DERNIERS TITRES PARUS

Contes des sages au fil de l'eau
Contes des sages du Japon
Contes des sages et facétieux
Djeha et Nasreddine Hodja
Contes des sages chamanes
Contes des sages nomades
Contes des sages peaux-rouges
Contes des sages de Corse
Contes des sages de Bretagne
Contes des sages de Provence
Contes des sages qui lisent dans les étoiles
Contes des sages de Sologne et du Berry
Contes des sages bêtes et animaux impertinents
Contes des sages samouraïs
Contes des sages tsiganes
Contes des sages de Mongolie
Contes des sages du Soleil
Contes des sages pèlerins
Contes des sages juifs
Contes des sages zen
Contes des sages de Polynésie
Contes des sages de l'Égypte antique
Contes des sages slaves
Contes des sages cuisiniers
Contes des sages de la Grèce antique
Contes des sages bouddhistes
Contes des sages du Maghreb

ISBN : 978-2-02-103104-1

© Éditions du Seuil, 25, bd Romain-Rolland, 75014 Paris, avril 2011.

Le Code de la propriété intellectuelle interdit les copies ou reproductions destinées à une utilisation collective. Toute représentation ou reproduction intégrale ou partielle faite par quelque procédé que ce soit, sans le consentement de l'auteur ou de ses ayants cause, est illicite et constitue une contrefaçon sanctionnée par les articles L.335-2 et suivants du Code de la propriété intellectuelle.

www.seuil.com

# Contes des sages jardiniers

PASCAL FAULIOT
PATRICK FISCHMANN

Seuil

# Sommaire

# Le vieux jardinier et le Roi des Rois

PERSE ANTIQUE

Ce soir-là, le *Sāhān šāh*, le Roi des Rois de Perse, se promenait dans son enceinte verte, le *pairidaeza*, paradis aux quatre jardins semblables aux quatre quartiers du monde. La fontaine, de ses quatre bouches, murmurait le nom des quatre fleuves. Le grenadier arbre de vie irradiait la terrasse. Le souverain traversa l'allée, suivit le canal, dépassa le bassin carré. Il aimait flâner le soir, seul dans le jardin délicieux, dilaté par le chant de l'eau, la brise et les gazouillis d'oiseaux. Purifié par les senteurs de myrrhe, de nard et de rose, il se sentait proche de la Divinité. *Pairidaeza* était un havre de sensualité, les sens exaltés y rencontraient la nature magnifiée, ils goûtaient à la géométrie sacrée, car il était tel l'univers. Pour le roi qui aimait chevaucher le désert, l'oasis était une louange.

Avant de faire quérir une jeune fille du harem, et de prolonger ces délices par les jeux de l'amour, il aperçut un vieux jardinier qui plantait des arbres, profitant de la fraîcheur du soir. Il s'approcha.
– Est-ce une heure raisonnable pour soigner la terre ? Ne ressens-tu pas la soif du repos et ignores-tu que j'aime être seul dans le jardin, le soir, pour y méditer ?
– Je plante les dattiers de mon roi. Ce jour et cette heure leur sont propices pour penser à l'avenir. Bénis sont ceux qui donneront un jour les fruits de leurs rêves.
– Et, dis-moi, combien faudra-t-il de temps à tes dattiers pour honorer leur songe et ta générosité ?

– Il faudra bien vingt ans !
– Penses-tu vivre assez vieux pour récolter les fruits de la patience ? N'y a-t-il pas de la folie, à semer dans la terre une réponse qui ne viendra que bien trop tard ?
– Les anciens ont planté les grands dattiers qui me nourrissent aujourd'hui, je fais comme eux : je mets le couvert pour nos enfants.

La réponse du vieux jardinier émut le Roi des Rois. Il tira de sa bourse une pièce d'or, l'autre se prosterna.
– Pourquoi t'abaisser ainsi, je ne te le demande pas.
– Je remercie la terre. Il n'a fallu que quelques instants à de si jeunes arbres pour donner leurs fruits.
La réponse du vieux jardinier plut au Roi des Rois. Il prit de sa bourse une autre pièce d'or et le vieil homme réitéra sa révérence.
– Cette fois, je remercie mon souverain. Ces dattiers prodigieux viennent de porter deux récoltes la même année.

Touché encore une fois, le Roi des Rois sortit une autre pièce dorée et demanda :
– Quel âge as-tu ? La sagesse se mesure-t-elle en hivers ou en printemps ?
– J'ai tout juste douze ans, répondit le vieillard en souriant.
– Quelle est cette nouvelle fantaisie, jardinier ?
– Quand votre devancier gouvernait, nous vivions dans l'intrigue et les guerres, le jardin était beau, mais triste. Depuis douze ans que vous régnez, la joie est venue en ces lieux et ma vie a vraiment débuté avec votre règne.

Le Roi des Rois fut reconnaissant, il reçut le compliment et, tout en riant, puisa une quatrième pièce d'or de sa bourse :
– Si je persévère à discuter avec toi, j'aurai bientôt cueilli tous mes fruits pour te les donner !
– Quatre sont les jardins et les quartiers du monde, quatre encore sont les bouches de la fontaine ainsi que les fleuves.

Ces pièces me suffisent, car elles sont autant que le Tout.

Le Roi des Rois rangea sa bourse en hommage au sage, et ce geste de retenue fut encore un don. Puis il s'éloigna en croquant des pistaches, s'abandonnant au chant de l'eau, aux saveurs et aux arômes du soir.

*Prends, les fruits des dieux sont pour toi*
*Les ondes bienfaisantes, le ruisseau,*
*Le gazon, les figues et le vin.*
*Vois la beauté et tète les grenades,*
*Sois attentif, donne et deviens le jardin.*

# Le philosophe et le jardinier

D'APRÈS TCHOUANG TSEU
ET AUTRES CONTES CHINOIS

Tseu-Kong, brillant disciple de Confucius, aimait déambuler dans les villes et les campagnes avec le cortège de ses élèves. Il cherchait des situations édifiantes, provoquait des rencontres susceptibles de mettre en application les principes de la sublime philosophie de son maître.

À la sortie d'un village, le philosophe aperçut un jour un homme aux cheveux de neige qui travaillait dans son potager. Il remarqua que le vieux jardinier tirait de l'eau de son puits avec une jarre pour arroser ses plates-bandes. Le récipient était rapidement vidé et le malheureux devait faire d'incessants allers-retours. Le professeur, toujours aux aguets, tenait là une excellente occasion d'accomplir une bonne action qui fût aussi une leçon pour ses étudiants. Il cita les paroles de jade de l'incomparable Confucius : *Agissez envers autrui comme vous aimeriez qu'on agisse envers vous*. Après quoi, il dodelina des épaules, fit entendre le froissement de ses longues manches et héla le vieux paysan en levant un index solennel :

– Oncle vénérable, veuillez pardonner un humble voyageur d'interrompre votre labeur. Me permettez-vous de vous donner un conseil pour soulager votre peine ?

Le jardinier, fronçant la broussaille d'un sourcil grognon vers l'aréopage de citadins, posa sa jarre et demanda :

– Un conseil ? Monsieur le Lettré s'y connaît donc en jardinage ?

– Mes modestes connaissances s'appliquent à tout. J'ai beaucoup étudié, voyagé,

et suis au courant de bien des choses. Et notamment celle-ci, vieil homme : *C'est par le bien-faire que se crée le bien-être.*
– Comment ? Ne rien faire crée le bien-être ?
Le lettré, forçant sa voix fluette, répéta sa maxime, ses mains fines aux ongles aussi longs que ses doigts en porte-voix.
– Ah ! Vous feriez bien de venir ici pour me parler alors, car avec l'âge mon ouïe n'est plus aussi fine.
Le philosophe s'aventura dans les allées du potager, engagea la conversation avec le vieillard narquois, sous les yeux de ses admirateurs attroupés devant la clôture, désappointés de ne rien entendre de leur dialogue apparemment très animé. Un nuage blanc traversa nonchalamment la vallée.
Le philosophe sortit enfin du jardin et, la mine déconfite, reprit la route pour quitter le village. Le troupeau de ses disciples se pressait autour de lui, impatient d'avoir un compte rendu de l'entrevue.

Après une marche de dix *li* où, le visage cramoisi, Tseu-Kong ne desserra pas les dents, il finit par se laisser choir sur un rocher. Depuis qu'il avait quitté le vieillard, il était visiblement en proie aux plus sombres ruminations. Ses élèves s'assirent aussitôt dans l'herbe, faisant cercle autour de lui, avides de boire le nectar de ses paroles.

– Mes pauvres amis, il m'a fallu tout ce chemin pour encaisser le coup de tonnerre que j'ai reçu sur la tête. Je croyais jusqu'à ce jour que mon vénéré maître était le plus grand des sages, mais j'en ai rencontré un autre sous les traits de ce modeste jardinier. Pensez donc, c'est à peine croyable, un homme qui n'a jamais étudié les Classiques, qui ne connaît des proverbes que ceux qu'il a hérités de son père, qui ne sait sans doute pas déchiffrer le moindre idéogramme, eh bien, il cache toute une science sous son aspect rustique !

Le lettré secoua longuement et douloureusement la tête sous les yeux ébahis de son auditoire avant de poursuivre :

– Quand je lui ai expliqué qu'il pourrait creuser une rigole dans son terrain en pente pour irriguer les sillons de son potager et puiser de l'eau à l'aide d'un balancier, il a éclaté de rire et m'a répondu, justement avec un proverbe : *Le grand défaut des hommes est de délaisser leur jardin pour retirer les mauvaises herbes dans celui du voisin*. Comme je le pressais de m'en dire plus, il s'indigna : « Pour qui vous prenez-vous ? Croyez-vous m'apprendre quelque chose ?! Vous connaissez-vous assez vous-même pour voir la réalité ou comprendre les autres ? Tenez, a-t-il ajouté, je vais vous poser une question. J'ai une voisine qui rapportait chaque jour de l'eau du fond de son jardin pour ses besoins domestiques. Elle avait deux seaux. L'un était neuf, l'autre usagé et fendu. Quand elle arrivait chez elle, le vieux seau était à moitié vide. Qu'auriez-vous fait à sa place ? » Je répondis au jardinier que j'en aurais acheté un autre. Il se gaussa encore de moi. « On voit bien que vous n'êtes pas dans le besoin ! Elle n'en avait pas les moyens ! Elle sut pourtant se servir du défaut de son vieux seau : elle sema sur son chemin une rangée de légumes que la fuite d'eau arrosait à son passage. Voyez-vous, monsieur le Lettré, il n'est pas facile de marcher dans les traces d'un autre et, pour qui sait agir en accord avec le Tao, rien ne se perd, sauf, peut-être, les paroles versées dans les oreilles d'un âne ! »

Le philosophe s'épongea le front d'un revers de manche, passa négligemment la main dans sa soyeuse barbiche et, pressé de continuer par ses disciples, il reprit :

– Je l'ai ensuite supplié de me dire pourquoi il ne voulait pas irriguer son potager à l'aide d'un balancier. Il me rit encore au nez en cueillant ce proverbe : *Nourrir l'ambition dans son cœur, c'est porter un tigre dans ses bras.* Comme j'insistais pour saisir, le priant de m'éclairer, le patriarche me dévoila la profondeur insondable de son esprit. Il me démontra qu'utiliser une machine, c'était mettre le doigt dans un engrenage vicieux, provoquant inéluctablement un enchaînement mécanique de catastrophes : la rentabilité, le profit, le chômage, l'asservissement de l'homme et le pillage de la nature. Il me dit ensuite qu'il préférait arroser un à un ses choux et leur parler ! Il m'affirma que cela les faisait mieux pousser tout en leur donnant meilleur goût sans gaspiller trop d'eau. Alors que j'allais prendre congé et le remercier pour cette édifiante leçon, il me demanda qui j'étais. Quand j'eus dit que Confucius était mon maître, le jardinier s'esclaffa : « Ce vieux fou qui cherche la gloire en prodiguant des conseils aux puissants pour gouverner le monde ? Il aurait mieux fait de vous enseigner à vous gouverner vous-même et d'apprendre à ses élèves de ne pas importuner les braves gens ! » Il hocha la tête, ramassa sa jarre et me décocha un dernier trait : « Décidément, votre science confirme ce qu'on dit par ici : *Un savant qui sait tout ne vaut pas quelqu'un qui sait faire quelque chose de ses mains.* »

Le philosophe regarda ses ongles de lettré dont il avait été si fier, leva les yeux au ciel et, dans un soupir, un poème fleurit sur ses lèvres :

*Seules les eaux tranquilles du lac*
*Peuvent capturer la lune*
*Le nuage de l'ignorance passe*
*Sans abreuver la terre*
*Le Roi Dragon garde la perle*
*De la Connaissance véritable.*

# Le jardin des mots

## HOMMAGE À SHÉHÉRAZADE

Parmi les graines des sages, celles de Shéhérazade ont levé en terre saccagée. La jeune fille épandit ses mots mille et une nuits, labourant le cœur d'un tyran cerné d'épines et rongé par la cruauté. Quand elle entreprit sa tâche, nul sentiment ne traversait plus la glaise inculte et désolée du despote. Les ronces, les entrelacs de branches et de lierre étouffaient toute espérance de rose, la lumière ne pouvait entrer dans l'inextricable forêt de sa colère. Elle choisit ses premières histoires pour le débroussailler, puis d'autres, faites pour juguler les poisons de haine qui rendent stérile la terre d'un homme. Elle en conta d'étranges, de drôles, de lumineuses, celles qui éclosent en touffes verdoyantes là où rien ne pousse plus. Promise à l'arrachement prématuré, celle qui devait être tuée à l'aube de chaque matin devint, à force de persévérance, de ruse et d'amour, la sultane d'un monde abondant et pacifié.

Six ans plus tôt, le jardin du palais avait été témoin d'une tragédie. Par la fenêtre, le frère du Roi avait assisté aux ébats torrides de la Reine et des esclaves. Mis au courant, ravagé par la nouvelle, le sultan fut saisi de barbarie et fit décapiter son épouse et tous les serviteurs. Durant trois ans il déflora chaque nuit une vierge, qu'il faisait tuer dès l'aube, pour ne plus jamais sentir la brûlure de la trahison. Shéhérazade s'offrit pour sauver les jeunes filles et le royaume, se livra sereine au redoutable désir du Roi. Et comme elle avait la vue et la voix de la Nature, elle agit patiemment avec les mots comme avec les graines, cassant les mottes, aspergeant les brindilles, gagnant à chaque aube nouvelle la grâce de vivre un jour de plus et, la nuit venant, celle de semer encore. Les deux dernières, elle conta *Le Prince Jasmin et la princesse Amande*.

Shéhérazade leva les sourcils comme on écarte les buissons, elle ouvrit sa main et fit ruisseler sa voix sur le tapis de la nuit.
« Il était un vieux roi qui avait sept fils pareils aux sept feux des Pléiades. Le plus jeune était le plus brillant, dans ses habits rose et blanc : le prince Jasmin, qui avait le regard clair, la taille d'un jeune cyprès, la douceur et les façons d'un lis... »
Le sultan remonta ses coussins, gage pour la conteuse qu'il buvait chaque goutte telle une fleur assoiffée. Elle reprit, sarclant la terre qui écoute et se laisse faire.
« ...Un jour qu'il jouait de la flûte à ses gazelles, il vit venir un saint derviche, qui lui demanda du lait...
– Garçon délicieux, tu n'as pas nourri une terre stérile mais abreuvé un messager de

l'Amour. J'ai traversé maints déserts pour chercher l'être digne de la jeune fille que j'ai aperçue au paradis-jardin. Elle vit en ce royaume attenant au tien et attend un signe. J'ai vu frémir son corps délicat, sa taille fine, sa bouche taillée dans un rubis d'Orient. Le soleil ferme les yeux quand il passe, pour ne pas jeter l'ancre afin d'admirer ses dents. Sa voix évoque les

abricotiers du Khorassan, ses pieds exquis, la saveur du gingembre. C'est la fille du roi Akbar, princesse Amande, bénis soient ces deux noms. Mais la pauvre a fait un rêve et se désole : puissent mes mots, comme des graines, t'inciter au départ ! »
Shéhérazade savait ce qu'elle disait, l'imagination du sultan courait déjà comme un liseron sur une allée. Il était Jasmin et elle,

Amande. Il écoutait et il allait nu-tête au milieu d'un verger.

« Le garçon partit tel un poète du Darat Jouljoul, ivre de vin, pris par des visions de chamelles, rêvant à de grandes felouques, voiles gonflées au vent sur l'oued, voguant vers la sublime Amande au sein lisse et rond. Aurait-il croisé la neige, qu'elle eût été incapable de le rafraîchir. Le rêve dicté par les génies avait laissé la princesse Amande en grande détresse. Elle qui allait sans souci, vive, prompte à discuter de tout, restait prostrée. La vision du prince Jasmin l'avait effarouchée. Elle avait l'âme collée sur l'autre côté du voile et elle semblait absente. Quand approcha sa favorite...

– Sache, ma princesse, qu'un joueur de flûte venu d'Hazara est sur nos terres. Il a pour nom Jasmin. On dit que son chant charme les grues cendrées, que l'eau des oueds babille sans plus vouloir couler, que les fleurs roses défaillent en le voyant

paraître. Il est l'étoile des Pléiades, il a le regard clair, la taille d'un jeune cyprès, ses habits ont la douceur du lis. Il a bravé mille dangers avant d'arriver, traversé des torrents impétueux, des sables mouvants. Il est si jeune ! On n'agit pas ainsi sans avoir une raison secrète ou une sainte image accrochée à son cœur.
À ces mots, Amande fut joyeuse comme jamais, son entrain, sa grâce revenaient du pays des songes. Elle se mit à danser, ivre de bon miel, entra dans sa chambre, saisit une plume de flamant rose et écrivit. »

À la première lueur de l'aube du mille et unième jour, Shéhérazade se tut. Les yeux brillants, le sultan était plein de sa nuit blanche, tel un arum baigné par la lune, attendant déjà qu'elle lui revienne. Il était telle la fleur qui replie au soir ses pétales, espérant le soleil de minuit. Pour la millième fois, d'un ton presque joyeux, il repoussa la sentence royale et s'endormit.

La nuit venue, Shéhérazade leva les sourcils, ouvrit sa main et reprit d'une voix chantante le fil de son histoire.

« Elle saisit une plume et écrivit : "Voici ce qu'accomplit le maître des existences quand il devient jardin : on m'a parlé de toi, mon cœur a glissé dans mes mains. J'ai vu ton image en songe, elle m'a menée si loin que je me crus perdue. Viens, ô viens que je te voie sur cette terre, que tu surprennes aussi celle qui brûle devant ton image et y danse comme de l'eau." Elle plia les ailes de la lettre, la parfuma de son sourire et la tendit à sa favorite. La jeune fille porta le pli à ses lèvres et à son front, le plaça sur son cœur et fila, comme une gazelle du djebel, au lieu où Jasmin chantait...

... Lui, fort comme quatre lions, relut cent fois le pli, touchant la lune avec sa tête. Quand il se calma, elle lui dit le moyen d'approcher sa bien-aimée. Au moment arrangé par les djinns, il prit le chemin de la princesse Amande, entra dans ce morceau de vert tombé du paradis. Le couchant rougeoyait d'un côté, la lune blanche en face se levait. Il vit l'arbre dont la suivante lui avait parlé, monta se mêler à ses branches. Alors elle vint, telle la biche, leva sa tête vers les ramures. Elle ne sut si le beau visage était la pleine lune ou le prince des nuits. Comme un fruit il tomba près d'elle, plus beau qu'un rêve, et sut que le derviche n'avait rien embelli. »

Le sultan sentait que l'arbre du conte vivait dans sa poitrine et qu'il bourgeonnait, ses paumes humides étaient des rameaux gagnés par la rosée, son ventre aspirait au pardon, il ressemblait au chardon cherchant le regard aimant du soleil. La peur de donner devint un tas de feuilles sèches, bonnes à faire brûler. Jamais il ne s'était senti autant choyé et malmené, tel un jardin livré aux mains expertes.

« ... Bénis par le Maître de l'amour, ils reçurent la manne des étoiles. Il restait à demander au roi Akbar d'accorder sa bénédiction. La jeune fille courut au palais, se fit rossignol et même mieux : voletant papillon et ardent dauphin. Elle supplia le roi son père, méridien des deux mondes, d'engager le bel étranger pour mener ses troupeaux, lui dit que ce doux joueur de flûte était aussi un pasteur de lions. À peine eut-il rétorqué qu'il voulait d'abord le voir qu'elle diffusa sa joie autour du palais, fut sous l'arbre, riante, prit par la main Jasmin, le mena à son père, qui le nomma au milieu de la nuit berger de ses troupeaux.

Mais elle avait un oncle nuisible qui l'accusa de félonie. Le roi Akbar, gagné par l'ire aveugle qui s'abat invariablement sur les croyants, renvoya sa fille derrière les moucharabiés du harem, appela ses fils.

– Arrangez-vous, tuez le gardien des bestiaux ! »

Le sultan était comme un bouleau pris dans la tempête, essayant de retenir ses chatons, priant que le roi du conte soit moins cruel, qu'il éloigne sa folie et qu'il épargne l'amoureux. Il se racla la gorge pour en retirer lui-même les dernières broussailles, sans se rendre compte qu'il donnait la main à Shéhérazade, qu'il se rendait enfin, qu'il agissait comme un apprenti qui nettoie une allée, que des mots doux attendaient à la porte des lèvres pour éclore.

« ... Il y avait près de la ville un bois en tout point contraire au jardin. Son nom sonnait l'effroi, ses habitants étaient des monstres. Les frères y dépêchèrent Jasmin, ignorant tout de l'infortune d'Amande et du sort qu'on lui réservait. Il entra de nuit, marchant devant ses bêtes sous l'astre aux deux cornes, étendit une peau blanche sur la terre et fit résonner sa flûte. Deux monstres cochons-daims chargèrent la clairière. Quand il les vit venir, il continua de jouer. Ils s'arrêtèrent charmés, puis, quand il sortit de la forêt, le suivirent, à sa droite et sa gauche, le troupeau derrière jusque sous les fenêtres du roi Akbar. Il fit entrer les monstres dans une cage de fer et les offrit au roi. Devant le peuple, le souverain leva sa sentence.»

Le sultan soupira. Il se laissa aller à rêver qu'il était lui-même un roi magnanime et bon. Que revenir sur un jugement absurde pouvait être une grande décision. Il était parcouru des picotements familiers à la terre quand elle couvre de fleurs ses prairies. Il attendait le dénouement, comme l'été qui attend son heure pour faire tomber ses fruits.

«... Mais les frères, inquiets devant sa popularité, obtinrent qu'Amande épouse séance tenante leur cousin. Ils eurent beau faire, préparer la noce en buissons de roses, leur sœur semblait morte de son vivant. Au jour fatidique, au milieu des ors sans saveur, elle croisa le regard confiant de Jasmin. Quand vint la nuit, elle fut conduite dans la chambre nuptiale, s'y retrouva seule, sortit sur le balcon où l'attendait son bien-aimé. Se donnant la main, ils s'évanouirent dans la nature. Nul ne les revit que ceux dont l'amour véritable mène au bonheur.»

Ainsi furent les derniers mots-jardin de Shéhérazade, dits en cette ultime nuit de floraison mémorable, où l'amour a gagné. Ils demeurèrent dans le silence de la fin des nuits.
Quand l'aube arriva, la longue maturation du sultan-jardin portait ses fruits : elle avait fait de lui en trois ans un jardinier. Il laissa jaillir un mot d'amour. Comme ses fruits avaient mûri, Shéhérazade montra au roi les trois enfants qu'elle avait eus de lui, en secret. La terre sauvage ennoblie, les fleurs du pardon et le calice du bonheur exhalèrent leur paix dans le sillage des mots qui guérissent un royaume.

*Prends donc une poignée de bonne terre.*
*Y trouves-tu une semence et peut-être*
*un ver ?*
*Si ta main était assez grande*
*et assez patiente,*
*La semence pourrait devenir une forêt,*
*Et le ver une troupe d'anges.*

Khalil Gibran, *Le Jardin du Prophète*

# Le jardin d'Alchemia

D'APRÈS DES SOURCES DE LA RENAISSANCE

Adelphe Duchesne trottait au bord de la route comme un poulain fougueux. Les quinze derniers jours avaient été longs, la perspective de revoir le vieux sage qui l'avait accepté pour disciple l'enflammait. Il n'avait pas trouvé de réponses aux questions qui le tourmentaient depuis le congé que lui avait donné l'alchimiste et il se repassait en boucle leur dernier dialogue.

– Alors comme ça, tu veux trouver la pierre des philosophes ?

– Oh oui, maître !

– C'est la septième fois que tu le demandes.

C'est bien. Il faut être têtu et patient. Tu rêves donc de cornues et de Grand Œuvre ?

– Je veux apprendre !

– Il faut un long chemin pour que le vieil homme devienne jeune.

– ?

– Alors écoute-moi, je vais te donner une adresse. Il faudra t'y rendre au premier jour du printemps et au petit matin. C'est à ce moment que commencera ton apprentissage. D'ici là, fais ce qu'il faut pour être libre de tes attaches et prépare-toi à vivre une chose peu commune. Ne reviens pas. Adieu. Nous nous reverrons là où tu sais, à l'été de ta propre terre.

Le maître parlait la langue verte et usait de métaphores et de tournures d'oiseau. Adelphe rageait car il ne comprenait rien. Quand le vieillard conversait avec un adepte en visite, sa langue feuillue tenait du chant du rossignol. Elle jouait un art subtil rompu aux énigmes et aux déguisements. Jusqu'à ce jour, le jeune homme

avait servi de commis, glanant tel un moineau des miettes, de petites étincelles éphémères de science prometteuses mais hermétiques. Il avait attrapé au vol des mots grecs et latins, des noms d'astres et de métaux et il n'avait fait qu'entrevoir la fumée des alambics.

Adelphe avait dormi dans une grange, pour être à l'aube au lieu convenu. Il était arrivé la veille au soir le cœur battant, étonné de se trouver loin des faubourgs de Paris. Il avait traversé des hameaux, des villages qui ne collaient pas avec l'idée qu'il se faisait d'un lieu où miroite un atelier d'alchimiste. Il imagina qu'il allait apercevoir sur le chemin une forge ou un château aux fortes murailles. Pourtant, lorsqu'il fut sur place, qu'il emprunta *l'allée de l'or*, il ne vit qu'une bicoque et un jardin en friche. Il heurta le marteau de la porte où figurait une tête de singe, attendit. Un homme apparut avec un tablier de jardinier.

– Vous êtes Adelphe.
– Oui, mon maître est-il là ?
– Il vous attend, répondit l'homme en montrant la terre.
– Vous voulez dire à l'intérieur de la maison ?
– Ou plutôt, *visita interiorem terrae rectificando invenies occultum lapidem !*
– ?!??
– Ici, il n'y a qu'une maison verte et c'est toi le jardin.
– ?
– Si tu viens pour bidouiller les cornues, les formules... tout le grand tintouin, il te faudra patienter, passer par ce jardin et verdir.
– Mais...
– Explore, rectifie... L'Art consiste à imiter la nature et parachever ce qu'elle lui donne, comme fait le vigneron.
– Je viens pour...
– Avant de faire germer de l'or et d'en voir les arborescences, tu vas apprendre à cueillir la rosée au creux des feuilles

d'alchémille, étudier les simples, la vie des fleurs, des arbres. Avant de parachever ce que la nature te propose de parfaire, tu dois humer ses secrets au jardin des transformations. Tu as dit au maître vouloir apprendre. Si tu veux devenir un labourant et entrevoir un jour la terre feuillée du Grand Œuvre, tu es là où tu dois être : au jardin de Mater Alchemia.

– Vous êtes donc aussi un...

– ... jardinier, ton guide florentin. Le jardin est notre oratoire et notre laboratoire, nous y prierons, tout en travaillant. Je vais te montrer comment cueillir ces orties et les laisser putréfier dans l'eau. Ici, tu apprendras la chanson de l'humus et tu y connaîtras le devenir de l'homme. C'est au jardin que tout commence et que tout s'illumine. Celui qui peut approcher la licorne et parvient jusqu'aux roses rouges aura su apprécier la secrète beauté du grand cycle. Le moment venu, tu reverras ton maître sous l'Opus Magnum au pied de l'arbre aux oiseaux. Ce jour-là où la tête du corbeau sera blanche, tu seras un sage et un jardinier.

*Dans mes cheveux il posa des lis*
*Sur mes sourcils, des roses incarnats,*
*Dans son jardin d'or on humait*
*Tout ce qui fait son bon plaisir.*

William Blake

# Le trésor d'Amenhotep

D'APRÈS DES LÉGENDES
DE L'ÉGYPTE ANCIENNE

Les sandales du grand jardinier de Pharaon claquaient joyeusement. Il avait tenu les délais, tout était divinement paré pour le retour d'Amenhotep III. L'ensemble naturel dont il avait dirigé la composition répondait aux désirs du souverain. Il honorait et comblait les dieux, il ferait l'admiration des vivants et des morts, des êtres de chair comme des âmes-oiseaux. Il estima les colonnes du temple, arbres de pierre ciselés d'ornements, lotus, papyrus et palmiers, semblables aux trésors verts de l'Égypte.

Longeant les pergolas et les pièces d'eau, il croisa un esclave aux jarres fraîchement remplies et sourit, quand il aperçut le bassin rectangulaire et les poissons colorés s'égaillant parmi les lotus. Il avait combiné l'abondance et l'économie, en écho parfait à cette vie du Nil, faite de canicule et de renaissance fertile. À bonne distance des plates-bandes à damiers et des piscines, se tenaient les puits à balancier, les kiosques de vannerie. Les esclaves viendraient chercher là de quoi transporter le vin, les jujubes et les figues. Ils chargeraient leurs têtes de paniers d'olives, de sacs de grenades et de pommes, de pêches, de laitues, de cumin et de coriandre. De part et d'autre de la villa étaient plantés des vignes, les figuiers sycomores de la déesse Hathor et des arbres à noix de ben. Au pied de l'escalier chatoyaient des fleurs de sesbanie, des buissons d'arbustes rapportés de Nubie. Sur la terrasse, Pharaon contemplait un couple d'ibis et de jeunes babouins. Il se retourna vers le maître de l'ouvrage avec un sourire qui en disait long sur sa satisfaction.

– Jardinier, tu es inspiré par les dieux! Ton jardin sort de l'île des Merveilles.
– Les désirs de Pharaon m'ont guidé.
– J'ai fait quérir mon conteur, qu'il honore cet instant d'une fable juste.

Le conteur s'approcha.
« Aux temps anciens, un navigateur envoyé par Pharaon partit en mer avec ses matelots. Une nuit, l'équipage affronta la tempête. Elle tournoyait, comme si le harpon d'Horus les avait pris pour Seth. D'une déferlante, Sobek, dieu des eaux, prit le navire. Le voyageur se trouva seul au milieu des vagues, lié à un morceau d'épave. Il résista jusqu'à l'aube, veillé par Hathor, puis fut déposé sur un rivage. Exténué, il rampa vers les arbres, où il délira, avant de reprendre des forces et de visiter sa terre d'asile.

L'île appartenait au roi-Serpent, ce souverain du lointain Sud qui parlait, dit-on, le langage des hommes. Elle était couverte de figuiers, de palmiers odorants. Les fleurs embaumaient leur mélange d'arômes, montant vers la Divinité. Le saule et l'acacia poussaient à côté du tamaris, du perséa. Le naufragé se sustenta de fruits juteux, pastèques, concombres, mangues, but aux sources abondantes. Il pêcha à pleines mains aux ruisseaux transparents, se délecta du concert des oiseaux rieurs. L'herbe était fournie, toutes sortes d'insectes y bourdonnaient. C'était un jardin sans pareil, entretenu par une invisible manne, puisqu'il n'y avait ni jardinier, ni âme qui vive pour l'aimer.

Le naufragé emporta des provisions dans une haie, bâtit une cabane de branches et alluma un feu pour remercier Rê de l'avoir épargné.

Il observait les flammes, quand un fracas se répercuta dans l'océan, jusqu'au ciel et sous la terre. La haie s'agita telle une plume d'autruche. Le voyageur terrorisé vit paraître le maître-Serpent. Il était long comme une piscine, portait une barbe interminable. Son corps était couvert d'un trésor d'écailles, ses yeux étaient des perles d'améthyste. L'homme se prosterna, vacillant d'effroi, tandis que le régent l'encerclait et dressait sa tête pour lui parler.

– Humain, qui t'a indiqué le chemin de mon île ? Si tu me dis la vérité, tu n'auras rien à craindre de moi. Le roi de tous les Serpents peut te déchirer ou te porter délicatement, comme un iris, dans sa gueule. Parle !

L'homme fut secoué d'une terreur sacrée. Quand il voulut parler, un râle mourut sur ses lèvres. Le Serpent le saisit telle une fleur d'iris et glissa, dans un grand froissement d'écailles, jusqu'à sa grotte.

– Qui t'a indiqué le chemin de mon île ? On ne peut venir ici en nageant.

La voix fébrile de l'homme perlait entre deux tressaillements, encouragée par le serpent, qui promit de l'épargner. Alors il conta son histoire et vit de l'émoi dans les yeux scintillants. Le roi soupira :

– Remercie Rê, qui t'a conduit sur cette île. J'ai connu jadis un sort semblable au tien. Une étoile de feu a dévoré ici ma fille et tous les miens. À la lune suivante, Khonsou guidera un vaisseau jusqu'au rivage et tu rentreras chez toi.

Le voyageur salua son hôte et goûta une lune entière au paradis vert de l'île, puis il aperçut au loin un vaisseau. Il alla jusqu'à la grotte, pour prendre congé.

– Humain, tu salueras Pharaon et la terre d'Égypte.

– Je dirai à Pharaon combien est généreux le roi-Serpent. J'affréterai un vaisseau pour t'offrir...

– ... Peut-on ajouter une plume à l'abondance ? Ici sont tous les fruits de la terre, les fleurs, toutes les essences, jardins épanouis, bêtes sacrées, pierres précieuses. Tu ne retrouveras pas la route de cette île qui va s'enfoncer dans les profondeurs et

disparaître. J'irai bientôt, avec elle, là où niche le royaume des serpents.
Puis, il siffla sur un rocher et la pierre s'ouvrit sur une vaste caverne aux trésors. C'était un jardin rempli de pierres précieuses où la vie tout entière étincelait. Le roi donna la myrte, les huiles, les encens rares, les bulbes de roses trémières. Il offrit le bois de santal, les babouins sacrés, les paons à l'effigie de Rê, les fruits, toutes sortes d'arbres. Le voyageur s'inclina, chargea les trésors sur le vaisseau, prit congé. De retour, il confia la précieuse cargaison à l'homme qui était digne de la recevoir et de l'honorer : cet homme était le jardinier de Pharaon. »

Le conteur se courba devant ses auditeurs et disparut dans l'allée.

– Toi aussi, tu as reçu les trésors de l'île-jardin, dit Amenhotep, tu as mis au jour le trésor caché.
– Pas encore, Pharaon. Je n'ai pas atteint

la sagesse du prêtre Djadjaemankh, je ne possède pas le secret qui commande aux éléments de servir la beauté.
– Quel secret ?
– Celui du mage. Pharaon sait comme l'on s'ennuie parfois dans un palais. Pour se divertir, le grand Snefrou suivit un matin le conseil de son prêtre-lecteur et fit sa promenade sur l'étang. Vingt jeunes femmes aux cheveux ondulants, cuisses vives et belles poitrines ramaient tandis que le jardin saluait Pharaon. Femmes et fleurs provenant d'une même essence, bras-fruits délectables saluaient la déesse-arbre qui étanche la soif des morts. Voilà qu'une jeune fille, assise à l'arrière du bateau, tressa sa natte. Et sa boucle d'oreille, faite d'une belle turquoise, tomba à l'eau. La jeune beauté délaissa sa rame et bientôt toutes en firent autant. Quand Snefrou comprit ce qu'il se passait, que la jeune fille tenait à sa boucle plus qu'à mille autres, il fit quérir Djadjaemankh. Le mage murmura à l'onde une langue douce

et il prononça des formules de prodige. Alors, la moitié de l'étang vint se poser sur l'autre. Le prêtre chemina dans le lit rocailleux où brillait le bijou et remonta, le rendit à la belle rameuse. Puis, reprenant ses incantations, il rétablit le cours habituel du bassin. Voilà un homme qui met à jour les trésors cachés.

– Vois-tu, jardinier, je suis comblé par ton humilité et ta sagesse, par ta profonde reconnaissance pour les lois qui gouvernent la beauté.

Le grand jardinier de Pharaon s'inclina, puis il s'éloigna, sous l'œil bienveillant des iris blanc et bleu, des euphorbes aux belles robes et des genévriers, dans la paix du soir.

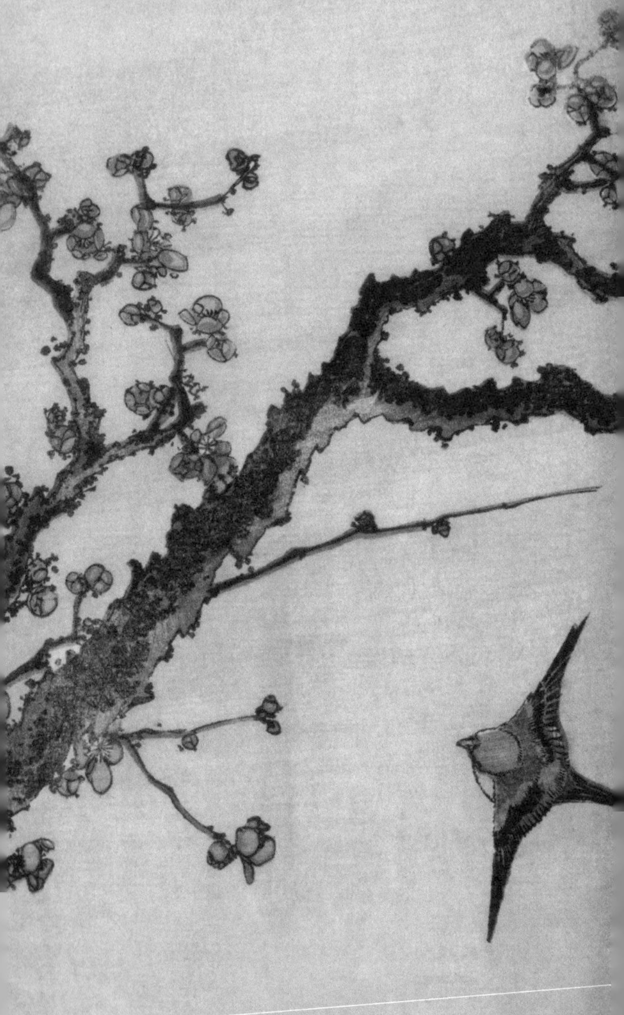

# Celle qui savait parler aux arbres

LÉGENDE JAPONAISE

Le gouverneur de la province de Kaga aimait se reposer des tracas du monde dans le parc de son palais. Dès que son emploi du temps le permettait, trop rarement, hélas, il s'y enfonçait seul, suivait les sentiers, accordant le rythme de ses pas et de sa respiration à celui des dalles de pierre qui serpentaient entre les bosquets de bambous nains ou de pivoines arborescentes. Elles le menaient dans les futaies de pins, les bois de chênes et les boqueteaux d'érables. Il ne se lassait pas de s'émerveiller devant la science que des générations de maîtres jardiniers avaient déployée pour perfectionner le jardin. Ponctuant la marche du temps, l'éclosion sans cesse renouvelée d'un nuancier de fleurs le ravissait : chrysanthèmes blancs, jaunes et or, camélias et asters roses, gentianes bleues, azalées rouges, écarlates... Le cycle des feuillus se métamorphosant au rythme des saisons concourait aussi à observer la transmutation perpétuelle des éléments, à méditer sur l'impermanence, à cueillir la fleur unique qu'offrait chaque instant. Au détour d'un chemin, il n'était pas rare qu'il soit surpris par l'envol d'une grue ou d'un héron, le chant du rossignol, le reflet de la lune capturé par le miroir de l'étang. Autant de messagers qui annonçaient la présence d'un autre monde.

À force d'arpenter les sentiers du parc, le gouverneur de Kaga avait compris que les maîtres jardiniers le guidaient sur le chemin de l'Éveil. Pas à pas, il s'apaisait, se dépouillait du superflu, s'ouvrait à une vision plus profonde, plus sensible, entrait en résonance avec la nature. Quand il débouchait devant la butte où se dressait la pierre levée entourée d'une coulée de roches, il sentait bien qu'il était prêt à entendre la parole du Bouddha exposant le nectar de la Loi à ses disciples. Et là, assis sur la pierre de méditation, il pouvait admirer la cascade qui illustrait une parabole zen : le rocher dressé sous la chute d'eau figurait la carpe qui remonte le courant pour se métamorphoser en dragon. Contournant le lac, il pouvait enfin traverser l'élégant pont arqué qui enjambait les eaux constellées de lotus, symboles mêmes de la fleur de la compassion émergeant de l'eau boueuse des passions humaines. Il accédait alors à l'île centrale pareille aux vergers célestes des Immortels. Toutes les espèces d'arbres fruitiers s'y côtoyaient : pruniers, cerisiers, abricotiers, pêchers, pommiers, kakis, poiriers, cognassiers, néfliers... C'était un régal des sens avec, au printemps, les myriades de fleurs aux parfums envoûtants et, l'été, des fruits divinement savoureux.

Au centre du verger trônait un cerisier centenaire. Le *daimyô* de Kaga vouait à l'arbre vénérable une affection particulière. Il aimait venir y contempler sa floraison, s'asseoir à son ombre et, parfois, se confier à lui comme à un vieil ami. Or, depuis quelque temps, le patriarche du verger dépérissait. Malgré les soins attentifs qu'on lui prodiguait, il ne donnait plus beaucoup de fleurs. La vie semblait irrémédiablement le quitter.

Le gouverneur fit un jour venir au chevet du cerisier moribond le maître jardinier d'un monastère de Kaga, réputé pour sa main verte. Le vieux moine ausculta longuement le malade, allant même jusqu'à coller son oreille contre son tronc comme s'il voulait écouter les battements de son cœur. Le vieillard délivra enfin son ordonnance aux jardiniers du palais : des instructions pour la taille, une décoction à vaporiser sur les feuilles, un emplâtre au bas du tronc et un fertilisant pour les racines.

Au printemps suivant, le vieux moine revint au palais pour vérifier si ses remèdes avaient fait leur effet. Force fut de constater qu'il n'en était rien : le cerisier chenu n'arborait plus que de rares fleurs. Le maître jardinier se tourna vers le gouverneur :

– Son Excellence n'est pas sans savoir que les arbres ont une âme. Si le malade n'a plus le goût de vivre, le traitement ne peut agir efficacement. Peut-être que l'esprit de ce vieux cerisier s'est lassé de ce monde impermanent.

– Il n'y a donc plus d'espoir ? demanda le seigneur, visiblement affecté.

Le moine à la barbiche blanche, un sourire malicieux effleurant ses lèvres, répondit :

– J'ai déjà pu vérifier de mes propres yeux que les arbres, tout comme nous, ne sont pas insensibles aux charmes des fleurs du monde flottant.

Pour *setsubun*, la fête du premier jour du printemps, le gouverneur invita donc dans ses jardins les plus belles geishas de sa

province. Au son des *shamisen* et des voix cristallines, les sublimes beautés dansèrent autour du vieil arbre, déployant les soies colorées de leurs kimonos comme des ailes de papillons.
Cette année-là, jamais les jardins du palais n'offrirent des fleurs et des fruits aussi éclatants, parfumés, savoureux. Sauf le vieux cerisier récalcitrant...

Quand le moine jardinier vint constater le nouvel échec de son traitement, il soupira puis il empoigna délicatement une branche du cerisier comme s'il lui prenait le pouls. Il hocha longuement la tête et finit par déclarer :
– Ce vieil arbre n'a plus beaucoup de souffle vital. Il s'endort, se laisse aller. Je ne sais plus trop ce qui pourrait encore toucher son âme...
Le gouverneur, les yeux embués de la rosée des larmes, laissa échapper ces mots :
– Il me faut donc dire adieu à ce vieil ami ? !

臥龍梅

Le moine demeura pensif un moment avant de dire :

– Vous connaissez le talent de Chiyo la poétesse.

– Bien sûr, s'exclama le *daimyô*, son art fait honneur à notre province. Ses poèmes figurent déjà dans maintes anthologies. Sa renommée a couru jusqu'à Edo. Il y a peu, le Shogun en personne s'est extasié en me citant ses vers :

*Traces des rêves*
*Des papillons*
*Les fleurs dans les champs.*

Elle est venue autrefois dans ce jardin participer à des *renga*, des joutes de haïkus. Dans sa jeunesse, elle brillait déjà par son *fûga*, l'élégance de sa poésie qui, d'ailleurs, était à l'égal de sa beauté. J'ai encore en mémoire les vers que le poète Rokyo composa pour la chanter :

*Ne fais pas tomber*
*Le cavalier de sa monture*
*Belle fleur !*

Le maître jardinier tenta de reprendre le fil de son discours sur un ton sentencieux :
– Sa beauté est grande certes, mais éphémère telle la fleur de cerisier. Par contre, son art la rendra immortelle.
Le gouverneur, qui était en verve, et sans doute inspiré par le souvenir de la poétesse, l'interrompit de nouveau :
– C'est vrai que ses haïkus atteignent des sommets inégalés. Il faut dire qu'elle fut très tôt à bonne école. Son père avait un atelier de montage de *kakémonos* fréquenté par les plus grands artistes de la province. On m'a rapporté qu'à six ans, elle écrivit ses premiers poèmes. À douze ans, elle entra au service de Hansui, un disciple de Bashô... Peu de femmes ont brillé sur la Voie étroite du haïku. Sa poésie est incomparable. Elle n'est d'ailleurs pas dénuée de sensualité. Il me revient à l'esprit ce poème :

*La fleur de courge*
*S'ouvre à la lune*
*Peau de femme qui se dénude.*

Mais dites-moi, qu'est-elle devenue ? Voilà longtemps que je n'ai pas eu de ses nouvelles.
– Sachez qu'elle a beaucoup souffert. Tous ses proches parents sont morts. Elle a trouvé refuge dans la doctrine de la Terre Pure du Bouddha Amida. Depuis peu, elle a revêtu la robe des nonnes. Mais, pour notre bonheur, elle n'a pas renoncé à la poésie, bien au contraire ! Tenez, le jour de son ordination, alors qu'on lui rasait les cheveux, elle improvisa ces vers :

*Le rouge à lèvres*
*Ma bouche a oublié*
*Ah ! l'eau de la source.*

– Excellent ! s'exclama le gouverneur. Mais, dites-moi, au fait, pourquoi me parlez-vous d'elle ? Où voulez-vous en venir ?
– Sa poésie est aussi pure que le jade. Peu d'hommes ont atteint un tel dépouillement, sont capables d'une telle union avec la nature. Peut-être parviendra-t-elle à trouver le chemin du cœur de votre vieux cerisier...

– Eh bien, soit ! Invitez-la à me rendre visite.

La nonne Chiyo se présenta aux portes du palais dans sa robe austère qui faisait ressortir la finesse de ses traits. Le seigneur la trouva plus belle encore que dans ses souvenirs, comme si les années et les épreuves avaient fait resplendir sa lumière intérieure. Le *daimyô* de Kaga la conduisit en personne au chevet de l'arbre malade. Quelle ne fut pas sa surprise quand il entendit la sublime poétesse s'adresser aussi vertement au vieux cerisier :

*Le printemps reviendra*
*Sans fleurs, tu ne seras plus*
*Que bois de chauffage !*

Au retour du printemps, le gouverneur guetta fébrilement l'effet du haïku. Il avait peur qu'il eût porté un coup fatal à l'esprit du moribond. Mais il fut émerveillé de constater que ce traitement de choc avait stimulé sa sève : le vieux cerisier était auréolé d'une myriade de fleurs.

# La rose d'immortalité

D'APRÈS UN CONTE D'ARMÉNIE

En ce temps-là, au pays d'Hayastan, un roi possédait un jardin parfait, chanté par les *achough*, les troubadours arméniens. Dans sa jeunesse, il aimait aller parmi les scabieuses du Caucase, les grappes de muscaris et les bouquets d'abricotiers. Il chérissait plus que tout sa roseraie, il éprouvait pour sa partie la plus cachée un amour infini. Près du bassin où sa jeune épouse venait se baigner, à l'abri d'un labyrinthe de buis, il contemplait Anmahagan Vart : le rosier dont les légendes promettaient sa fleur d'immortalité au maître du jardin. Mais le roi avait fini par se détourner du joyau de sa roseraie, car aucun des jardiniers qu'il avait engagés n'avait su faire éclore la reine des roses. En vérité, la peur de la mort dévorait le roi. À chaque nouveau cheveu blanc, de rage, il faisait décapiter le jardinier et pour oublier le temps qui file, se grisait de plaisirs amers.

Malgré le salaire royal promis par le souverain, plus personne n'était candidat à l'entretien de la roseraie. Être nommé responsable de l'éclosion de la fleur des fleurs finissait invariablement sous la lame d'un *kindjal* affilé. Il arriva un temps où nul ne s'occupait du jardin, jusqu'à ce qu'un jeune va-nu-pieds vînt frapper à la porte du palais. Le roi, incrédule, voulut recevoir en personne l'audacieux.
– Que sais-tu de l'art du jardin, toi qui viens risquer ta tête ici ?
– Mon père disait qu'il tenait en trois

mots : connaissance, vigilance et patience.
– Et que préconises-tu pour faire naître un bouton sur un rosier récalcitrant ?
– D'arroser ces trois graines avec amour.
– Et pour ton audace, quel est ton prix ?
– Vivre au jardin et que le roi patiente trois printemps.
– Soit, que ta main honore tes paroles et que ta langue n'attire pas sur ton col la lame du bourreau.

Le jardinier donna à boire au rosier, il bêcha précautionneusement, étudia la terre et la nourrit d'un terreau dont il avait le secret. Il le pailla pour l'hiver, le tailla à la fin des gelées et il soigna ses feuilles. Il couchait au pied du rosier et dormait à peine, demeurant à son chevet comme l'amant qui guette le battement de cils de sa belle endormie. Un jour, aux premières lueurs de l'aube, il aperçut, scintillant de rosée, un bouton naissant. Soulagé, un sourire aux lèvres, il attendit la visite du roi.

– Ça y est, hurla le monarque, je vais vivre cent dix mille ans... tu as sauvé ta vie et la mienne !
– Mon père disait que nul ne sait si sa lumière brillera jusqu'à demain, répondit le jeune homme.
Le roi parti, le jardinier exténué et rassuré s'abandonna au sommeil, le temps de tourner en rêve une page de la légende d'Anmahagan Vart. Quand il ouvrit les yeux, le lendemain matin, le bouton avait disparu.
Une fois avisé, le roi tonna, éructa, déballa un tas de grossièretés. Mais il avait promis trois printemps au jardinier. Alors il fut hanté de grande inquiétude qu'il tenta de noyer dans un tourbillon de débauche.

Le jeune homme n'arrivait pas à saisir ce qui s'était produit durant son sommeil. Il avait beau tourner et retourner ses pensées comme une terre meuble, il se laissa gagner par l'incertitude. Avait-il suffisamment donné de son art ? Il songea alors aux paroles avisées que prononçait son père lorsque le résultat escompté ne venait pas : le doute est la clé de toute connaissance. Il refit chaque chose qu'il avait déjà faite, abreuva le rosier, bêcha, étudia la terre, la nourrit. Il pailla, tailla après les froidures, prit grand soin des feuilles. Il veilla auprès du rosier, dormit les yeux ouverts, son arc et ses flèches à portée de main, guettant l'intrus qui oserait forcer l'entrée de la roseraie et profaner le bouton espéré. Il scruta l'adversité tel un chevalier amoureux et protecteur.

Un jour, à l'aube, il découvrit scintillant de rosée un bouton entrouvert, redoubla sa garde, inspecta chaque buisson de l'enceinte, prêt à décocher une flèche sur l'intrus. Aux aguets, attendant la visite du roi, il se retourna vers le rosier et vit un gros ver finissant d'avaler la fleur. Il avait compris, mais il était trop tard pour cette année. Le roi faillit rompre son serment, il appela et décommanda vingt fois son bourreau, renversa des chaises, fit battre les valets et s'affala, épuisé, chancelant à l'idée de partir rejoindre ses aïeux. Puis, las, il fit quérir des filles légères, des jongleurs et des cracheurs de feu.

Pendant que le roi partait festoyer, le jeune homme suspendit son arc à un arbre et reprit ses soins saisonniers.
Il veilla inlassablement nuit et jour jusqu'à l'apparition du bouton aux premières lueurs du petit matin. Quand le ver sortit des entrailles de la terre, il s'en saisit. Alors qu'il l'observait dans le creux de sa main, un moineau surgit, le prit dans son bec et se posa en haut du rosier. Le jardinier vit un serpent s'enrouler autour du pied d'Anmahagan Vart. Alors, voulant protéger le bouton en train d'éclore à la lumière naissante, il courut vers l'arbre où il avait suspendu son arc, se jucha sur une branche et visa le serpent, qui dévorait déjà l'oiseau. Avant qu'il n'eût le temps de tirer sa flèche, un aigle avait glissé sur le

premier rayon du soleil pour emporter le serpent et le dévorer. Dans la lumière dorée de l'aube, au chant du rossignol, Anmahagan Vart déploya gracieusement ses pétales vermeils. Alors, au-dessus des buis, le jardinier vit venir la jeune reine, s'avançant telle l'Aurore, ses pieds blancs trempant la traîne de sa robe déjà tout imprégnée de rosée. Elle s'approcha du bassin, déboutonna son habit de pourpre et se glissa nue dans l'onde transparente. Il admira sa peau de nacre, l'harmonie vertigineuse de ses formes, sa grâce où se reflétait toute la beauté du monde.

L'arrivée tonnante du roi le sortit de sa contemplation. L'ire rendait Sa Majesté cramoisie. Ne voyant du jardinier qu'un insolent qui se repaissait des charmes de son épouse, aveuglé par la jalousie, il essaya de grimper dans l'arbre afin de déloger l'impudent. Une branche cassa et il se rompit le cou, roulant au pied du rosier, agonisant. Apercevant enfin Anmahagan Vart, il murmura :

– Dois-je ainsi mourir alors que je possède enfin la fleur d'immortalité ?
S'approchant, la reine se pencha à l'oreille du mourant et lui dit :
– Le véritable maître du jardin est celui qui connaît, qui veille et qui patiente.

*Dans le cœur doré de la rose immortelle*
*Qui se dilate et s'exalte,*
*Un parfum de louange s'exhale,*
*Au soleil de l'éternel printemps...*

Dante, *La Divine Comédie.*

# Les figues de Nasreddine

CONTE ORIENTAL

Nasreddine Hodja avait ses entrées au palais de Tamerlan. La légende affirme que le redoutable Conquérant des steppes en avait même fait son bouffon.

Pour conserver les faveurs de l'irascible souverain, le Hodja eut un jour l'idée de lui rapporter de son jardin un plein panier de figues savoureuses. Or, il ignorait que le Mongol détestait ces fruits. À peine les eut-il offerts que le Maître du Monde en choisit un bien mûr et le lui lança au visage.

– Allah est grand ! s'exclama le Hodja

hilare, le visage dégoulinant de jus rougeâtre.
Tamerlan prit une autre figue et lui fit suivre le même chemin.
Et Nasreddine, levant les bras au ciel, dansant d'un pied sur l'autre, tel un derviche hurleur, continua de plus belle :
– Allah est grand ! Allah est grand !
Exaspéré, Tamerlan lui lança alors :
– Arrête de rendre grâce à Dieu, triple idiot ! Ne vois-tu pas dans quel état j'ai mis ton turban et ton caftan ? !
– Peut-être, s'exclama Nasreddine, mais Allah est grand car il m'a inspiré juste au bon moment. Avant de partir, j'ai vu un rayon de soleil danser sur le figuier. J'ai posé mes gros sacs et rempli mon petit panier. Et dire que j'allais me mettre en route pour t'offrir d'énormes pastèques !

# Le paria aux mains fleuries

RÉCIT JAPONAIS

Tout au long de l'histoire du Japon, l'art du jardin ne cessa de se transformer. Son origine se confond avec les enceintes sacrées des temples shintos et des palais impériaux. Sous l'influence chinoise furent introduits les principes du feng shui, la reproduction en miniature de paysages célèbres ou mythiques comme les Îles-Montagnes des Immortels. Puis, avec le bouddhisme, le jardin symbolisa le paradis de la Terre Pure d'Amida où se réfugie l'adepte pour se libérer des vicissitudes de ce monde impermanent. Plus tard, l'esprit du zen aboutit à un dépouillement propice à la méditation sur le Vide dont la quintessence fut une forme d'abstraction de la nature avec la création de jardins minéraux.

Les premiers concepteurs de jardins furent des aristocrates, laïques puis entrés en religion. Comme les travaux manuels, et plus encore, le terrassement et le transport des pierres, considérés comme dégradants, étaient réservés aux plus basses castes, des moines de rangs inférieurs se spécialisèrent dans l'art du jardin. On les appelait *ishitatesô*, « moines dresseurs de pierres ». Ensuite, sous l'influence du zen, enseignement favorisé et souvent pratiqué par les shoguns et les samouraïs, les tâches quotidiennes, les activités les plus humbles furent réhabilitées. Cuisine, ménage, artisanat, jardinage furent considérés comme d'excellents supports à la méditation en mouvement. Le jardin devint le lieu par excellence de la contemplation de la nature du Bouddha présente dans tous les êtres vivants, y compris les arbres, les plantes et les pierres.

Les *kawaramono*, les « gens du fleuve », étaient des hors-castes qui travaillaient le cuir, équarrissaient les animaux, tannaient les peaux. Ils étaient considérés comme impurs et vivaient dans leurs ghettos au bord de l'eau. Certains d'entre eux devinrent les assistants des « moines dresseurs de pierres » en accomplissant les travaux de terrassement. À force de travailler à leurs côtés, ils acquirent de grandes connaissances dans l'art des jardins. Mais leurs mentors conservaient les secrets les plus profonds de leur science qu'ils se transmettaient oralement ou par écrit avec des *makimono*, des documents codés. Un artisan sellier du nom de Matashirô décida un jour de changer sa condition et de démontrer qu'un hors-caste comme lui pouvait devenir non seulement un maître jardinier mais également un créateur, un innovateur. Il entra au service des moines du Shôkoku-ji, l'un des plus importants monastères zen de Kyôto. Tout en travaillant à leurs côtés dans les jardins, il étudia sans relâche tant les traités de jardinage que les écritures saintes du bouddhisme. Sa réputation de jardinier hors pair finit par franchir l'enceinte du monastère. Des moines de toute obédience et de tout rang, même les fameux « dresseurs de pierres », le consultaient en secret pour avoir son avis, aussi bien sur les fertilisants, les traitements appropriés à telle plante, que sur l'esthétique ou la ré-harmonisation d'un lieu. Il trouvait toujours des solutions ingénieuses, semblait avoir réponse à tout. Sa renommée enjamba les enclos des moines. De riches marchands, de puissants seigneurs firent appel à lui pour créer ou redessiner leurs jardins. Et Matashirô se montra de plus en plus inventif, repoussant sans cesse les limites de son art, créant de petits paradis à la beauté inouïe. Les amateurs éclairés s'extasiaient devant la subtilité des formes, le nuancier des couleurs, le rythme et la symbolique de la disposition des pierres. Cela lui valut des éloges et, comme le veut une loi de ce monde impermanent, son lot de jalousie et de calomnie. Alors qu'il venait de recréer une partie du jardin d'un temple de Kyôto, un groupe d'*ishitatesô*, de « moines dresseurs de pierres », le prit à partie devant le supérieur du sanctuaire :

– Tous les traités de notre art, en accord avec les principes du feng shui, enseignent depuis des temps immémoriaux que les cours d'eau ne sont favorablement orientés que s'ils coulent du nord-est vers le sud-ouest, car le souffle du Dragon bleu doit purifier les mauvaises énergies apportées par la route du Tigre blanc. Comment avez-vous osé faire couler cette cascade en sens contraire ?!

Matashirô cloua leurs becs persifleurs par cette réponse renversante :

– Ô honorables moines, oseriez-vous affirmer que la parole du Bouddha qui s'est répandue d'ouest en est pour venir jusqu'à nous n'a pas été bénéfique ? Ne serait-il pas temps de nous libérer de ces vieux principes taoïstes pour nous mettre en accord avec notre foi ?

Un autre jour, un moine du Nanzen-ji, le monastère zen le plus prestigieux de Kyôto, vint trouver Matashirô pour lui demander comment faire revivre un arbre vénérable qui se desséchait irrémédiablement. Le paria érudit traça quelques calligraphies sur une feuille de papier. Il la roula, la tendit au moine et lui expliqua qu'il fallait l'enterrer au pied de l'arbre et l'arroser abondamment chaque jour pour que l'encre atteigne les racines. Un mois plus tard, l'arbre avait reverdi. L'histoire fit grand bruit. Beaucoup y virent un miracle, l'œuvre d'un saint homme. D'autres de la magie de bas étage du même acabit que celle des vendeurs de charmes de places publiques. De nouveau, le maître jardinier fut sommé de s'expliquer :

– Les vieux arbres ne sont-ils pas habités

par des *kami*, des dieux ? Ne peuvent-ils pas guérir eux aussi quand les paroles du Bouddha pénètrent leur cœur ? Méditez, je vous en prie, cet extrait du Soutra du Lotus que j'avais fait enterrer près des racines : « Versée sur eux, la pluie du nectar de la Loi élimine toutes les illusions qui obstruent le chemin vers l'éveil. »

Cette nouvelle joute philosophique dédoubla encore l'aura hors norme de notre jardinier iconoclaste. Plus rien d'important n'était désormais entrepris dans les jardins de la capitale sans ses conseils éclairés. Aristocrates et dignitaires ecclésiastiques se l'arrachaient dans leur désir d'éblouir leurs pairs à travers l'originalité esthétique et allégorique de leurs jardins. Même les jardiniers de l'Empereur venaient le consulter, brisant en cachette les interdits. Avoir notoirement recours à un hors-caste pour régir l'enceinte sacrée du descendant de la déesse solaire Amaterasu aurait pu leur coûter leur place et, peut-être, leur vie.

Pourtant, en 1504, le supérieur du Shôkoku-ji, le monastère zen où était rattaché Matashirô, brisa un tabou. Pour la première fois, il accueillit un hors-caste jardinier dans la communauté des moines ordonnés et lui donna un nom bouddhique : Jifuku.

Matashirô fit école. Il créa une nouvelle tradition de l'art des jardins, y forma d'autres parias. Par la suite, les jardiniers hors-castes supplantèrent les « moines dresseurs de pierres ». Certains entrèrent même au service du shogun et de l'empereur. Ainsi grandit la légende du paria aux mains fleuries.

# Les roseraies du roi Midas

MYTHOLOGIE BABYLONIENNE
ET GRECQUE

Le gardien du sanctuaire toisa son jeune élève : il comprenait vite et possédait le bon sens indispensable aux jardiniers. Il s'était fort bien acquitté des tâches qu'il lui avait confiées : entretien des myrtes, des figuiers, des bosquets de noisetiers et du verger, nettoyage et réparation des canalisations de bois. Comme chaque soir, l'adolescent attendait impatiemment ce moment où son mentor se faisait conteur et complétait ses connaissances des plantes par des récits. Les semaines passées avaient vu défiler un aréopage de héros, dieux de l'Olympe, simples mortels pris dans les tourments ou les délices des bois sacrés. Il avait aimé les assauts et les ruses déployés par Hercule pour rapporter les pommes d'or des Hespérides, les jardins d'Arcadie et tous ces lieux verdoyants et fabuleux des confins de la terre. Il avait été ému par le récit de Tammuz, fertile dieu-berger aimé d'Ishtar, déesse de l'amour et de la guerre, de la vie et de la mort, reine du ciel et des fruits de la terre. Descendue aux enfers pour ravir ce royaume à sa sœur, elle avait échoué et était morte, avec la fertilité. Le seigneur des dieux intervint pour sauver Ishtar et le monde, et elle dut choisir un vivant pour la remplacer : Tammuz juché sur son trône, le jeune dieu-épi assis près d'Orion, livré aux démons. La déesse, ressaisie, entendit l'appel du dieu-nature, son premier amour, arracha sa parure et répandit sa plainte douloureuse. La reine des enfers décréta qu'il resterait six mois sous terre, qu'Ishtar irait chaque année le

chercher, la sœur du dieu partageant le sort du frère, pour l'autre moitié. En été il meurt, la sécheresse lie la terre. Il est mis en croix sur le bois de vie tels Adonis et Dumuzi. Il va au séjour des morts, vivre le mystère du jardinier verdure, qui a sagement admis la loi de la vie.

L'adolescent, enthousiaste, attendait un nouveau récit.
Le conteur lui fit signe de le suivre et s'arrêta près d'un rosier odorant.
– Aujourd'hui je vais te parler des roseraies du roi Midas. Que sais-tu de lui ?
– Qu'il avait sauvé un satyre magicien, l'avait prié d'exaucer son vœu que tout ce qu'il toucherait se transformât en or. Mais ce don, il s'en était mordu les doigts. Il avait aussi perdu une joute musicale contre Apollon, fut mauvais perdant et s'en trouva puni par des oreilles d'âne.
– Je sais ce qu'on raconte, mon garçon, ce sont des fredaines pour ceux qui restent en dehors du jardin. Vois-tu, je préfère te dire

l'histoire du véritable Midas, celle du berger-roi de ses roses, dont le nom était une graine. Elle est moins connue et pourtant plus véridique que les fables. Ce roi de Macédoine, qui eut Orphée pour professeur, ne se faisait-il pas de la richesse une plus haute idée que celle qu'on lui prête? Vois-tu, quand il trouva Silène, le satyre magicien, saoul, endormi dans son jardin de roses, il le fit ligoter par ses jardiniers à des guirlandes de fleurs. N'est-ce pas curieux, as-tu déjà vu ça? L'autre se réveilla de bonne humeur, lui parla des doux rivages d'Hyperborée, évoqua les deux fleuves incomparables, bordés d'arbres. Au bord du premier, il lui dit que ceux-ci portaient les fruits qui font pleurer, gémir ceux qui les mangent. Au bord de l'autre, ils redonnaient la jeunesse et la beauté aux plus âgés, à tel point qu'ils retournaient à l'enfance, jusqu'à disparaître au lieu-mystère d'avant leur naissance. Ce genre d'histoire ravissait le roi Midas. Lui qui avait reçu d'Orphée le don de parler la langue des bêtes, qui charmait les nymphes et donnait du plaisir à ses fleurs, qu'aurait-il eu besoin de faire de l'or ? Ou bien... l'or désignait-il autre chose ? Quand il fut reçu par Dionysos qui voulut le récompenser d'avoir aidé Silène, il demanda que tout ce qu'il toucherait se transformât en or. Et que touchait le roi-jardinier Midas ?

– Ses roses ?

– Eh oui ! Ses oreilles étaient celles d'un roi-jardinier qui avait entendu les secrets d'un éminent fils d'Hermès, des oreilles incomparables qui percevaient le chant du monde. Quand Midas toucha ses fleurs, elles se dédoublèrent et leur parfum devint sublime. Elles étaient sorties des flots avec Aphrodite, s'étaient ouvertes au bois sacré, avaient maintenant soixante pétales. Midas passait des heures à les contempler. Si ses oreilles là s'allongèrent comme celles d'un âne, c'était pour mieux capter leur chant. Tu vas être étonné, mon garçon, car alors le roi sut qu'il devait boire l'eau de vie de ses roses. D'un simple toucher d'or, l'herbe flétrie et l'arbre mort reverdissaient.

Pour finir ce soir, sache que le même mot désigne la rose ou la rosée, qu'humus veut dire *à terre* et que c'est là qu'il te faut chercher.

# Le son du bambou

RÉCIT ZEN CHINOIS

*La faute la plus grave que tu puisses*
*commettre*
*Est de citer les Écritures et de donner*
*des explications*
*Pour prouver que tu « comprends ».*
*Peu importe que tu arranges les choses ;*
*En réalité, tu cherches un être vivant*
*parmi des fantômes !*

Da Hui Zong Gao, maître chan

Xiangyan était un moine particulièrement érudit, un discoureur infatigable et impénitent. Bien qu'il fût pendant des années le disciple de Baizhang, grand maître du zen en Chine, il confondait encore le savoir intellectuel avec la connaissance véritable. Incapable de se décoller du mental, il prenait toujours le doigt qui désigne la lune pour la lune elle-même. À la mort du maître, il demeura auprès de son assistant, Guishan.

Un jour, Guishan interpella Xiangyan et lui dit :

– Du temps de notre regretté maître, tu étais assez habile pour donner dix réponses à n'importe quelle question, mais je serais curieux de t'entendre sur ce *kôan* : quel est ton visage originel, celui que tu avais avant de naître ?

Xiangyan, perdu dans les méandres de sa mémoire, gratta son crâne luisant un long moment. Avec une grimace amère, il finit par bredouiller :

– Je dois méditer cette question.

Le moine savant retourna précipitamment à ses appartements où il s'enferma pour relire les soutras, les discours des patriarches et les notes qu'il avait prises sur les sermons de son maître. Il ne quitta pas sa chambre pendant une semaine. Finalement, le visage décomposé, il revint auprès de Guishan.

– Je n'ai trouvé aucune réponse à ton *kôan*. Je te prie humblement de me donner quelques explications qui pourraient me mettre sur la voie.

– Une peinture de gâteau de riz ne supprimera jamais ta faim.

De dépit, Xiangyan remisa les soutras dans la bibliothèque, brûla ses notes, fit son baluchon et quitta le monastère. Au cours de son errance dans les montagnes du Nanyang, il visita la tombe du maître national Huizong, disciple du sixième patriarche du zen. De hautes herbes cachaient le monument, le lierre le dévorait. Le moine pèlerin décida d'y construire son ermitage, de s'effacer derrière l'humble tâche de gardien de tombeau. Sa hutte de branchages terminée, il entreprit de désherber les alentours. Il creusa la terre pentue et l'aplanit pour former des terrasses. Il planta des haies de bambou, bêcha, sema des graines, repiqua des boutures, détourna l'eau d'un torrent. Dans ce lieu désert balayé par le vent, il réussit à faire fleurir tout un jardin.

Du soir au matin, pour échapper à la tyrannie du mental, il pliait son corps à la discipline éreintante du jardinier montagnard, appliquant inlassablement son esprit à percer le *kôan* du visage originel. Alors qu'un jour il balayait une allée du jardin en ruminant ses sombres pensées, désespérant de résoudre l'énigme, un caillou alla frapper la tige creuse d'un bambou. Ce petit choc sonna comme un coup de tonnerre, un rugissement de dragon. Le couvercle de son mental sauta, laissant enfin couler en lui la cataracte de l'esprit libéré. Son corps vibrait comme un bambou au souffle de l'univers, ivre de lumière et du parfum des fleurs. Le Ciel en fit une flûte pour faire retentir en ce monde le chant de l'Éveil.

*J'ai jeté cette chose misérable*
*Qu'on appelle « moi »*
*Et je suis devenu*
*Le vaste Univers.*

Musô Soseki

# Le chant du colatier

CONTE SÉNOUFO, CÔTE D'IVOIRE

Zwaconiyo Soro, le grand chef, disait à Samory, le combattant qui le menaçait :

– Je ne suis pas un guerrier mais un cultivateur. Je ne me bats avec personne, c'est avec la terre que je me dispute.

Pour les Sénoufos, Koulou Tyolo, le dieu qui dort, n'intervient plus dans la marche de l'univers. Katieleo la Mère protège le Poro, le bois sacré où vivent les génies qui soumettent les hommes. Ces derniers doivent arracher à la forêt leurs lopins de terre et respecter les esprits qui vivent là.

Noix de Cola avait essarté et gratté le sol, pour ses ignames. Il se servait de sa *daba*, sa houe en jujubier, dont il avait affûté la lame. Il lui fallait de l'endurance, de la persévérance pour venir à bout de la terre sèche et y faire pousser ses oignons, le sorgho et les ignames. Son « jardin », un champ minuscule, était bordé par un karité et un gros baobab où s'alignaient des piments et des aubergines.

À quelques pas, les génies attirés par les raclements de la houe lui dirent :

– *Nεani mεε faa ce yoo*, que le brave soit habile dans son travail, et ils ajoutèrent : qui cultive ce champ ?

– C'est moi, Noix de Cola, qui voulez-vous que ce soit, je brûle, je sarcle, je prépare ma terre pour les ignames.

Alors dix génies aidèrent Noix de Cola. À midi, l'homme regagna le village, salua le forgeron, passa devant la case du bouffon, avec sa *daba*, fièrement.

Le lendemain il revint planter ses ignames, vingt génies s'emparèrent des bouts

de tubercules, se rassemblèrent, l'aidèrent tout autant. À midi il rentra au village. Quand il retourna plus tard pour butter ses légumes-racines, les esprits attirés par les raclements de la houe réitérèrent :

– *Nɛani mɛɛ faa ce yoo*, qui cultive ce champ ?

– C'est moi, Noix de Cola, qui voulez-vous que ce soit, je butte ma terre pour les ignames.

Et quarante génies buttèrent promptement. Après ça, Noix de Cola laissa faire la terre. En attendant la récolte, il décida de voyager vers Niakaramandougou, confia la garde du champ-jardin à sa femme.

Un jour qu'elle était en train de le garder, son enfant se mit à pleurer. Elle déterra une petite igname et la lui tendit pour qu'il la suce. Les génies demandèrent :

– Qui fouille dans le champ ?

– C'est moi, la femme de Noix de Cola, j'ai sorti une petite igname pour apaiser la faim de mon enfant.

Ni une ni deux, quatre-vingts génies sortent les pousses et les entassent au bout du champ.
Elle est désespérée. À son retour, Noix de Cola la trouve là, en larmes : elle lui raconte. Il est si fâché qu'il la gifle... et réveille les esprits du bois sacré.
– *Nεani mεε faa ce yoo*, que le brave soit habile dans son travail, qui frappe ?
– C'est moi, Noix de Cola, qui voulez-vous que ce soit, je gifle ma femme, pour les ignames.
Cent soixante génies viennent pour l'aider, font si fort qu'ils la tuent. Noix de Cola pleure sa malchance. Un moustique profitant de son atterrement le pique au bras.
Alors, il donne un grand coup sur sa peau et rate l'insecte.
– *Nεani mεε faa ce yoo*, qui fouette, qui claque ?
– C'est moi, Noix de Cola, qui voulez-vous que ce soit, j'essaie de tuer le moustique sur ma peau.

Aussitôt, trois cent soixante génies s'en mêlent. Noix de Cola s'enfuit aussi vite qu'un chasseur dans les histoires de Kouassi, le joueur de balafon. Il bouscule le forgeron, saute au-dessus du bouffon et plonge dans la poche d'un vieux.

Voilà pourquoi il y a des noix de cola dans la poche des vieillards et des sages. Pour rappeler à ceux qui jardinent combien il est vital de craindre les esprits du bois sacré et de savoir dialoguer avec eux.

*J'ai ma* daba *à la main!*
*Les hommes disent*
*que rien ne me fait mal,*
*Mais c'est la futilité qui me blesse!*
*Ma parole est au fond des vieux canaris.*
*Je ne me bats avec personne,*
*Avec la terre, je me dispute,*
*Dans la paix.*

# L'oasis des quatre errants

CONTE SOUFI

Ils étaient quatre errants silencieux marchant en plein désert. Affamés, assoiffés, ils songeaient aux fruits sucrés des oasis. De temps en temps s'élevait la voix de l'un, offrant sa bouche sèche à ses rêves de grappes.

– Où êtes-vous *angûr*, que je vous croque, disait le Persan.

– Je préférerais qu'éclatent dans ma bouche des *inab*, murmurait l'Arabe.

– Et moi, je ne désire que le jus sublime et la chair des *uzum*, chantait le Turc.

Le Grec haussa les épaules et proclama :

– Seuls les *iztafil* feraient de moi un bienheureux !

Las de supporter les jérémiades des autres, qui n'y connaissaient rien, ils finirent par se quereller, s'attraper par la robe et en venir aux mains.

Or un voyageur, un lettré du Jardin des philosophes, croisa leur chemin. Il venait d'un pays blanc où les sages de son école concoctaient, pour les chercheurs de vérité de toutes confessions, des réflexions à même la terre, cela tout en soignant les fleurs, taillant les arbres, parmi les nectars qui favorisent l'intuition. Il assista à leur querelle, fit comme le Cheikh dans la volière, claqua dans ses mains.

– Arrêtez la dispute, vous êtes comme des oiseaux fous dans une cage ouverte.

– ?!!

– Vous parlez d'une même chose ! Vous rêvez au raisin qui se nomme *iztafil* en grec et *inab* en arabe. Vous espérez sur vos lèvres l'*uzum* turc et l'*angûr* persan.

Amis, vous qui errez dans le désert, votre faim est la même ! Allez vers le plaisir mais ne faites pas de vos désirs une tour de Babel. Tous ceux qui se déchirent et s'entretuent, piégés par les mots qui désignent le nom secret de Dieu, agissent comme des insensés.

Et les quatre burent la parole du philosophe, ils se comprirent, virent que la porte était ouverte, ils aperçurent l'oasis aux vignes innombrables, surent qu'une seule grappe exaucerait leur vœu.

# Le vieux portail

RÉCIT JAPONAIS

Sen no Rikyû, le grand réformateur de la cérémonie du thé au XVIe siècle, mit en avant le concept esthétique et spirituel du *wabi-sabi* qui influença les arts japonais, notamment celui du jardin. Le *wabi* évoque la simplicité rustique, le dépouillement, l'humilité. Le *sabi*, la patine du temps, la nostalgie, l'impermanence, la solitude...

Un jour, à l'invitation insistante d'un riche marchand, Rikyû se rendit à une cérémonie du thé en compagnie de Dô-an, son fils aîné, qui était aussi son disciple. Ils pénétrèrent dans le *roji*, le

« sentier de rosée » qui désigne le jardin entourant le pavillon de thé, en référence au Soutra du Lotus où il est écrit : « Échappant à la demeure brûlante des Trois Mondes des phénomènes, ils s'assirent sur la Terre de Rosée. » Ce sentier-jardin doit aider les invités à quitter le monde profane pour se dépouiller, faire le vide. Il évoque un layon de montagne qui serpente dans la forêt avant de déboucher à l'entrée du pavillon de thé semblable à la hutte d'un ermite.
Le maître des lieux s'était appliqué à respecter les règles de l'art pour y introduire la saveur du *wabi-sabi* : vieilles pierres patinées grignotées par la mousse, feuillus cramoisis en cette fin d'automne... Parvenus au milieu du jardin, ils se retrouvèrent face à un second enclos où trônait un vieux portail. Dô-an s'extasia devant le charme du bois vermoulu qui reflétait tout à fait le *sabi*, la saveur du temps qui passe. Et il improvisa un *waka*, une variation sur un thème

favori de Jien ou Saigyô, ces ermites poètes que son père aimait tant :

*Feuilles de chêne, d'érable*
*Dans leurs teintes automnales*
*Tombent et s'entassent*
*Sur le sentier solitaire*
*D'un vieux temple de montagne.*

Rikyû répliqua avec un sourire sarcastique :
– Fils, ta pensée s'est arrêtée en chemin. Cela ressemble au *sabi* mais contredit le *wabi*, la simplicité. Cette porte, en effet, ne provient pas des environs mais d'un vieux temple perdu en montagne. Le maître du jardin a dû dépenser une somme considérable pour la faire transporter jusqu'ici ! S'il comprenait vraiment ce qu'est le *wabi-sabi*, il aurait fait fabriquer une porte avec de vieilles planches. Le jardin reflète l'esprit de son propriétaire. Décidément, je n'ai pas du tout envie de boire le thé avec cet homme !

Sen no Rikyû, le maître des maîtres de thé, rebroussa chemin devant le portail et laissa son fils aller seul à la cérémonie. Il le pria de l'excuser auprès de leur hôte au prétexte qu'il venait d'être rappelé au service du *taikô* Hideyoshi.

Sen no Rikyû retraversa le *roji* sans plus vouloir le regarder, simplement et seul, dans l'esprit du *wabi-sabi*, se remémorant un poème de sa composition :

*Bien que le sentier de rosée*
*Soit un passage*
*Pour quitter ce monde profane,*
*Comment ces gens peuvent-ils encore*
*le ternir*
*Avec la poussière du mental ?*

# Les belles-de-jour

RÉCIT JAPONAIS

Un jour, un courtisan apprit au *taikô* Hideyoshi, le despote éclairé du Japon, que Sen no Rikyû, son maître de thé et l'un de ses favoris, avait réussi à faire pousser dans son jardin des *asagao** d'une beauté exceptionnelle. Irrité de ne pas avoir encore été convié à venir les contempler, il envoya aussitôt un message pour annoncer qu'il s'invitait le lendemain matin à une cérémonie du thé.

Quand Hideyoshi franchit le portail du *roji*, le jardin de thé, quelle ne fut pas sa surprise de n'apercevoir aucune de ces fleurs qu'il désirait tant admirer ! Il pensa que Sen no Rikyû les avait dérobées au premier regard afin qu'elles se dévoilent au détour du sentier pour mieux surprendre le visiteur. Mais au fur et à mesure que le redoutable *taikô* arpentait les dalles de pierre, rutilant dans son kimono extravagant, la colère le submergeait comme la marée montante. Il constatait que toutes les fleurs venaient d'être coupées ! Un rictus accentuait les traits simiesques de son visage, lui donnant l'allure d'un masque de démon grimaçant. Quel affront ! Traiter ainsi le maître du Japon ! Furibond, il pénétra dans la maison de thé pas plus grande que la cabane d'un ermite. Et là, sous le *kakémono* calligraphié, dans un modeste vase de bambou, trônait une belle-de-jour unique, une fleur sublime à l'éclat sans pareil rehaussé par le dépouillement austère de la pièce.

Désarçonnée par ce coup de maître, l'exaspération d'Hideyoshi se dissipa comme la brume dans les premiers rayons du soleil levant. Dans un silence plus vaste

que leurs personnes, l'hôte et l'invité se saluèrent. Un sourire flottait sur leurs visages.

Ce fut là l'un des fameux épisodes de la prodigieuse partie de go entre le maître de thé et son mentor. Un jeu redoutable, un duel sans merci que se livrèrent pouvoirs spirituel et temporel et que Sen no Rikyû,

jardinier exigeant à la fleur unique, finira par payer de sa vie...

*Comme ils sont silencieux,*
*L'hôte, l'invité*
*Et le chrysanthème blanc !*

Ôshima Ryôta

**Asagao* : belle-de-jour ou gloire-du-matin.

# La chemise verte

VARIATIONS SUR UN THÈME EUROPÉEN

Dans un ancien royaume, un souverain contemplait tristement les douves de son château. La guerre, la chasse ne le distrayaient plus. Les fêtes et les rendez-vous galants se révélaient impuissants à entamer sa morosité. Ses pensées étaient toutes accaparées par la santé chancelante de son fils. Depuis des lunes, il dépérissait. Le feu avait quitté ses joues, l'air ne pénétrait plus en lui que faiblement, l'eau semblait avoir déserté sa peau, ne baignant que ses grands yeux, ses os saillants se cassaient au moindre effort.

Le roi avait pourtant fait quérir les meilleurs médecins des onze provinces,

mais ils demeuraient impuissants et démunis, face à un mal dont ils ignoraient tout. Il avait consulté des mages et des sorciers, pourtant mis à l'index, mais en vain. Ce soir-là, son serviteur s'approcha et dit :
– Mon roi, il y a une vieille dans le bois au-delà du dernier faubourg, une drôlesse qui s'y connaît dans la magie des plantes. Pourquoi ne pas essayer ?
– Tu as raison, Dominique, va et ramène-la.
Quand le serviteur passa la clôture de ronces qui ceinturait le jardin, il la trouva, faisant sécher des racines d'aunée. Elle l'écouta, s'enquit des maux rongeant le prince, emporta un grand van, rempli de simples et de flacons.
Lorsqu'elle eut ausculté le malade, évalué sa peau, son souffle, écouté le garçon lui dire son humeur, elle le baisa au front, prépara des potions et dit au roi :
– Je le soulage, il sera plus vaillant mais pas guéri. Une seule chose pourrait lui rendre la beauté de son âge, c'est la chemise d'un homme heureux.

Mais où trouver une chose pareille? L'émeraude énorme, le rubis rare ou l'épée sertie de jade, bon, passe encore. Le cheval fougueux, l'oiseau parleur, l'adorable danseuse aux pieds menus venue d'Orient... toutes ces choses à portée de main d'un roi, bon oui, mais un homme heureux, où dénicher un tel spécimen?

Alors il ordonna que les soldats, les espions et les chevaliers se fissent chercheurs de bienheureux. Toute la crème du royaume se mit en quête de l'oiseau rare. Dès qu'on en avait déniché un, on l'envoyait au roi pour le soumettre à ses questions. On vit tout un défilé de princes, de prêtres, de lavandières, bandits et courtisans. Mais ils étaient encore gourmands de terres, d'oilles et de linges blancs, de bons coups à faire et d'avantages. On passa au crible les provinces les plus éloignées, les régions désertiques, montagneuses, les bords de l'océan. Chaque fois qu'on croyait avoir découvert la perle, un désir se rappelait à lui au dernier moment. Il lui manquait toujours une chose pour affirmer son contentement. On interrogea tout ce qu'un royaume comptait de gens frôlant le bonheur, mais on ne trouva pas le porteur de la chemise de médecine.

– Êtes-vous sûr qu'aucun sujet n'est passé à travers les mailles de nos filets ?

– Majesté, à part votre jardinier qui est simplet, personne.

– Mon roi, dit le serviteur, s'il n'en reste qu'un, pourquoi ne pas essayer ?

– Tu as raison, Dominique, va et ramène-le.

En fait d'être un simplet, l'homme était surtout simple. Comme ses plantes, il ne demandait rien de plus, juste la pluie et la bonne lumière, quand elles voulaient bien l'honorer, le tutoyer comme un petit frère.

– Es-tu certain d'être heureux ? bredouilla le roi.

– Si être heureux, c'est se réjouir de tout et de rien, oui. Un battement d'ailes, le va-et-vient des hirondelles, une fleur qui pointe son nez, un ver de terre, un escargot qui passe, un potiron dodu, un pois ou une abeille qui se pose. Tout cela qui va entre les doigts du vent et me parle, si c'est cela, oui.

– Et il ne te manque rien ?

– Quand on se régale du Tout, rien ne manque assurément.

– Donnerais-tu ta chemise à ton roi, pour qu'il en revêtît son fils agonisant ?

– Certainement, d'ailleurs je la gardais neuve pour une telle occasion.

En effet, le jardinier portait un tablier de moine. Il sortit et revint de sa masure avec une chemise verte, soigneusement pliée.

Tous entouraient le prince quand on l'habilla : le roi et son serviteur, la vieille, le grand chambellan et le jardinier. À peine le garçon eut-il passé la chemise que le feu colora ses joues, que l'air pénétra en lui, que l'eau irrigua sa peau, que ses os furent guéris de la faiblesse.

Tandis que le visage du roi s'éclairait, la liquette du jardinier recouvrit le monde et tout fut jardin.

# L'ivresse du derviche

TRADITION TURCO-PERSANE

Assis en tailleur au bord du chemin, un derviche ensoleillé souriait, les yeux clos tournés vers un pays caché. Un berger, attiré par la lumière, contemplait, radieux, cet homme au doux visage orné d'une belle barbe blanche. Il songeait, devant l'extase, aux sources d'*anna*, jardin du paradis. Quand il vit que le sage sortait de sa transe, il s'approcha et lui dit :

– As-tu vu *gannat al-mawa*, le refuge aux roses ?

– Bien au-delà du *bagh* de Samarkand, des jardins moghols du Cachemire et des

magnificences de la Perse, j'ai vu *ğannat al-ma'wa.*

– As-tu vu la fleur des fleurs, as-tu parlé au jardinier ?

– Celui qui voit *ğannat al-ma'wa* est la fleur des fleurs et le jardinier.

– Rapportes-tu des présents célestes, autres que ton ivresse ?

– Quand je suis entré, je suis allé de rosier en rosier pour chercher le plus sublime. Je voulais remplir les pans de ma robe de pétales divins pour en faire cadeau à mes frères. Je me suis approché d'une rose, embrasé par son parfum. Les fragrances m'ont enivré, alors j'ai quitté ma robe, en tournoyant.

Le berger s'en fut béat. N'avait-il pas entrevu la fleur et parlé au jardinier ?

# La piste des fleurs

MYTHE ABORIGÈNE D'AUSTRALIE

*Les pistes sont nos parents*
*L'une mène au jardin-pré de Baiame*
*Les autres en redescendent*
*Avec les shamans et les fleurs.*

Le Rêve est Tout. *Tjukurrpa*. Les étoiles du ciel, les sites sacrés, les plantes, les animaux, les humains sont liés par l'esprit. Je connais ma montagne, ses chants, ses bonnes peintures, je plante les récits anciens et je veille. Je danse et peins ce qui va maintenant. J'ai vu le chemin coloré, la piste des fleurs. Nous autres, ici, n'avons pas de jardinets pour domestiquer les pensées sauvages. Nos *banksia*, nos *hakéa*, nos *waratah* sont belles et farouches. Ce vaste continent est *le* jardin. Nos sages ont suivi les recommandations de Baiame, le grand esprit créateur. En repeuplant la terre de fleurs, ils ont choisi les lieux où les répandre. Voici comment les *malins*, nos shamans, ont jardiné la terre.

Bien avant le désastre et le déluge d'eau, les hommes vivaient en résonance avec les choses cachées. Quand arriva l'inondation, les survivants avaient déjà oublié le cœur du Rêve, la cruauté s'était emparée d'eux et elle empira après le cataclysme. Il subsista une poignée de sages pratiquant l'entraide et des groupes épars, désorientés et à l'abandon. Devant ces changements, Baiame se retira en haut de la montagne. L'être surnaturel se concentra, communiqua en esprit avec les créatures. Alors, fourmis, hannetons, kangourous, toutes créatures ayant survécu quittèrent les lieux où elles vivaient. Les oiseaux et les fleurs montèrent jusqu'au refuge de

Baiame esprit-ciel de la pluie, de la vie et de la mort. En une seule nuit, la terre fut déserte. Les shamans ayant reçu le message quittèrent leurs refuges, préoccupés par la disparition des abeilles et des fleurs. Ils allèrent vers la montagne qu'ils avaient vue en esprit et reconnue, comprirent ce qu'il était advenu des abeilles : elles bourdonnaient en multitude, sur les trois arbres sacrés, à la porte du désert. Les branches ployaient jusqu'au sol sous les fruits innombrables, devant les survivants affamés, confus, craintifs et repentants, et qui les désiraient. Les shamans parlèrent au peuple qui les écouta. Ils dirent où ils allaient, commandèrent de révérer le sanctuaire de vie gardé par les abeilles. Ils en appelèrent à la fraternité pour réintégrer le grand cercle des créatures. Pour la première fois depuis le désastre, cœurs et âmes étaient en paix.

Baiame, de sa retraite, reçut le vent frais de l'espérance, entrevit le sentier qu'il augurait. Il souleva les bras en coupe, fit germer des arbres inconnus sur la terre lézardée. Les eucalyptus furent bientôt immenses, rejoints par les abeilles.

– Cela est bon, dirent les shamans, avec ces arbres Baiame nous a rendu le miel.

Ils laissèrent le peuple et reprirent le chemin de la montagne.

Ils allèrent ainsi dans le désert aride durant des lunes. Leurs corps étaient brûlés, leurs barbes et leurs cheveux, broussailles, mais leurs yeux fatigués brillaient. Ils arrivèrent un jour devant le roc immense. La paroi était lisse, nul chemin visible pour grimper, alors ils en firent le tour. Après des jours de marche, ils virent une cavité, puis une autre, une autre encore, telles des marches creusées dans la paroi rocheuse. Ainsi débuta l'ascension hardie vers la retraite où l'Esprit appelait ses créatures. Le sommet semblait hors d'atteinte, avalé par un puits de brume. Pour les encourager, l'Être invita une ambassade d'aigles à s'élancer vers les hauteurs et piquer en des précipices verti-

gineux. Les shamans se hissèrent au-dessus des nuages et campèrent autour d'une source-rêve, dont l'eau montait. Après avoir bu, ils furent ragaillardis.
– Cela est bon, avec cette eau Baiame nous a rendu la force.
Un peu plus haut ils virent un grand cercle fait de lourdes pierres et pénétrèrent dans l'enceinte. Alors, ils entendirent la voix puissante, sans savoir si elle venait du dehors, de l'intérieur d'eux-mêmes ou des deux à la fois.
– Que faites-vous dans la paume de ma main ?
Et ils furent secoués comme les feuilles d'un arbre par la tempête.
Le plus âgé se releva et répondit :
– Nous avons reçu un message dans nos esprits, nous sommes venus. Nous avons vu tes arbres sacrés porter les derniers fruits, compris et transmis la signification au peuple. Nous avons vu pousser leurs frères géants, nous te remercions de les avoir donnés aux nôtres, mais nous

sommes inquiets pour les animaux et surtout pour les fleurs.

– Les animaux sont en route, voyez !

Et ils virent des oiseaux descendre comme pluie et des koalas, des wombats, des kangourous, opossums, varans, dingos, ornithorynques, lézards, émeus...

– Que pourriez-vous faire des fleurs ?

– Elles nous inspirent, elles habillent nos songes, nos chants, nos danses. Depuis qu'elles se sont enfuies, les contes ont déserté nos lèvres, nos maux sont sans remède, nous n'avons plus de pigments ni de parures pour nous protéger et nous embellir. Si nos corps sont sans beauté, comment nos âmes auraient-elles le désir d'y demeurer ? Tu nous as donné des géants, rends-nous ces naines incomparables.

– Qu'il en soit ainsi, suivez donc la piste des fleurs, emportez-les !

À ce moment, la nuit étant venue, les étoiles brillaient. Une ouverture lumineuse se dessina dans le firmament, pointée par le sommet. Les shamans montèrent les dernières marches et ils passèrent la porte des étoiles. Un pré verdoyant et infini, jonché d'innombrables fleurs aux formes ingénieuses, composait un parterre aux couleurs inouïes.

Les *malins*, pris dans un bouquet de parfums, ramassèrent les bulbes avec un soin sacré, récoltèrent les graines, prenant leur temps pour ne pas oublier une seule espèce.

Quand ils furent revenus dans le cercle de pierre, Baiame leur dit :
– Je vous ai appelés pour vous aider à surmonter l'épreuve et réveiller les chants. Asseyez-vous, formez le cercle sacré, rappelez-vous qu'il est mon corps. Contez la Piste des fleurs, cultivez-la, sinon elles repartiront. Choisissez avec sagesse le lieu où vous irez les planter. Faites de la terre un reflet du jardin. Soignez avec l'eau des fleurs vos peurs, votre colère : le souvenir du désastre vous poursuivra longtemps. N'oubliez pas la prairie céleste, protégez les abeilles et rejoignez le cercle des étoiles.

L'Être sourit en esprit et se retira dans les territoires du Rêve.

*Les pistes sont nos parents*
*L'une mène au jardin-pré de Baiame*
*Les autres en redescendent*
*Avec les shamans et les fleurs.*

# Nasreddine et les courges

CONTE ORIENTAL

Nasreddine Hodja, l'incomparable maître oriental de la Folle Sagesse, était aussi jardinier. Et c'est dans son jardin qu'il récolta quelques-unes des plus belles graines de ces sublimes vérités qui ne cessent d'éclairer nos lanternes.

Un jour, Nasreddine ronchonnait tout en s'échinant à ramasser d'énormes courges qu'il avait réussi à faire pousser :

– La création est loin d'être parfaite ! Ces gros légumes prospèrent sur des tiges maigrelettes qui doivent ramper sur le sol. Ce serait tout de même moins éreintant de les cueillir dans les arbres ! Eh bien, non, les grosses branches, elles, ne portent que des fruits rabougris ! Comme Dieu a fait sa Création en six jours pour se reposer le septième, Il n'a pas eu le temps de s'occuper de tous les détails !

Épuisé, le dos brisé, le Hodja finit par s'allonger à l'ombre d'un figuier. Après avoir retiré son turban pour s'en faire un oreiller, il ne tarda pas à s'endormir avec l'insouciance d'un ravi.

Un coup sur le front le réveilla en sursaut. Il se redressa en maugréant, darda des yeux furibonds à droite et à gauche pour débusquer le malotru qui avait osé le tirer d'un rêve sucré où il dégustait le vin céleste en compagnie des houris du paradis. C'est alors qu'il reçut un autre choc sur sa tête dégarnie. Une figue bien mûre rebondit devant lui avant de rouler dans l'herbe. Nasreddine se mit aussitôt à genoux et s'écria :

– Que le Miséricordieux pardonne le mécréant que je suis ! Sa création est bien faite. S'Il avait fait pousser des citrouilles dans les arbres, j'aurais maintenant le crâne aussi fendu que ce fruit !

# Le paradis du frère Anselme

LÉGENDE MÉDIÉVALE

*Tu trouveras bien plus dans les forêts que dans les livres.*

Bernard de Clairvaux

Le frère Anselme reposa le manuscrit du jardin de santé de sainte Hildegarde. Il aimait à se replonger dans l'étude, que ce soit l'*Hortus Deliciarum* d'Herrade de Landsberg, les écrits de saint Bernard relatifs à la création, à la germination et la récolte, ou les odes dédiées à la nature de saint François. L'univers créé reposait bel et bien sur quatre éléments et la santé sur quatre humeurs. Le frère jardinier consacrait la majeure partie [illegible] son temps aux travaux extérieurs et au[illegible]xpériences. Plus que les rituels religie[illegible] lui importait la méditation sur les v[illegible]us secrètes, cachées dans la nature. Là [illegible] d'autres dénichaient des empreinte[illegible]e pollen, lui trouvait partout des trace[illegible]Éden. Il avait non seulement en char[illegible] l'*Hortus* et l'*Herbolarius* situés dans l'[illegible]ceinte du monastère mais s'occupait [illegible] l'*Incultum*, l'espace sacré en forêt où[illegible]oussent les espèces sauvages. Face à [illegible]*ngluvies ventri*, les ripailleries de ce [illegible]onde, il cultivait dévotement *caritas*, l'amour du prochain. Le commerce avec le vent, les abeilles, les oiseaux et les fleurs lui procurait une intense joie d'être.

Le matin, après sa lecture, il avait récolté l'absinthe, l'hysope et la joubarbe aux vertus souveraines. Après avoir pilé les simples, il avait pris sa cognée et quitté le monastère dans l'intention de couper des jets de chêne en forêt pour aménager le potager des frères.

Tout en respirant l'odeur de mousse et d'humus, il guettait la forme et la mesure convenables d'un feuillu pour tailler ses piquets. Bientôt, il surprit un jeune chêne qui semblait attendre, pris en amitié par des papillons. Frère Anselme éloigna les drôles, leva sa cognée. Mais à l'instant, un chant d'oiseau retentit, pur gazouillis d'un pinson du paradis. Le moine reposa son outil, saisi d'une vision céleste. C'était le premier jardin, celui planté par Dieu, pour le premier jardinier. Adam veillait sur la nature, faite de fraîcheur et d'enfance. Les bocages étaient emplis d'arbres, d'odeurs suaves et de fruits-soleils. D'une fontaine de saphir s'écoulait un fleuve qui arrosait le jardin et reliait ce havre au monde par quatre bras : l'un de miel, les autres de lait, de vin et d'encens. Un chœur d'anges bourdonnait un chant profond sur lequel l'oiseau improvisait. L'Arbre de Vie était au milieu et l'Arbre de la Connaissance aussi.

Le frère Anselme était agenouillé, devenu lui-même prière sortant du fleuve, eau de jouvence et terre de sagesse, composé des quatre éléments. Il n'était plus pris dans les replis du temps, tout occupé par le lieu d'avant l'exil. Puis d'un coup, l'oiseau battit des ailes, se tut. Frère Anselme, revenu au monde, serra le manche de sa cognée qui fondit en poussière. Quand il regarda devant lui le jeune chêne, il fut surpris de voir un arbre vénérable, âgé de trois cents années. Il avait la peau rugueuse des vieux sages, que sont les régents des forêts. Comme le soir venait, le jardinier congédia l'énigme pour se rendre à l'office et prolonger sa vision de paix. Mais le chemin était obstrué par des ronces et il dut batailler pour retrouver l'abbaye. Lorsqu'il la vit dans le couchant, il peina pour reconnaître la silhouette familière. Puis le frère portier ouvrit, et cette impression se mua en une soudaine étrangeté face au moine, à son accoutrement et au jardin lui-même, qu'il trouva d'une beauté

baroque. On le fit asseoir, il conta son histoire, alla vers la chapelle où il aimait prier, puis au jardin.
Tandis que les moines chuchotaient, que le père abbé allait consulter les heures de l'abbaye à la bibliothèque, y apprenait la disparition d'Anselme trois cents ans plus tôt, le frère sans âge, souriant aux angelots, fondit en poussière lactescente entre deux ancolies.

Devant l'assemblée troublée des moines, le père abbé cita Marie-Madeleine qui avait appelé Jésus près du tombeau ouvert.
– *Adonaï, est-ce toi qui l'as emporté, dis-moi où tu l'as mis, je le prendrai.*
Puis elle avait aperçu un homme, une bêche en main, c'était un jardinier. Il avait simplement répondu : *Marie !*
Alors, elle l'avait reconnu et lui avait dit : *Rabbouni, je te vois.*
– Mes frères, nous avons vu le jardinier, le frère Anselme, revenu et ressuscité.

*Ma maison petite est un gland*
*Mon univers un chêne géant*
*Je me promène entre les deux*
*Sur la barque du temps.*

# Le taoïste et le bambou

CONTE CHINOIS

*Jeune, je n'avais aucun penchant pour*
*les affaires du monde.*
*Mon cœur me portait vers les collines*
*et les montagnes.*
*Pourtant je me laissais prendre dans*
*les filets du monde.*
*Quand je m'éveillai, treize années*
*de ma vie s'étaient envolées.*

*L'oiseau prisonnier pleure sa forêt natale,*
*Le poisson du bassin, sa rivière*
*profonde.*
*J'ai défriché une lande au sud.*
*Pour cultiver ma nature, je suis revenu*
*au jardin.*

*Mon domaine ne fait pas plus*
*de dix arpents,*
*Mon toit de chaume couvre huit*
*ou neuf travées.*
*Ormes et saules font de l'ombre à*
*l'arrière,*
*Pêchers et pruniers ornent la façade.*

*Dans les volutes de fumée qui*
*s'échappent des toitures,*
*S'effacent au loin les autres maisons.*
*Seuls me parviennent, du fond des*
*ruelles, les aboiements des chiens*
*Et le chant d'un coq juché sur un mûrier.*

*Chez moi n'entrent plus les poussières*
*du monde,*
*Plus rien n'encombre mes pièces vides.*
*Ayant trop longtemps vécu en cage,*
*J'ai pu enfin revenir à ma nature*
*véritable.*

Tao Yuanming

Un Lettré vivait retiré dans un village de montagne, loin de la vie mondaine. Il avait été autrefois un puissant mandarin au service du Fils du Ciel, avait eu des charges officielles d'importance. Lassé des intrigues de la Cour, fuyant les compromissions, écœuré par les injustices, il avait démissionné de l'administration impériale. Il préférait désormais se consacrer à l'étude des Classiques et des traités taoïstes, composer des poèmes, peindre des paysages, cultiver son jardin, pratiquer le qi gong et s'absorber dans la méditation. Parfois, des amis venaient le visiter et il passait avec eux des heures à boire du thé et du vin, à chanter, jouer du *qin*, la cithare à sept cordes, réciter des vers.

*On peut faire le tour de la terre*
*Et ne rien comprendre.*
*De son ermitage*
*On peut tout connaître.*

Lao Tseu

Depuis qu'il avait quitté les sentiers poussiéreux du monde, le taoïste s'était fait bâtir une modeste demeure à flanc de montagne et avait consacré la majeure partie de son temps à son jardin. Fidèle à l'art de vivre des Lettrés, il en avait fait une reproduction miniature de l'univers en accord avec les principes du feng shui et en résonance avec sa propre sensibilité. Après avoir longuement observé le terrain en friche, ressenti les veines et les nœuds des dragons, il avait fait dresser des pierres, planter des arbres, creuser un étang, bâtir des kiosques afin de capter les énergies du Ciel et de la Terre, de réharmoniser les lieux. Comme un médecin acupuncteur qui sait où placer ses aiguilles, il avait rééquilibré le yin et le yang. Tout en respectant la nature du terrain, il avait retiré le superflu et rajouté l'indispensable. Peintre de talent, il avait dessiné le jardin en jouant subtilement du vide et du plein, de la complémentarité des couleurs, soucieux que pas un seul

trait de pinceau ne détonne dans le tableau. En fin Lettré, il avait fait de son jardin un poème où chaque mot, chaque image, chaque sonorité devait jouer son rôle dans la composition finale.

Sur le versant sud d'un promontoire, il avait construit sa demeure afin de la protéger du vent et des influences néfastes du nord. Sur le terrain pentu à l'arrière, il avait fait dresser de grands rochers dont les formes évoquaient les montures des Hommes-Montagnes, les Immortels : grues, tortues, tigres, dragons, phénix. Ces gardiens hiératiques propres à repousser les mauvais esprits semblaient s'animer dans les lambeaux de brume ou dans la lumière de la lune qui jouait avec les nuages et les ombres dansantes des arbres. En haut du promontoire, il avait aménagé en terrain découvert la Terrasse du Vide Azuré d'où l'on pouvait contempler, de jour, le paysage et, la nuit, les étoiles.

À l'ouest, captant l'eau d'un torrent et profitant du dénivelé, il avait fait bondir une cascade qui alimentait l'étang au sud. Les fenêtres de la salle de séjour s'ouvraient sur ses berges où tout le monde aquatique était convié : roseaux, lotus, châtaignes d'eau, saules pleureurs. Au milieu de l'étang, trois magnifiques pierres du lac Taihu évoquaient les mythiques Îles des Immortels. L'ensemble était si réussi que, malgré la présence humaine, les oies et les canards sauvages s'y posaient. Rien n'avait été laissé au hasard, tout était calculé pour produire son effet : la profondeur et la pureté de l'eau, la distance des bâtiments et de la végétation. Le miroir émeraude de l'étang pouvait ainsi refléter tour à tour chaque partie du jardin suivant la course du soleil. Un kiosque érigé à moitié sur l'eau permettait de voyager immobile dans le paysage. Le bassin agissait aussi comme un prisme. Les reflets de jade sombres ou clairs des feuillages, l'azur du ciel, les nuages, les scintillements dorés des vaguelettes ou des carpes coloraient à leur tour les végétaux, les murs, les balustrades, les toitures. Ce chatoiement sans cesse renouvelé faisait entrer le jardin dans la danse perpétuelle de la mutation des éléments.

Quelle que fût la saison, la lumière du soleil ou de la lune, dans l'écran de la brume, la grisaille de la pluie, les métamorphoses du jardin ne pouvaient laisser indifférent et appelaient un nouveau sentiment.

L'ouïe et l'odorat n'étaient pas en reste. Le Sentier de Brocart Parfumé permettait de humer le subtil mélange des orchidées, des angéliques ou des pivoines. Le bruissement des feuillages, les murmures de l'eau et les chants des oiseaux se répondaient pour composer la mélodie secrète de l'esprit des lieux.

Une galerie en zigzag permettait d'aller, abrité du soleil ou de la pluie, jusqu'au kiosque de l'étang. Chaque travée laissait voir une partie du jardin, comme une peinture. Les murs de clôture blanchis à la chaux renforçaient cette impression

d'être devant un rouleau peint. Certaines cloisons étaient percées de portes ou de fenêtres de formes variées qui, tels des cadres, montraient un détail, découvraient une perspective sur lesquels le maître du jardin voulait attirer l'attention : l'évocation d'un paysage ou d'un poème célèbre, d'une légende, d'un symbole...
Des sentiers qui bifurquaient, se rapprochaient et s'éloignaient au travers d'une végétation touffue évoquaient la vie sur la terre, les méandres de la Voie. La maison, les kiosques, les points de vue, les berges de l'étang étaient difficilement accessibles. Qui croyait s'approcher était soudain renvoyé en arrière. Qui apercevait une porte ou parlait à une personne ne comprenait pas comment la rejoindre. Qui se croyait arrivé, soudain se perdait. Seul le maître du jardin en connaissait à fond tous les sentiers, les recoins les plus secrets. Et il était un endroit caché où il se rendait seul pour méditer. Nul ne pouvait le trouver. Il fallait suivre un layon étroit qui serpentait

sur le flanc escarpé de la montagne, traverser une passerelle suspendue sans rampe et aux planches disjointes qui surplombait une gorge vertigineuse. Seule la maîtrise du souffle et de l'esprit permettait d'y marcher. Sur l'autre versant, on débouchait dans la Forêt des Dix Mille Bambous de Jade. Nul chemin, nul repère ne signalait l'Ermitage du Vieux à la Jarre, la cabane où se réfugiait le taoïste et à laquelle il avait donné un nom qui évoque un conte de Tchouang-Tseu. Et là, il aimait interpréter sur sa cithare l'air de la Robe Arc-en-Ciel. La mélodie se déployait, montait et redescendait le long des fûts des bambous où le vent jouait en contrepoint de l'orgue à bouche.

*Assis solitaire dans le bosquet de*
*bambous,*
*Je joue de la cithare et mon chant s'élève.*
*Dans la profonde forêt inconnue*
*des hommes,*
*La lune me rend visite : illumination !*

Wang Wei

Quand le Maître du jardin s'approchait de sa cabane cachée au cœur du bosquet de bambous, et qu'il apercevait le plus élancé d'entre eux, il avait le sentiment de retrouver un vieil ami. Il aimait contempler sa danse gracieuse dans le vent, écouter le bruissement des feuilles qui murmuraient comme des langues. Au fil des ans, ayant raffiné le *cinabre* au creuset de son corps, l'alchimiste taoïste pouvait comprendre la vénérable plante et dialoguer avec elle. C'est au cours de ces échanges qu'il avait percé maints secrets sur la nature et les éléments. Le bambou lui avait parlé de son irrépressible aspiration pour la lumière, un désir d'élévation qui respectait la vie communautaire du bosquet. Cette ascension ne portait ombrage à personne, au contraire, la solidarité du groupe aidait à résister aux tempêtes. Il avait exprimé sa joie de savoir concilier les contraires : le vent et l'humidité, la force et la souplesse, la droiture et l'humilité. Les nœuds de la tige marquaient la respiration, le rythme, les étapes du Tao, symbolisaient les traits d'union entre le Ciel et la Terre. La permanence de son feuillage toujours vert témoignait qu'il avait acquis toutes les qualités d'un Immortel.

*Mon ami habite sur les hautes*
*montagnes de l'est*
*Il affectionne par-dessus tout les collines*
*et les vallées.*
*Au printemps verdoyant, il dort*
*dans les forêts désertes*
*Où le soleil en son zénith le trouve*
*endormi.*
*Le vent entre les pins époussette*
*ses vêtements,*
*Un torrent lave ses oreilles et son cœur.*
*Libéré des bruits de ce monde,*
*Il repose sur son oreiller de nuage bleu.*

Li Po

Un matin qu'ils se saluaient comme deux gentilshommes, le bambou s'inquiéta du silence du Maître du jardin :

– Ami, il y a longtemps que tu n'es pas venu me rendre visite. Je me languissais de toi. Tu n'as pas apporté ta cithare. Comme tu as l'air soucieux, ton esprit est bien sombre !
– Cher bambou, j'attendais de savoir comment tourneraient les choses... J'ai un grand service à te demander. Toi seul peux m'aider mais mon cœur se fend à l'idée de t'en parler.
– N'aie crainte, entre amis véritables, l'entraide est un devoir sacré. N'hésite pas à me dire ce que tu attends de moi et, si c'est en mon pouvoir, je le ferai.
– Tu sais combien compte pour moi mon jardin. C'est l'œuvre de ma vie, j'y ai mis toute mon âme. Une terrible sécheresse s'est abattue sur le pays. Les devins prédisent qu'elle sera longue.
– Ah, c'est donc ça, murmura le bambou, ces soupirs végétaux que m'apporte le vent.
– Oui, ami, les torrents sont à sec, l'étang n'est plus qu'une flaque où agonisent les

poissons. Les arbres, les plantes, les fleurs se dessèchent irrémédiablement. Aucun d'entre eux ne survivra à cette soif mortelle. Seul ici, dans ton bosquet, ton peuple est encore verdoyant grâce à la source qui continue de couler à tes pieds. Si je veux sauver mon jardin, je n'ai d'autre choix que de la capter. Et pour que l'eau franchisse le ravin, il me faut une grande canalisation. Toi seul, hélas, cher compagnon, as la taille qui convient.

Le vénérable bambou frissonna des racines jusqu'à la pointe des feuilles.

– Ô mon inestimable ami, que me demandes-tu là ? Quel grand sacrifice ! Ivre de lumière, je n'ai pas fini mon ascension. Amoureux de ta cithare, mon cœur est toujours assoiffé de l'entendre. Es-tu certain qu'il n'y a d'autre issue ? Avez-vous, frères humains, fait assez d'offrandes aux Rois-Dragons qui président à la pluie ?

– Écoute, si tu n'es pas prêt, n'en parlons plus. Je ne t'utiliserai pas sans ton consen-

tement. Ton sacrifice serait d'une cruelle inutilité si ta souffrance faisait éclater tes fibres et si ta tige se fendait.
– Attends, parlons encore. Que deviendra ma beauté ? Que restera-t-il de ma grandeur ? Notre lien ne sera-t-il pas brisé ?
– Tout n'est que nécessaire transformation. Ton corps connaîtra une autre vie, ton esprit continuera de vibrer à l'unisson avec le mien. Jusqu'ici tu n'as vécu que pour toi-même et pour ton clan. Ta descendance est assurée. Il t'est proposé de sauver tout un monde.
– Reviens demain, je méditerai tes paroles à la lumière de la lune.

Quand le taoïste déboucha au petit matin dans le bosquet, il trouva son ami le bambou, ruisselant des gouttes de rosée, transfiguré dans la lumière dorée. La graminée géante s'inclina humblement devant lui.
– Ô précieux compagnon, je n'ai pas oublié que je te dois la vie. N'est-ce pas toi qui as planté ma jeune pousse au bord de

cette source ? Ma vie t'appartient. Je suis prêt à te servir. Fais de moi ce que tu voudras.

Le Maître du jardin salua le bambou et, la main tremblante, il prit sa hache. Le patriarche de la bambouseraie se coucha parmi les siens dans un dernier souffle qui leur arracha un long gémissement. Après l'avoir ébranché, le taoïste le fendit en deux et creusa en pleurant son tendre cœur.

Quand le tronc évidé du bambou fut placé en travers du ravin, la course joyeuse de l'eau lui donna une seconde vie. Son sacrifice avait fait reverdir le jardin. Son esprit immortel logeait dans l'étang, imprégnait chaque feuille, chaque fleur, chaque brindille.

Le Maître du jardin ne retourna plus jamais dans la Forêt des Dix Mille Bambous de Jade. La Cabane du Vieux à la Jarre tomba en poussière. Le taoïste ne jouait plus de la cithare que dans le kiosque au bord de l'eau dont la toiture gracieuse se déployait comme les ailes d'une grue. Et là, au clair de lune, il voyait danser les volutes de brume qu'exhalait l'âme de son ami de jade.

# Le secret du buis

INSPIRÉ DE CONTES JUIFS HASSIDIQUES ET SÉPHARADES

*Et Eloah prit Adam*
*Le déposa dans le jardin*
*Pour qu'il danse avec l'Arbre.*

Nourris d'images d'Éden, les frères jardiniers ont chéri les parterres fleuris et les vergers conquis sur le désert et la forêt. L'Arbre de Vie prodigua ses fruits, passant de mains en mains, du Bédouin silencieux au druide, puis dans les leurs. L'esprit du jardin demeura vivace, emprunta des voies secrètes et arborescentes, voilées par le temps. Il s'en-

seigna de bouche à oreille, murmura les trésors d'*etz chaim*, l'Arbre de Vie.
Dans le récit biblique, il a été planté au milieu de l'Éden, jardin des délices.
Le fleuve qui l'arrose a quatre bras ou directions, révérés par les peuples qui se savent encore être des arbres, tels les Cheyennes, les Bushmen, les Pygmées, les Mayas... Mais, comme l'enseignait Rabbi Na'hman, le sage conteur de Breslev, innombrables sont ceux tombés dans le sommeil. À ceux-là il faut dire des contes pour qu'ils se réveillent.

C'est donc arrivé, puisque je l'ai vu. Et quand je l'ai dit aux gens sur ma route, ils ont écouté et dit *alevie*, ça devrait nous arriver, à moi, à vous.

Quand le fer surgit sur la terre, les arbres des forêts, des vergers sauvages et des premiers jardins frissonnèrent. La Création avait introduit un ennemi plus cruel et coriace que le vent le plus emporté.

*Car quand l'homme se tiendra*
*Aussi droit que l'Arbre,*
*Montera sa sève d'intelligence.*
*Il en viendra à imaginer la hache*
*Plutôt que l'Esprit,*
*Pour faire sa charpente.*
*Et comme il risque aussi de suivre*
*La pente mauvaise,*
*De qui se croit supérieur,*
*Différent, séparé du Jardin,*
*Il n'aura plus de retenue*
*Pour nous mettre à terre.*
*L'homme : celui qui n'est pas encore*
*un arbre.*

– Qu'à cela ne tienne, dit le fer, cessez de trembler comme des feuilles. N'êtes-vous pas les maîtres de vos destins ? Demeurez solidaires, unis, ne vous offrez pas pour être taillés, ne devenez pas des manches de haches, des poignées de scies, des pommeaux de cognées. Alors moi le fer, contre vous, je ne pourrai rien. Mais si certains se désunissent et deviennent mes alliés,

alors je taillerai sans retenue vos troncs et vos branches dans un fracas qui vous laissera pour longtemps dans la servitude.
Ainsi commença l'âge du fer, quand l'intégrité fut perdue, que la discorde laissa les hommes étêter leurs semblables, aux portes du jardin. Les grands mélèzes se rirent des cerisiers. Le poirier se gaussa du chêne aux glands amers, le charme et l'if se querellèrent, le peuplier argenté se glorifia d'être l'unique à jouer dans la lumière. Mais les cèdres pleuraient et l'homme n'était pas encore un arbre.
Les fruitiers furent mieux traités que les espèces sauvages promises au tranchant implacable. Mais de sages arbousiers se laissèrent corrompre : qu'on fasse d'eux des pelles, des houx, des serpes et ce, afin que l'homme s'intéresse un peu plus au jardin !

*Car quand l'homme se tiendra*
*Ainsi penché vers le sol,*
*Retournant humblement*
*Vers le lieu de la graine,*

*Montera une sève d'entendement*
*Tournée vers l'Esprit.*
*Il fera sa charpente*
*Là où sont ses pieds,*
*Et sa tête fleurira.*

Or il advint qu'un bûcheron entendit murmurer dans ses mains le manche bavard d'un arbousier. Et comme l'arbre qui porte des fruits en toutes saisons savait que ceux qui sont dans le sommeil ont besoin d'entendre des contes, il lui mit l'eau à la bouche, devant un buis avisé.
– Aïe aïe, comme il est triste de mourir en emportant un grand secret !
– Va, parle, dit le bûcheron, retenant le fer de sa cognée.
– C'est que mon secret ne peut être dit, répondit le buis, que devant une grande assemblée d'arbres et d'hommes, au jardin où l'on fera venir leurs rois, le fer en personne et le *chochem* verdoyant, le plus sage des jardiniers.
Le bûcheron passa sa main dans les

broussailles de sa barbe, posa sa hache et compta sur ses doigts. La fête du fer était dans dix jours, il fallait organiser ça !

Ils arrivèrent des quatre directions. Les deux rois, leur suite, le fer en personne et le long cortège des conifères, des feuillus, les quatre races humaines et l'homme vert aux sourcils herbeux.

– Alors ? dit le bûcheron au buis. Alors ? firent les deux rois.

– C'est que, répondit le buis, je sais comment semer la graine d'un grenadier pour qu'il devienne en une nuit un arbre.

– Ah çà, firent les majestés, est-ce possible ?

– *Voï voï*, mais seule une branche ou un bras qui n'a jamais rien dérobé est à même de réussir le prodige. Moi, je ne peux pas, j'ai volé la mort au moment de mon sacrifice et c'est pour ça que je suis encore là.

Le roi des hommes fit signe au bûcheron d'officier. La cérémonie fut simple et belle, la graine confiée à *Adama* la terre. Il n'y avait plus qu'à aller dormir.

Mais au matin, le sol était nu et le roi contrarié.

– Aurais-tu menti, buis, pour te sauver ?

– Non. Si ton serviteur a échoué, c'est qu'il ne remplit pas les conditions.

– Oh, avoua le bûcheron, j'ai volé dix stères de bois à votre majesté.

Le roi des arbres désigna un châtaignier géant pour semer la graine.

Mais au matin suivant, le sol était nu, le roi contrarié.

– Te moquerais-tu de nous, buis, pour gagner du temps ?

– Non. Si ton serviteur a échoué, c'est qu'il n'a pas le bras taillé pour le prodige.

– C'est que j'ai volé à mon tronc ses branches pour confectionner des manches de haches, admit l'arbre, et je m'en mors les doigts qui me restent.

On se tourna vers le fer en personne.

– N'y pensez même pas, siffla le fer.

Alors, on comprit pourquoi le buis avait fait venir le *chochem* verdoyant. Le jardinier s'avança.
– Que fit le renard quand il voulut entrer dans le jardin clos ?...
Il avait l'œil filou et poursuivit lui-même, pour répondre à sa propre question.
– ... Il attendit d'être assez maigre pour se faufiler par un trou étroit, venir picorer des figues et du raisin. Mais quand il voulut partir, il était si replet qu'il lui fallut tout rendre. Il en est ressorti sans avoir rien donné, aussi maigre qu'un coucou.
L'éveillé jardinier savait que ceux qui sont dans le sommeil ont besoin de boire le nectar des contes et d'être bien secoués. Et comme en hébreu le mot *ma' assim* désigne un acte comme un récit, il se leva, prit une cognée et se coupa le bras en riant.

*Lui, l'homme qui était un arbre.*

– Couper est familier, mais réunir et recoller ?

Alors il se baissa, prit une poignée de terre promise où scintillaient les étincelles divines perdues et dispersées. Là où était sa blessure se posa la *Chekhina*, visage féminin du Sans Nom qui parcourt les univers. La *Chekhina* versa ses larmes sur le moignon, sur le tronc de l'homme. Alors un bouquet de lettres sacrées vint, en grappes de contes naissants, et s'égailla pour libérer les étincelles prisonnières.
Alors qu'il contait les nouveaux récits, où il était question de la connaissance du Bon et de son contraire, le bras perdu se recollait. De ce bras, il planta la graine.
– *Voï voï*, dit le manche d'arbousier au buis, cela est bon, ce *mentsh** est un as, c'est ainsi qu'on s'y prend pour semer un arbre qui pousse en une nuit !
– Hé oui, répondit le buis, le secret, c'est de recoudre le bras qui plante !

Au matin, les deux souriaient devant le grenadier et se donnèrent l'accolade, heureux de voir les hommes soulever leurs racines et mêler leurs feuillages au jardin. Les deux rois rirent, ne furent plus qu'un. Tous dansèrent, bras branches entrelacés autour de la *Chekhina*, entonnèrent des chants de joie, décoiffés par les tourbillons de l'Arbre et le souffle puissant d'Eloah.

*Car quand l'homme fera sa greffe*
*Il sera telle l'étoile d'une pomme*
*Jonglant avec les dix balles de l'Arbre*
*Une toupie joyeuse.*

* *Mentsh* : un individu vraiment admirable.

# Le jardin de Baudoin

D'APRÈS DES SOURCES MÉDIÉVALES

Ce jour étincelant de mai, le chevalier Thierry fit ses adieux à sa fille au pied du beffroi. En passant devant la chapelle et les logis, il redit combien il était désolé de la laisser seule au château. Pour se rassurer, il fixait les chemises et les braies de l'enceinte fortifiée. L'un et l'autre pensaient aux prétendants venus demander sa main. En vain, car chacun avait émis ses réserves et fait siennes celles de l'autre. Il songeait qu'il avait été trop exigeant ou pas assez autoritaire, elle pensait avoir un haut idéal et de l'indocilité. Ils firent silence, s'étreignirent et se séparèrent. Le chevalier salua ses gardes, ses gens de maison et ses tailleurs de pierre, fit ses recommandations et partit au grand galop rejoindre ses soldats et les seigneurs qui l'attendaient au pied de la colline.

Durant son absence, le comte Thierry avait autorisé sa fille à se promener dans la cour de la chapelle, l'allée des douves et l'*hortus conclusus*, le jardin clos reçu pour ses seize ans. C'était au château le joyau-écrin d'Emma, paradis dédié aussi à sa mère défunte, dont le chevalier disait effleurer l'âme en frôlant le lis et le bleuet. Ainsi, le lait de Junon versé sur la terre et les remèdes de Chiron rendaient le lieu fécond et doux. La jeune fille passait des heures dans cet écrin, l'esprit et les sens avivés par la beauté. Entourée de haies, plessis de saules et châtaigniers, elle aimait s'asseoir sur une banquette de gazon fleuri. Elle entrait par la porte étroite finement taillée dans le buis par le jardinier. C'était le seul jeune homme qu'elle apercevait et

elle feignit longtemps d'ignorer combien cela la contentait.

Baudoin avait succédé au vieil abbé qui avait créé le jardin et l'avait initié à son art. Qu'il fût penché sur les simples ou entretînt les neuf carrés du potager, qu'il taillât un pommier, s'occupât de la volière, de la fontaine, des rosiers, il sentait s'épanouir le cœur d'Emma. Accompagné par les saisons, les feuilles dorées et les flocons, veillant aux formes du jardin qui élèvent l'âme, sa présence devenait senteur et son art était peu à peu dédié à une femme. L'amour humain les gagnait l'un et l'autre, fondu à la félicité du jardin clos.

Or, le chevalier Thierry revint un soir, le front barré par les épreuves, les mains ouvertes. Blessé, fait prisonnier et libéré, à son tour vainqueur, il rentrait sans prétendre avoir perdu ou gagné. Si ce n'est un ami. Un ennemi qui vous épargne et vous revient les mains liées. Un frère, hors de toute norme, qu'il ramenait sur ses terres, par-delà les mers et à son côté. Il avait vu tant de bassesse, tant de fanatisme parmi les puissants, qu'il revenait avec l'œil neuf de celui qui a brisé le miroir des apparences. Après avoir étreint sa fille, il présenta Abdallah, son ami, un sage qu'il lui demandait d'aimer comme un oncle.

Une semaine passa et un soir Abdallah vint s'asseoir près de Thierry, déjà en train d'échafauder des projets pour marier Emma à un chevalier.

– Mon ami, puis-je te parler sincèrement ?

– Va, dis-moi ce que tu as sur le cœur.

– N'as-tu pas vu comment ta fille regarde vers le jardin ?

– ?

– Il y a un garçon dans ce cœur et là-bas un jeune et beau jardinier.

– Tu veux dire...

– Que ces deux-là s'aiment et qu'ils sont patients comme un vieux figuier.

– Mais...

– ... Ce n'est qu'un modeste et elle, une perle, n'est-ce pas ?
– Oui, on peut le dire comme ça, mon ami.
– On dit chez moi qu'un homme riche est recouvert de fruits. Tu le sais, certains chevaliers ne méritent même pas un cheval. Peut-être un manant ferait-il un bon roi. Dans mon pays, il y a des vizirs jardiniers. La noblesse ne tient pas dans la parenté, l'or qui brille sur la langue et sur les mains vaut mieux qu'un cœur vide.
– Certes.
– La serrure défend la porte, la sagesse protégera ta fille.
– Comment savoir ?
– Mets-le à l'épreuve. Demande-lui quelles sont ses vertus, mais pas la couleur de sa peau.
– Tu as raison.

Dans la grande salle, sous la tapisserie à côté des trophées, Thierry et Abdallah étaient assis dans des fauteuils de velours,

Emma frissonnait. Son père venait de lui demander si elle aimait le jeune homme qui soignait l'*hortus conclusus* et si elle avait durant tous ces mois éprouvé envers lui un amour vertueux. Elle avait répondu sans détour et vu dans le regard de son père qu'il ne lui en voulait pas. Il avait fait quérir le jardinier, lui offrit de s'asseoir et lui parla franchement.

– Il est clair que ma fille t'aime et probable que tu l'aimes autant. Encore faut-il savoir de quoi est fait cet amour-là et puis, qui tu es. Pour ton avantage, tu as le par-

fum qui monte ici le soir et la géométrie parfaite des bordures que j'admire le matin. Tu as l'espoir que je lis dans les yeux d'Emma et ta propre flamme. Mais pour devenir un maître jardinier et hériter un jour de ces terres et de ce château, j'ai dans l'idée que seules ta sagesse et la hauteur où peut aller ton âme peuvent te servir en cet instant. Écoute attentivement Abdallah, mon frère, et réponds-lui comme si c'était moi qui te parlais.

– Je suis prêt, répondit Baudoin.

– Voici, dit le Maure. Quand j'en fais le tour, je fais le tour de l'infini. Il soulage, nourrit, honore votre croix et est aussi mon paradis. À l'horizon, à l'azur, il tient la main des femmes en couches, délivre et garde ses secrets. Qui est-ce ?

– Seigneur, c'est le jardin et c'est moi-même. Quand je fais le tour de mon amour, je ressens l'infini et je bois à sa source. Ce jardin clos soulage les maux et il me nourrit, les allées vont en croix comme aux paradis des croisés et des sarrasins, là à l'horizon, là à l'azur, terrestre et céleste à la fois. Ses plantes tiennent la main des femmes en couches comme je tiendrai celle d'Emma, si je plante en elle une graine et qu'elle en fait un fruit. Celui-là qui est jardin délivre, garde ses secrets comme je vous parle, essayant d'habiller des mots éternels, qui fanent aussi vite que des fleurs.

Le chevalier se leva, prit la main de sa fille et de son gendre pour les conduire au jardin.

*Je me lève moi-même pour ouvrir*
*à mon amant.*
*Mes mains dégoulinent de myrrhe,*
*mes doigts de myrrhe ruisselante,*
*sur les paumes du loquet.*

Cantique des cantiques

# Balayer le jardin de thé

RÉCIT JAPONAIS

Quand Sen no Rikyû étudiait encore le *Chadô*, son maître lui demanda d'aller nettoyer le *roji*, le jardin qui entoure la maison de thé. Le disciple entra dans l'enclos et constata que le « Sentier de Rosée » venait d'être soigneusement balayé ! C'était l'automne et pas la moindre feuille morte ne jonchait le sol... Il était devant un véritable *kôan*, une énigme zen.

Sen no Rikyû resta un moment interloqué. Puis, esquissant un sourire comme s'il devinait la pensée de son maître, il se dirigea vers un arbre. Il agrippa une grosse branche, secoua vigoureusement.

*Para-para*, quelques feuilles mordorées voltigèrent avant de venir émailler les dalles de pierre.
Le maître traversa peu après le *roji*. Un sourire flottait sur ses lèvres. Son disciple avait ajouté la touche de *sabi* qui manquait : la saveur du temps qui passe, le dépouillement que symbolise l'automne.

*Une nuit d'automne où j'étais éveillé,*
*Je pris mon bâton et sortis dans*
*le jardin.*
*Les criquets chantaient*
*Sous les anciennes tuiles.*
*Les feuilles mortes dansaient*
*Autour des arbres frissonnants.*
*Au loin murmurait le torrent.*
*La lune s'élevait lentement au-dessus*
*des pins.*
*Tout conspirait pour me plonger*
*Dans une profonde méditation.*
*La lumière de l'aurore me surprit*
*Dans ma robe imprégnée de rosée.*

Ryôkan

# La carotte et les ânes

CONTE ORIENTAL

Tamerlan, le Conquérant des steppes, était aussi, dit-on, un despote éclairé. Il avait réuni à Samarkand, la capitale de son empire, les plus grands artistes et savants de ses vastes terres. Une tradition orale bien établie prétend que Nasreddine Hodja fut un temps son bouffon et son confident.

Un jour, le souverain fit venir le philosophe excentrique pour un entretien privé.

– Cher ami, susurra l'Émir de fer qui tentait de donner à sa voix rauque la douceur du miel, j'ai un petit service à te demander. Je sais que sous tes manières extravagantes, tu caches bien ton jeu. Mes informateurs prétendent que tu es en réalité un initié de haute volée, une espèce de fou divin qui converse avec Dieu. Ils m'ont même parlé d'une confrérie soufie dont tu serais l'un des maîtres secrets : l'ordre des Malamatis, les Gens du Blâme. De saints derviches qui cacheraient leur sagesse sous une conduite scandaleuse...

– Oh, là, là, éclata de rire le Hodja, certains sont prêts à inventer n'importe quoi pour se rendre intéressants ! Si je vous rapportais tout ce qu'on raconte sur vous...

– Peu importe ! le coupa sèchement Tamerlan dont le regard était redevenu aussi étincelant qu'un sabre. Ne joue pas au plus malin avec moi. Il est de notoriété publique qu'on te donne le titre de Mollah. Tu sais lire, tu as fait des études coraniques et, de toute façon, tu as réponse à tout.

– Réponse à tout ? s'interrogea Nasreddine à haute voix en se caressant la barbe. Je me souviens d'une fois où je n'ai vraiment pas su quoi répondre.

– Ah bon, toi, l'impénitent discoureur ?
– Oui, quand mon voisin me surprit un soir dans son jardin alors que j'étais en train d'arracher l'un de ses poireaux. Il me traita de voleur et, levant son bâton, il était sur le point de me frapper. Je lui dis de ne pas se méprendre, qu'un violent coup de vent m'avait fait passer par-dessus la haie et que je m'étais accroché où j'avais pu pour ne pas être emporté plus loin. Il me demanda alors pourquoi il y avait d'autres poireaux dans le panier derrière moi. Et là, je n'ai pas su quoi répondre !
Le redoutable Mongol laissa fuser un rire retentissant puis, prenant le Hodja par l'épaule, il lui dit :
– Décidément, tu as le don de me distraire des soucis du monde. Tu sais mieux que personne soulager le fardeau que Dieu a placé sur mes épaules. Mais revenons à la raison pour laquelle je t'ai fait venir. Figure-toi qu'hier, lors d'une causerie avec des savants, ceux-ci ont parlé d'« ésoté-

risme ». Comme je ne connais pas ce mot, je n'ai rien compris à leur charabia et, ne voulant pas paraître idiot, je n'ai pas posé de question. N'ayant pas le temps de faire des recherches à ce sujet, je compte donc sur toi pour trouver une définition claire et précise de ce terme. J'ai donné des instructions pour que tu puisses accéder à ma bibliothèque. Et que cela reste entre nous !

– Vos désirs sont des ordres, répondit Nasreddine avant de saluer et de se retirer avec un air entendu.

Quatre jours plus tard, le Hodja fut de nouveau appelé auprès de Tamerlan. Le Conquérant patibulaire, visiblement courroucé, l'apostropha vertement :

– Tu devrais savoir que je suis très bien informé, sinon comment aurais-je tenu si longtemps les rênes d'un empire, déjoué tant de complots ? On m'a rapporté que tu n'as pas mis les pieds une seule fois dans ma bibliothèque, ni dans aucune

autre, d'ailleurs. Il paraît que tu passes tes journées dans ton jardin. Tu sembles avoir oublié ce que je t'ai demandé. Sache que ma patience a des limites ! Si tu veux encore te payer ma tête, la tienne ira bientôt rejoindre tes babouches !

– Ne vous fiez pas aux apparences, Votre Majesté. Vous savez que j'ai des méthodes peu orthodoxes mais très efficaces. J'en sais déjà assez sur l'ésotérisme mais c'est une science subtile et complexe. Il me faut encore un peu de temps pour digérer cette doctrine de façon à en extraire le suc. Vous m'avez bien demandé une définition claire et concise ?

– Oui, mais crois-tu que bêcher ton potager soit l'occupation idéale pour réfléchir à un tel sujet ? Tu ferais mieux de t'enfermer chez toi avec un calame et de l'encre !

– Détrompez-vous, Votre Grandeur, le jardinage m'aide à méditer.

– Comme tu voudras, lui lança le Maître du Monde d'une voix menaçante, je te laisse encore deux jours. Et pas un de plus !

Au jour dit, Nasreddine se présenta devant le redoutable Tamerlan. Le visage illuminé d'un sourire triomphant, il s'exclama :

– Le jardin m'a inspiré. Ma définition tient en deux mots : âne et carotte !

– Cette fois, tu dévoiles ta vraie nature. Tu n'es qu'un ignorant doublé d'un charlatan, un faux derviche, un parasite. Tu as dépassé les bornes de l'insolence !

– Pas du tout, répondit le Hodja. Laissez-moi seulement préciser ma définition : l'ésotérisme est comme une carotte en pleine terre, la meilleure partie est bien cachée et il y a beaucoup d'ânes qui s'y intéressent !

# Le Fou des Fleurs

LÉGENDE CHINOISE

*Si tu veux être heureux une heure,*
*bois une coupe de vin.*
*Si tu veux être heureux une journée,*
*marie-toi.*
*Si tu veux être heureux toute ta vie,*
*fais-toi jardinier !*

Proverbe chinois

Sous la dynastie des Song, au sud du fleuve Yangtsé, non loin du paisible village Joie Éternelle, il y avait un manoir qui était la possession campagnarde d'un puissant mandarin. Le cadet de la famille, un certain Zhang Wei, s'y était installé depuis peu avec quelques-uns de ses compères. N'ayant aucun goût pour les études, il avait depuis longtemps renoncé à passer les examens de Lettré. Adepte des arts martiaux externes*, buveur impénitent, d'une arrogance démesurée, il cherchait querelle sans raison. Comme l'une de ses rixes avait mal tourné et qu'il avait été piteusement rossé par un véritable maître de kung-fu, de honte il s'était réfugié à la campagne. Il avait en tête de prendre sa revanche mais, au lieu de s'exercer sans relâche à l'art du poing, il passait le plus clair de son temps à boire et à jouer des tours pendables à ses rustiques voisins.

Un jour radieux de printemps, alors que le jeune Zhang Wei se pavanait dans ses habits de brocart avec sa basse-cour de mauvais garçons aux abords du village Joie Éternelle, il passa le long de la clôture d'un jardin. Il remarqua une profusion de branches fleuries qui exhalaient un parfum envoûtant. Jamais il n'avait vu autant d'essences réunies dans le même verger. Hélant un passant, il lui demanda à qui appartenait ce domaine.

– À un certain Qiu Xian. On le surnomme le Fou des Fleurs.
– Vraiment ? Et pourquoi donc ? En fait-il collection ?
– Oui, Jeune Seigneur, en quelque sorte. C'est un vieil original qui a une passion immodérée pour les fleurs. Il ne vit que pour elles. Il dépense tout son argent à en acheter de nouvelles. Il en détient même de fort rares. Il s'échine du matin au soir à les semer, les repiquer, les nourrir et les arroser. Il leur parle, les encourage, s'extasie à chaque éclosion, les contemple pendant des heures et fait des libations aux esprits de la nature pour les remercier de tant de beauté. Il lui arrive de dormir au milieu de ses fleurs et de passer la nuit dehors pour pouvoir contempler à l'aube leur éclosion.
– Ce Qiu Xian ne serait-il pas un riche mandarin retiré du monde ?
– Pas du tout ! C'est un vieux paysan qui ne cultive plus que son jardin. Comme il possède toutes les variétés d'arbres frui-

tiers, il en tire de quoi subsister et, surtout, il peut compléter sa collection de fleurs en achetant des graines qui proviennent des plus lointaines provinces, même d'autres pays.

– J'ai bien envie d'aller admirer ces raretés.

– N'y comptez pas ! De peur que des visiteurs ne les piétinent ou les cueillent, il ne laisse plus personne entrer dans son jardin.

– Cela m'étonnerait qu'un simple manant ait l'audace de claquer sa porte au nez d'un digne représentant de la famille Zhang !

Et avec un rire tonitruant, déjà quelque peu imbibé, l'arrogant cadet se dirigea vers le portail, suivi par son cortège de vauriens. Il cogna contre le vantail, vociféra, jusqu'à temps qu'on lui ouvre. Un vieillard se montra, hirsute, les cheveux de neige en broussaille, la tenue négligée.

– Pourquoi ce tapage ? Vous vous êtes trompés d'adresse. Je n'attends personne !

– Tout doux, mon brave, laisse-moi t'expliquer le motif de ma visite. Je viens contempler ton jardin dont la renommée est venue jusqu'à moi, Zhang Wei, qui ai l'honneur d'habiter le manoir à la sortie du village.

– Mon jardin n'a rien de remarquable, il n'y pousse que des légumes. Vous perdez votre temps, passez votre chemin !

Dressé sur ses ergots, le jeune coq s'indigna :

– Monsieur le Fou des Fleurs pense que j'ai le nez bouché. D'où provient donc ce capiteux parfum de pivoine ? De ces carrés de choux ? De ces parterres de navets ou de radis ? Allons, misérable insolent, laisse-moi jeter un œil avant que ma bile ne s'échauffe !

Le vieillard leva les bras pour l'empêcher d'entrer mais le jeune freluquet força le passage, le faisant tournoyer comme un tourniquet. Le maître du jardin vacilla, se retint à la porte pendant que le reste de la bande s'engouffrait dans l'allée. Les gredins firent quelques pas entre deux haies de bambous et ne tardèrent pas à déboucher devant un immense massif de pivoines, la reine des fleurs. Le jeune Zhang Wei se mit à siffler avant de s'extasier :

– C'est incroyable ! Il y a ici toutes les espèces de pivoines, même les plus rares. Je croyais que seul l'Empereur en possédait autant.

Il y avait là en effet la quarantaine de variétés qui existent : pivoines herbacées ou arbustives, à fleurs simples ou doubles, aux teintes et aux nuances les plus diverses. Certaines étaient aussi larges que des soucoupes, portaient des noms poétiques comme Pavillon de Jade, Papillon Émeraude, Pulpe de Pastèque, Lion Noir Dansant, Tête de Dragon Rouge.

La troupe s'égailla dans les allées pour admirer et respirer les fleurs, les toucher de leurs mains indélicates, les respirer en les incommodant avec leurs haleines avinées. Le vieux jardinier enrageait, s'arrachait les cheveux, allait de l'un à l'autre pour tenter de les raisonner :

– Malheureux, que faites-vous ? Atten-

tion, vous les piétinez ! Elles sont si fragiles. Vous allez les effaroucher avec vos manières et, demain, elles n'oseront plus déboutonner leurs robes !

Le meneur de la bande cria à tue-tête :

– Il faut fêter un si beau spectacle. Amis, buvons !

Ils sortirent de leurs sacs un flacon et des coupes, s'assirent au milieu des fleurs pour se servir à boire, trinquer et entonner en chœur des chansons de Li Po :

*La neige ne charge plus les branches*
*de l'abricotier ;*
*Le souffle du printemps renaît parmi*
*les rameaux du saule.*
*Les chants amoureux de l'oiseau yng*
*portent l'ivresse dans les sens ;*
*L'hirondelle est de retour et voltige*
*au bord des toits,*
*en poussant son petit cri.*
*C'est le temps des longs jours,*
*c'est le temps où le soleil*
*éclaire la natte des joyeux convives ;*

*C'est le temps où fleurs nouvellement*
*écloses*
*et danseuses élégamment parées se font*
*valoir mutuellement...*

*Sur les bords du Jo-yeh, les jeunes filles*
*cueillent la fleur du nénuphar.*
*Des touffes de fleurs et de feuilles*
*les séparent ;*
*Elles rient et, sans se voir, échangent*
*de gais propos :*
*Un brillant soleil reflète au fond de l'eau*
*leurs coquettes parures ;*
*Le vent, qui se parfume dans leurs*
*manches, en soulève le tissu léger...*

Soudain, le cadet Zhang fit taire ses compagnons de beuverie et s'adressa au vieillard qui se morfondait dans son coin :
– Vieux Fou des Fleurs, viens donc te joindre à nous pour fêter le printemps et la beauté de ton jardin !
Le jardinier, furibond, se contenta de secouer la tête en faisant la grimace. Alors,

le jeune gredin chanta un autre poème de Li Po :

*Seigneur, ne voyez-vous donc point*
*les eaux du fleuve Jaune ?*
*Elles descendent du ciel et coulent vers*
*la mer sans jamais revenir.*
*Seigneur, ne regardez-vous donc point*
*dans les miroirs*
*qui ornent votre noble demeure,*
*Et ne gémissez-vous pas en apercevant*
*vos cheveux blancs ?*
*Ils étaient ce matin comme les fils de soie*
*noire,*
*Et, ce soir, les voilà déjà mêlés de neige.*
*L'homme qui sait comprendre la vie*
*doit se réjouir chaque fois qu'il le peut,*
*En ayant soin que jamais sa tasse*
*ne reste vide*
*en face de la lune...*

Puis le vaurien s'adressa de nouveau au vieillard :
– Tu n'es pas un joyeux compagnon mais

tu es un bon jardinier. Ton jardin me plaît. Je voudrais l'acheter pour y organiser de grandes fêtes avec mes amis de la ville. Combien me le vendrais-tu ? Demande-moi un prix raisonnable et tu pourras prendre une retraite bien méritée.

Le vieux Qiu Xian réussit à contenir sa colère et, pour se débarrasser au plus vite de ces fâcheux visiteurs, il eut l'idée de répondre :

– Pourquoi pas, Jeune Seigneur ? Laissez-moi le temps de la réflexion et revenez demain.

– Très bien mais, avant de partir, cueillons quelques fleurs pour aller les offrir aux charmantes hôtesses de la taverne du bord de l'eau !

Et les malotrus de se précipiter pour arracher sans vergogne les plus belles pivoines. Le vieillard les supplia :

– Arrêtez, par pitié ! Vous leur faites mal. Comme vous êtes cruels ! Elles ont patienté trois saisons avant de pouvoir naître et, maintenant, vous les privez de

leur heure de gloire, de leur joie éphémère. Voyant que les vauriens restaient insensibles à ses arguments, le patriarche explosa de rage. Muni d'un gros râteau, il fondit sur le chef de la bande, lui donna un grand coup par-derrière, sur le crâne. Déjà bien éméché, le seigneur Zhang tomba en avant de toute sa hauteur, le nez dans les plates-bandes. Tandis que certains le relevaient, les autres se ruèrent sur le vieux jardinier qui savait bien manier son râteau. Ils reçurent quelques coups, poussèrent force jurons, avant de pouvoir le désarmer. C'est alors que les voisins accoururent, alarmés par les cris, brandissant des faux et des fourches. Inférieurs en nombre, les canailles optèrent pour un repli stratégique. Ils disparurent par le portail en soutenant leur camarade titubant.

Devant le spectacle de ses massifs de pivoines dévastés, le vieux Qiu Xian fut inconsolable. Les villageois tentèrent de le réconforter mais rien n'y fit. À la nuit tombée, ils durent le laisser à son chagrin. Sous le lampion de la lune, il ramassait les pétales en les humectant de la rosée de ses larmes tout en demandant pardon à ses chères fleurs de n'avoir pu éviter ce malheur. Soudain, une voix aussi pure que le chant du rossignol lui fit lever la tête :

– Grand-père, pourquoi pleurez-vous ainsi ?

Devant lui se tenait une jeune fille dont le visage de nacre étincelait dans la lumière fantomatique de l'astre nocturne. Elle était d'une beauté peu commune et sa robe de brocart laissait flotter un parfum enivrant.

– J'ai élevé ces fleurs comme mes propres filles et voyez comment le jeune seigneur Zhang et sa meute de chiens enragés les ont violentées. Mais, dites-moi, aimable demoiselle, qui êtes-vous ? Que venez-vous faire ici ?

– Je suis l'une de vos proches voisines. Émue par vos pleurs, je suis venue vous consoler.

Comme le vieillard ne fréquentait plus grand monde depuis des années, il pensa qu'elle était nouvelle dans le village. Il répondit en pleurnichant :

– Laissez-moi à mon deuil. Il me faut maintenant rendre les derniers honneurs à mes chères fleurs.

– N'aimeriez vous pas qu'elles retrouvent leur beauté ?

– Si, mais je n'ai d'autre choix que de souffrir jusqu'au prochain printemps.

Illuminée d'un sourire dont l'éclat rivalisait avec la clarté de la lune, la jeune fille affirma :

– Grand-père, j'ai le pouvoir de redonner vie à vos pivoines, cette nuit même.

– Comment est-ce possible ? Êtes-vous magicienne ?

– Mon père est un Immortel qui m'a enseigné quelques tours de magie. Pour celui-là, j'ai besoin d'un bol rempli d'eau.

Partagé entre la joie et le doute, le vieux jardinier courut en chercher un dans sa chaumière. Quand il revint, la jeune beauté n'était plus là. Il n'en croyait pas ses yeux : les parterres de pivoines étaient intacts, plus aucun pétale ne jonchait le sol.

Au petit matin, quand les voisins vinrent prendre des nouvelles du vieux Qiu Xian, il leur montra le prodige. Le miracle fit le tour du village. Le prêtre taoïste affirma que c'était la Déesse des Fleurs qui était venue en personne soulager la peine de son plus fervent dévot. Entendant cela, le vieux jardinier alluma des bâtons d'encens et se prosterna pour remercier la divinité. Puis, touché par la grâce, il se dit que c'était son égoïsme qui avait provoqué ce malheur. Dorénavant, il laisserait son portail ouvert et permettrait à tous de contempler ses fleurs.

Sachant que l'insolent Zhang Wei allait revenir avec sa bande de scélérats, les villageois montèrent la garde à la porte du jardin. Quand il arriva, il proposa d'acheter le domaine pour un prix ridicule et menaça, sinon, de porter plainte pour coups et blessures sur un fils de grande famille... Tous prirent la défense du Fou des Fleurs, affirmèrent qu'ils témoigneraient pour lui.

Le trublion rebroussa chemin en fulminant. Rentré dans son manoir, une idée lui vint pour se venger. Ayant entendu dire que le préfet avait ordonné l'arrestation des membres d'une secte de magiciens taoïstes qui avaient fomenté une révolte dans la province, il dénonça le jardinier comme faisant partie du complot. Après une enquête expéditive, le vieux Qiu Xian fut arrêté. En récompense de la dénonciation, le cadet Zhang obtint la somme de trois mille sapèques et la propriété du prétendu conjuré.

Pendant l'interrogatoire, le préfet fut pris de vertige et dut ajourner le procès. La nuit, il vit en rêve la Déesse des Fleurs qui le menaça des foudres de l'Empereur de Jade s'il ne relâchait pas l'innocent jardinier. Le mandarin, aussi pieux que super-

stitieux, craignant de s'attirer des ennuis avec l'administration céleste, ne voulut prendre aucun risque et fit libérer le vieux jardinier au petit matin.

Quand le Fou des Fleurs passa son portail avec ses voisins qui l'escortaient, ils trouvèrent un serviteur du jeune seigneur Zhang qui déambulait dans le jardin, les yeux hallucinés. Il leur tint des propos extravagants :
– Mon maître a disparu. Cette nuit, lui et ses amis buvaient dans le jardin quand de jeunes beautés sont venues leur rendre visite. Elles ont dansé pour eux, les ont aguichés et ils se sont mis à leur courir après. C'était une vraie partie de cache-cache dans les vergers, entre les haies, dans les bosquets. Puis, passé l'heure du Rat, les choses ont mal tourné. On a entendu des hurlements, des cavalcades. On a vu mon maître et ses amis s'enfuir, poursuivis par les jeunes filles grimaçantes qui les fouettaient avec leurs longues

manches. On eût dit qu'ils étaient pourchassés par des femmes-renardes ou des revenantes. Les malheureux sont rentrés en piteux état au manoir, les vêtements et la peau en lambeaux. Seul le jeune seigneur Zhang n'a pas réapparu. Je suis donc à sa recherche.
Au cours des battues, on a fini par retrouver le corps sans vie du fils de noble famille qui était planté, tel un oignon, la tête la première dans une fosse d'aisances.

La nuit venue, au clair de lune, la Déesse des Fleurs rendit visite au vieux jardinier. Il se prosterna à ses pieds, la remercia d'être intervenue pour le sauver et d'avoir envoyé ses suivantes punir les voyous.
– Cher grand-père, ta dévotion envers mes protégées te promet à un grand destin. Il te faut maintenant t'y préparer. Pour cela, tu ne boiras plus que la rosée au calice des fleurs et tu ne te nourriras que de leurs pollens.

Ce régime fut pour le vieillard une cure de jouvence. Son corps se redressa, ses rides s'estompèrent et ses cheveux de neige retrouvèrent leur teinte de jais originelle. Le quinzième jour du huitième mois, le jour de la Fête de la Lune, une musique céleste retentit au-dessus du paisible village Joie Éternelle. Un phénix bleu et une grue blanche tournoyèrent entre les arbres du jardin du Fou des Fleurs. Des nuages colorés s'entrouvrirent pour laisser apparaître, rayonnantes de lumière, la déesse et ses suivantes, les fées des fleurs. De sa voix cristalline, la divinité prononça ces paroles :

– L'Empereur de Jade m'envoie te chercher, ô noble Qiu Xian. Il t'invite à séjourner parmi les Immortels. Il te confie la tâche de récompenser ceux qui respectent mes filles-fleurs et de punir ceux qui les offensent.

Soudain, sous les yeux ébahis des villageois, le jardin et la chaumière du vieillard qui avait rajeuni se détachèrent du sol. Sur son tapis volant de brocart parfumé, le Fou des Fleurs traversa les nuages de ce monde impermanent pour entrer dans les vergers célestes.

** Les arts martiaux externes s'appuient davantage sur la force physique et une gestuelle acrobatique, les styles internes sur la décontraction et la respiration pour laisser œuvrer le Qi, l'énergie intérieure.*

# La greffe universelle

CONTE D'AUJOURD'HUI

Était-ce pour avoir été nourrie de contes de femmes-fleurs qu'elle était devenue jardinière ? Elle préservait ces images, celles d'un lieu rare où l'union des forces contraires est possible, malgré la grêle, les orages et les dormances du temps.

Au fil des ans, elle avait appris à aimer les fleurs sauvages, coquelicot, ancolie, cœur saignant, sceau de Salomon et rose trémière. Elles vivaient avec le liseron, le ciste et la scabieuse entre les lilas et le potager, d'où elles pouvaient converser paisiblement avec les choux et les cardes.

À une époque où les jardineries regorgeaient de produits toxiques, désherbants, anti-limaces et répulsifs, confier la santé des choux à des *sauvages* relevait sinon du défi, du moins d'une grande clairvoyance. Celles qu'on appelait couramment *les mauvaises herbes* rivalisaient de beauté, inventivité, énergie. Elles détenaient de grandes vertus médicinales qu'il convenait de manier sagement. Certaines fleurs ou herbes se révélaient redoutables, d'autres se mangeaient ou protégeaient le sol ou leurs semblables. Ici, les mondes sauvages et cultivés s'appréciaient, tels les désirs farouches et raffinés du jardin secret de leur jardinière.

Ce jour-là, il y eut deux visiteurs : un asphodèle bleu apparu près des petits buis, et l'ingénieur départemental missionné pour le tracé de la future autoroute, entré pour faire relevés et repérages. La cohabitation des mondes sauvages et civilisés montrait ici toutes ses limites.

Elle l'invita à boire le thé, versa un philtre puissant de sa composition.

– C'est délicieux, c'est quoi cette tisane ? fit l'ingénieur qui n'était pas insensible aux charmes de la belle jardinière.

– Est-ce que je peux vous parler franchement ? dit-elle en attendant que la mixture produise son effet, car comme toute jardinière, elle était un peu sorcière.

– Euh, oui.

– Comment pourrez-vous prendre une décision, sans avoir d'abord demandé leur avis aux pierres, plantes, fleurs, bêtes et gens qui vivent ici ?

– ? ? ! !

– Avant de bavarder, je dois vous présenter au jardin.

– Me...

Elle ne plaisantait pas. Elle l'entraîna dehors. Ce fut une singulière promenade, qu'elle entama par un petit discours au peuple rassemblé des cailloux, herbes, brindilles, fleurs, civilisations de coccinelles, de fourmis et d'oiseaux. L'*herbe à voir* commençait à faire son effet. L'homme eut le sentiment que les papillons le suivaient, que les geais commentaient les échanges entre la femme et les occupants du jardin, que les branches des arbres et la lumière participaient à cet étrange et vibrant entretien. L'air fut vivifié, le temps sembla se démultiplier. Alors, il défit sa cravate, éteignit son portable, ouvrit ses boutons de chemise, soupira d'aise. Il était ennobli par la dive mixture, mûr pour voir, réentendre la voix du plantain et de la berce, surprendre *le petit peuple* à l'œuvre, goûter aux horizons quantiques. Alors, il vit les mondes qui coexistent et interagissent, il sentit le lien entre les créatures. Il perçut le chant de l'asphodèle comme celui des astres. L'ingénieur pensa joyeusement : « *L'homme est une sorte d'arbre.* » Bouche bée, il buvait à la régalade un enseignement que ni l'école ni ses parents n'avaient pu lui offrir. L'*herbe à voir* enfonçait les vieilles portes, faisait voler les verrous, entraînait l'enfant-sans-nature dans une danse. Elle secouait vigoureusement ses croyances désuètes et ses élans domestiqués : elle laissait sa place au Grand Mystère. Quelle salutaire greffe d'arbre ! Le suc clarifié des éons offrit à l'ignorant qui s'était cru civilisé un nom, écrit en lettres d'homme : il était un *gardien de la terre*.

Cela dura des heures et, comme on ne peut sortir indemne d'une telle expérience, lorsque l'effet psychotrope s'estompa, l'ingénieur demeura béat, fessier au frais sur le carrelage et magnifié. Alors, la jardinière sortit un cahier. Elle lui montra des photos de cristallisation sensible. On pouvait admirer la rosace harmonieuse d'une goutte de jus de pomme naturel et, à côté, le chaos d'un jus terrassé par les traitements chimiques ou irradié. Il vit ce qu'une goutte de lait d'une vache des alpages produisait de beauté et ce que l'ignorance, la folie des hommes générait, lorsque les cornes des bêtes étaient coupées ou qu'on leur donnait à manger des farines d'origine animale. Il vit des images montrant des cristaux de glace ayant reçu de l'*eau de bruit* et d'autres, somptueux, confiés à des sonates de Beethoven ou aux romances des merles. La nature était vivante, sensible à l'environnement, aux intentions humaines, prête à répondre à la conscience qui observait. Dans l'atelier, elle lui montra un liquide vert doré qu'elle avait préparé quatorze jours avant. Elle commença en son honneur la dynamisation des pétales d'ombelles, brassa le tout dans de l'eau tiède, ajouta de la bouse et de la silice de corne, parla des soins qu'elle prodiguait au jardin, posa sa main sur son épaule, lui fit cadeau d'un plein panier de fioles d'*herbe à voir*, cligna de l'œil, lui donna un baiser.

Le soleil avait triché, la journée dura un printemps.
Le temps qu'il fallait pour consulter la vie,

avant de jouer inconsidérément avec elle. Le temps d'agir, avant que Terre ne secoue toutes ses puces à la lumière.

L'homme s'en fut léger, changé, illuminé dans la brise du soir et la jardinière sut que la greffe avait pris, que l'arbre humain portait en ville de bons fruits. Il était venu en conquérant de l'asphalte, il repartait Merlin parmi les décoiffés, un plein panier de vie à déverser dans la tasse des têtes raides. Elle, caressant la vie qui remuait dans son ventre, songea que la sagesse était contagieuse, quand elle était enseignée au jardin. Sur le chemin, lui se mit à rire entre deux elfes et songea qu'il était devenu à son tour un jardinier, soucieux de l'avenir d'une graine qu'il avait semée dans sa femme jardin. Il alla d'un pas joyeux pour verser le contenu des fioles dans le grand réservoir des villes. Bientôt les robinets allaient cracher une nouvelle eau de vie et réveiller les fontaines des *gardiens de la terre*.

*Il a ceint son front d'une charmille,*
*Fait un nœud d'eau à sa ceinture,*
*Il a libéré une horde de frères*
*Entre ses doigts de buis.*

*Vers le sol il a baissé sa tête*
*Et laissé monter les écureuils*
*de l'Amour.*

*Quand il s'est avancé vers la ville*
*Un edelweiss entre les dents,*
*La terre-mère a soufflé sur lui*
*Comme une jardinière.*

# Remerciements

Pascal Fauliot remercie les personnes suivantes pour leurs précieuses informations et certaines versions orales de contes :

Mme Shi Qiao Fang, architecte et paysagiste, créatrice du merveilleux jardin de Lettré chinois « Yi Li ».

Mme Nobuko Matsumiya, musicienne, maître de thé et d'ikebana.

M. Jacques Normand, maître de kyûdô (7e dan) et autres budô traditionnels.

M. Dominique Buisson, photographe et écrivain spécialiste du Japon.

# Sources écrites

– *Les Paradis naturels, jardins chinois en prose*, anthologie réunie et traduite par Martine Vallette-Hémery, Philippe Picquier, Arles, 2001.
– *Récits classiques*, coll. « Panda », Bai Wang Zhuang, Pékin, 1985.
– Baridon Michel, *Les Jardins*, coll. « Bouquins », Robert Laffont, Paris, 1998.
– Bournaud Michel, *Contes du jardin*, Hesse, Saint-Claude-de-Diray, 1999.
– Buisson Dominique, *L'Esprit du bambou*, Philippe Picquier, Arles, 2004.
– Chikamatsu Shigenori, *Stories from a Tea-Room Window*, Tuttle Publishing, Tôkyô, 1982.
– Chiyo-Ni, *Bonzesse au jardin nu*, Moundarren, Millemont, 2005.
– Espinassou Louis, *Contes et légendes*

*de l'arbre*, Éditions Hesse, Bonchamps, 2005.
– Impelluso Lucia, *La Nature et ses symboles*, Hazan, Paris, 2004.
– Itoh Teiji, *Jardins du Japon*, Herscher, Paris, 1984.
– Ji Tomek, *Légendes et Contes des pharaons*, Gründ, Paris, 1985.
– Jodorowsky, *La Sagesse des contes*, Vivez Soleil, Genève, 1997.
– Gaster Théodore H., *Les Plus Anciens Contes de l'humanité*, Payot, Paris, 1953.
– Harrison Robert, *Jardins*, Le Pommier, Paris, 2007.
– Mardrus J.-C., *Les Mille et Une Nuits*, coll. « Bouquins », Robert Laffont, Paris, 1980.
– Muecke Stephen et Shoemaker Adam, *Les Aborigènes d'Australie*, coll. « Découvertes » Gallimard, Paris, 2002.
– Pinguilly Yves, *Contes et Légendes d'Afrique d'Ouest en Est*, Nathan, Paris, 1997.

– Roob Alexander, *Alchimie et Mystique*, Taschen, Bonn, 1996.
– Sadler A.L., *The Japanese Tea Ceremony*, Tuttle Publishing, Tôkyô, 2008.
– Schmidt, *Les Mou allaqât*, L'Esprit des péninsules, Paris, 1998.
– Sen Sôshitsu, *Vie du thé, esprit du thé*, Jean-Cyrille Godefroy, Paris, 1994.
– Serych Jiri, *Légendes du soleil, de la lune et des étoiles*, Gründ, Paris, 1977.
– Suzuki D. T., *Essais sur le bouddhisme zen*, Albin Michel, Paris, 1972.
– Suzuki D. T., *Zen and Japanese Culture*, Princeton University Press, Princeton, 1970.
– Takei Jirô & Keane Marc P., *Sakuteiki, Visions of the Japanese Garden*, Tuttle Publishing, Tôkyô, 2008.
– Tchouang-Tseu, *Œuvre complète*, Gallimard, Paris, 1973.
– Voisin André, *Les Contes du Roi Singe*, Sophon, Strasbourg, 1988.

## Crédits des textes

Les traductions des poèmes sont celles des auteurs excepté pour les contes suivants :

– « Le Fou des Fleurs » : Poèmes de Li Po traduits par le marquis d'Hervey-Saint-Denys (1822-1892).

– « Le son du bambou » : Poème de Da Hui Zong Gao traduit par Yen Chan dans *La Voie du Bambou*, © Éditions Almora, Paris, 2008.

– « Celle qui savait parler aux arbres » : Deux haïkus de Chiyo-Ni : « Traces des rêves... » et « Le rouge à lèvres... » traduits par Hervé Collet & Cheng Wing Fun dans *Bonzesse au jardin nu*, © Éditions Moundarren, Millemont, 2005.

– « Le jardin de Baudouin » : *Cantique des cantiques*, traduit par A. Chouraqui, © Desclée de Brouwer, Paris, 1950.

## Crédits photographiques

AKG : 129 (détail) ; British Library : 192 ; De Agostini Pict. Li. : 46 (détail) ; R. et S. Michaud : 110, 197 ; © Sotheby's : 225.
BnF, Paris : 78 (détail), 140 (détail), 143 (détail).
**Bridgeman** : 28-29, 68, 104-105, 170, 187 ; © British Library Board, All Rights Reserved : 146-147 ; © John Piper/NTPL/J. Hammond : 122 ; © World Religions Photo Library : 133.
Corbis : © Asian Art & Archeology Inc. : 80.
**Leemage** : © Aisa : 151 ; © Electa : 183 ; © Josse : 41 ; © North Wind Pictures : 91.
© The Metropolitan Museum of Art/Dist. RMN : 10 (détail), 120-121 ; photo B. Hanson : 115.
RMN : J.-G. Berizzi : 137 ; H. Bréjat : 56 (détail) ; T. Ollivier : 63 (détail) ; G. Vanneste : 16, 96 (détail), 152, 157, 169 (détail), 200, 207, 212, 218.

Iconographie rassemblée
par Karine Benzaquin-Laidain
et Caroline Fuchs-Sabolo

Photogravure : APS Chromostyle, Tours, France
Impression : Lego, Vicenza, Italie
Dépôt légal : avril 2011. N° 103104-3